Everything That Makes Us Feel

CHUCK MURPHREE

Ten|16 PRESS

www.ten16press.com - Waukesha, WI

To Karen, who has held my hand since we were fifteen, and that is all I have ever needed. Your love is a gift.

Mom, thank you for teaching me resilience and allowing me to always explore.

David, you have become a memory and, even with the pain, one I'm thankful I have.

To my students—past, current, and future— you give me purpose and have ridden on my shoulders as I typed every word in this book.

For all of you who grapple with the darkness in your mind, you are not alone.

The First Day of School, Again

FRIDAYS TYPICALLY SIGNIFY ENDINGS, NOT BEGINNINGS, BUT
to me it was easier to start my new school on a Friday and then take
the weekend off to process the day. I gently stirred through my bowl
of Frosted Flakes until it started to become soggy. My legs felt heavy
at the table as I looked directly across from me where David used
to sit. I was still waiting for him to come back. He was the one who
was supposed to help me navigate high school. Mom walked by me,
taking me out of my daze, and brushed her fingers through my hair
like she has been doing since I was little.

"Time to go, sweetheart," she said. "You don't want to be late on
your first day."

I didn't answer. Instead, I stood, dumped my cereal into the
garbage disposal, looked over at David's chair one more time, and
then went to my room and got my backpack. I had packed my
backpack the night before and made sure that I had folders for each
class. I didn't need to write new class names on any of them because
they were the same as the ones at my last school from a week ago.

As I stood in front of the mirror that hung on the inside of my
door, I immediately judged my body. I had grown enough over the
past summer that when I registered for my new school, they had to
look twice to see that I was a freshman. However, my giraffe-like

growth spurt brought with it lanky arms and legs that seemed to barely hold up the pair of faded jeans and hoodie that I was wearing. My hair was all over, but I stopped trying to comb it after it grew past my ears, and then it seemed to have a mind of its own and fell wherever it wanted no matter what I did to it.

My mom drove me to school. There was nothing more embarrassing than getting out of an old minivan and having your mom lean over to kiss you goodbye. I already didn't fit in at any school, and if these new kids saw my mom kissing me goodbye, that would be my death. I literally had the door open and jumped out as she was rolling to a stop.

"Neil." Mom said my name in a way that I knew she was about to tell me something important. "This one is going to work for you. I can feel it. Just be yourself and open up to people." She finished by saying, "I love you." I didn't say it back, but I immediately regretted it as I shut the door. I glanced back, and Mom was still there, hesitant to leave, tears in her eyes. I kept walking.

When I reached the entrance of the school, I immediately saw a teacher that stood outside greeting all of the kids, high-fiving and fist-bumping and goofing around with them. Some of the kids circled around him and laughed while some just passed by, trying to be cool, but even they had smiles on their faces. I tried to avoid him by walking into the door furthest away, but it was locked, and the only door to enter through was the one he was near. Out of the corner of my eye, I saw him break free of the circle and walk toward me with a slow stroll. It was almost like he was waiting for me to arrive. I didn't know what to expect as he approached. He stuck his hand out for me to shake.

"I'm Mr. C," he said. *That's it? Where's the rest of his name?* I shook his hand but didn't say anything or make any expression. "My last name is spelled C-E-A, but it sounds just like the letter C. Most people just write the letter though." He laughed, creating wrinkles on the sides of his eyes. He wasn't old, probably in his mid-thirties. His hair was a little longer than I'd seen on other teachers, but only down to his collar. His clothes were baggy and wrinkled.

"Welcome to our school. What's your name?" he asked.

I didn't say anything. Usually around this time, whoever tried to carry on the conversation with me found the silence awkward and invented a reason to walk away. Not this guy. He just gave me a slanted grin.

"Yeah, I would stay quiet too. Take the Fifth. Don't implicate yourself on day one. You can never get what you said back. Believe me, these teachers and kids remember everything you say and can hold it against you."

He was grinning and making a joke of my silence. I guess I could have been insulted but it actually made me feel normal. I didn't feel like a freak, just a boy who preferred to stay quiet.

"Well, I will see you around, Neil." *Holy shit! How does he know my name already?* Mr. C smiled and went back to shuffling the kids into the school, and as I followed him in with the rest of the students, he was making cattle noises like he was in a herd. This guy was a bit off.

I went to the office to check in and pick up my schedule. *Perhaps this'll be a new start*, I thought, optimistic for just a moment before my anxiety started to grow and I suddenly wanted to flee. I glanced through the door towards the parking lot beyond. The busses were gone, and I was across town from home. The anxiety was making me sweat. The kids would be staring at me, and the teachers would want to introduce me and ask me questions. The lunch lady would want me to order my food and give her my I.D. Everyone would want something from me. They would want to hear my voice. I took a step toward the door.

"Neil," the secretary said. She was an older woman with her gray hair in braids, and she wore a flowered dress and about five bracelets on each wrist. "The counselor wants to see you before you head to class."

"Do I have to?" I whispered. It was starting already. They wanted me to see a counselor. Maybe my mom had called and told the school how messed up I was, or that I refused to talk, or that my brother hung himself.

"He likes to see all the new students before they go to their first class," she told me, a strange grin on her face. "You can get there through those doors." She pointed toward the back of the office to a dark room. I looked back at her and shook my head. "It's okay, hon. He's waiting for you."

I walked back through a doorway toward the dark room. When I got there, another set of doors awaited, leading into an office. I gently knocked and stepped inside. The room had a fish tank and three bright orange lamps and two yellow lamps with little pictures of the Beatles on the lampshades. There was an old futon against one wall with a faded cushion, along with three other chairs that looked like they had been picked up from a garage sale of a family that had used them for years. "What kind of school is this?" I whispered to myself. Normally, I only let myself talk aloud in the woods or when Mom and Dad weren't home, but apparently now I did in this crazy place too. Were they sending me toward a trap to get rid of the mute kid with the dead brother?

When I cleared my throat, I heard a familiar voice. "Enter . . . if you dare." Then, an evil laugh rang out. It was Mr. C. He was at his desk typing with his back toward me. *Shit!* This guy was the counselor?

I hesitantly walked further into his office. Since I felt like an easy target standing in the middle of the room, I hurried to the futon against the wall and sat back down, fidgeting with my backpack strap. There was a coffee pot next to his desk that smelled strong and like chocolate, a bunch of board games lay across a large, wooden coffee table, magazines were stacked in a lopsided pile near the coffee pot, and a shelf of books stood tall against the wall opposite of Mr. C's desk. I anxiously started to rub the worn cloth of the futon cushion. The color was fading to a lighter shade of blue. The pillows on either end were brown and seemed new, which were totally out of place on the musty, old piece of furniture that had probably been around since the year I was born. I figured I was coming in to be examined, to answer a bunch of questions that I have been asked a million times before:

> *How did your brother's suicide affect you?*
> *Is that when you stopped talking?*
> *Do you know what Selective Mutism is?*
> *How do you get along with your parents?*
> *Do you ever want to talk again?*
> *Do you think medication would help?*

The list went on and on. I hated therapy. I hated feeling like a freak and being judged. I knew the therapists had all thought they were helping, but I didn't want their help. I just wanted to feel normal! I was screaming in my head, eyes closed, and for a moment, I was nervous that I was actually screaming aloud. But all I heard was the music Mr. C had playing: something mellow, one guy singing while playing guitar. I looked over to the iPod dock that sat on his desk.

"You like the music?" Mr. C turned and faced me, and I just shrugged. "It's Iron & Wine. It's mellow, and it helps me relax. I love the lyrics. I can burn you some music if you like it." I shrugged again. "Elliott Smith is great, and of course there's the older stuff like Dylan and The Byrds." Had this guy really dragged me in here to talk about music? My eyes moved across the room without moving my head and noticed a guitar in the corner. Mr. C smiled. "Taking the Fifth again. Smart man! Never let them break you." Was this guy for real?

"So here's the thing, Neil," Mr. C rolled his chair closer to me and leaned in. "You can come and see me whenever you want. You will probably see me more than you'd like because I like to get out in the hallways with the kids. The school sticks me back here away from everyone because I'm nuts." He giggled at his own attempt at a joke. "I'm kidding!"

I still didn't say a word. Mr. C seemed different, but in a good way. To my surprise, he didn't ask me any questions about my brother or my parents or past schools. He just went over my schedule and told me about the different teachers and how to work with them. "Your math teacher, Mr. Peters, is pretty strict and old-school. He teaches from a text that's so old it's growing mold." He laughed at his own joke. "Mr. Davis is your American History teacher. He's cool. He's

a friend of mine, so if he's being a pain in the ass, come and see me."
Did he just say "ass"? Mr. C got this boyish smile on his face, like he
had just gotten away with something. "Sorry, I'm a counselor. I get a
few privileges, like swearing every so often. My boss said I am allowed
two per day." The more he talked, the more I thought this guy should
be the one in counseling. Finally, Mr. C handed me my schedule, and
I was off to class. "Keep taking the Fifth, Neil!" he yelled down the
hall as I exited his office. "Don't let them break you down. Not even
if they stick toothpicks under your fingernails!" The secretary just
rolled her eyes and chuckled.

I walked down the hallway to my history class. Mr. C had
confused me enough that I'd forgotten all about wanting to dash
out the front door and run. I found Room 211, which said "Mr.
Davis" on the door under a poster of an old car, a Volkswagen Beetle.
It reminded me of when my family would take road trips and my
brother, David, and I would look for that car just so we could hit each
other on the arms and say, "Slug bug." I shook the memory from my
mind and opened the door.

When I stepped into the room, Mr. Davis waved, and I
immediately looked down at the floor. "Sit anywhere," he said.
The rest of the class glanced at me, then back toward Mr. Davis. I
was introduced, but not required to speak. For the next forty-five
minutes, I sat in a daze as Mr. Davis tried to make the Industrial
Revolution interesting. Instead of the boring lesson I'd expected, he
taught us about privilege and the working class, big chain stores and
monopolies. The class was over before I knew it, and my silent secret
stayed intact.

The next class was math, with the strict teacher Mr. C had warned me about. I hated math. There were too many rules, and rules pissed me off. The worry that I would be called on to speak made my anxiety spike, and I started to sweat in anticipation. My hands got clammy, and my throat went dry. But luckily, it never happened. The teacher stayed at the front of the room and lectured the entire class, and we took notes and attempted to solve the problems. It was boring, but I didn't have to worry about being asked to talk because no one dared say a word or ask a question with this teacher. He seemed too old and worn out to care whether we paid attention anyway.

After math, I walked toward the office, still searching for my escape route, wondering which way I should turn when I reached the parking lot. Then I spotted the principal heading toward me. At least, I assumed he was the principal because he wore a suit and tie. I turned around to look for another escape route when I nearly ran into Mr. C.

"Neil." He shook my hand and gently grabbed my shoulder. "Getting lost or getting found? Do you have to do one before the other, and if you do, which one first? Or does it matter?" His questions threw me for a loop, and I had no idea what he was talking about, but I let him lead me toward the library as we talked, or, I should say, as he talked. "Let me show you my favorite part of the school."

I followed Mr. C's lead and crouched down as we snuck through the library. He motioned for me to stay quiet, which I couldn't help but laugh at; me staying quiet was definitely not a problem. Mr. C smiled. I wasn't really sure why we were sneaking around at all. I figured the school library was open for everyone.

The librarian stepped away from her desk, and we made a mad

dash for a side room. "That was close," Mr. C muttered to me. "We can't get caught. She doesn't like anyone in here unless it's a class doing research or checking out books." That seemed strange. Books should be for anyone at any time. It made me angry, and my frown must have spoken volumes. "Makes me mad too," said Mr. C, seeing the look on my face. We crept into the "secret" room, and when we walked in, I saw wall-to-wall books: modern novels, the classics, and even a couple rare books too which were locked up on one of the shelves and seemed like they were more for display than for reading. I loved the smell of books, and the room made me smile.

"Pretty cool, right?" said Mr. C.

I nodded my head, and my eyes roamed around the room. There was an old copy of *The Great Gatsby* and another of *The Catcher in the Rye* sitting on a dark wood bookshelf. Plastic covers protected the book jackets. There were also books from authors I had never heard of. Then, a halting voice sounded from behind me.

"What are you doing in here?" It was the librarian. "The library is closed, and this room is only open by appointment."

Mr. C looked at me and grinned. "I just wanted to show the new lad your prized possession of books and how lovely our, I mean, *your* library is. It's just so impressive."

"I will not take any of your sarcasm today or you bringing a student in here. What kind of modeling are you doing? What are you teaching him?"

Usually when someone asks a question like that, they don't expect a response, but Mr. C gave her one. "That libraries should be open for everyone, and books should be enjoyed by all." He offered her a big smile.

The librarian cleared her throat, angrily adjusted the purple scarf around her neck, and said, "These books can be enjoyed by appointment only." She gestured for us to leave. Mr. C went to give her a high five, but she kept her hands tight to her sides.

We left the library, and Mr. C walked me to my next class. He gave the teacher a wave to indicate that I was with him so I wouldn't be marked tardy, then said, "Until our next adventure." I'd never snuck around or broken any rules with a teacher before. Something told me I would be seeing a lot of him.

After fifth hour was the worst time of day for me: lunch. It's the most social part of the day, when the "cool" kids clump together and all the other cliques spread out around them. The geeks are off at one table talking about their games. The goths cluster in another corner to act as opposite from everyone else as possible. The jocks act like they run the school, along with the rich kids. Then, there are the loners who don't talk to anyone, plus everyone else in between, who I always figured were the ones who either didn't care or had the confidence enough to remain their own person no matter what. There are also the lost kids that haven't transformed themselves to fit in at all, who sneak through the cracks of the school walls and go unnoticed. That was me. Lost.

I didn't have a lunch but managed to throw an apple in my backpack before I left this morning. I tried as hard as I could not to make eye contact with anyone. If my secret got out during lunch, who knew what would happen. Maybe there would be laughter and heckling. Maybe they would whisper about me and start rumors. Or maybe they would find out that I was the brother of the kid who hung himself across town last year. After all, David's death had been in all the papers, I guess because they'd investigated whether it was more than a suicide. They said it wasn't the "typical suicide," whatever that meant.

All I knew was that they'd taken all of our computers and searched our house. They even went to my dad's work and questioned him at his office. That hadn't gone over well. See, my dad is well-known around town. He was an advisor to the mayor and had helped him get reelected, which was why my dad had been so embarrassed when David killed himself, and even more embarrassed when I stopped talking. He would often yell at me, "You have to start talking, Neil! It's just not normal," before stalking away and ignoring me. Mom would come up and rub my back after he yelled at me, pretending to comfort me but really just protecting my dad. "He's just upset, dear. You understand?" *Fuck you!* No, I didn't understand. I understood that they both had left me after David was gone, maybe not physically, but emotionally. I understood that they blamed me in some weird way because I was the one who found him and had to tell them that their oldest son was hanging in the basement. But I didn't understand why they thought they could make me talk and why they'd stopped being my parents. These questions plagued my mind, and I often screamed them to my parents in my head.

I escaped the school day without anyone finding out about my secret. I wandered past the office and peeked in to see if Mr. C was there, but he wasn't.

Once I walked out the front door, I heard, "There's my partner in crime." It was Mr. C standing in front of me, surrounded by the same kids that had surrounded him this morning. I just smiled and kept walking toward the parking lot. "Neil, can I introduce you to some of these knuckleheads?" Part of me wanted to meet the kids he was with. I wanted friends, but I just shook my head and kept moving. Meeting new people seemed dangerous. I heard Mr. C say, "See you tomorrow. Maybe we can harass the librarian again." The kids that surrounded him laughed. He must have taken them on his little journey through the library too.

Day one was over, and I hoped I would have the courage to come back. I wanted to thank Mr. C for making me normal. I hadn't felt that way in a long time.

Family Time

I LOVED WATCHING OLD SHOWS ON TELEVISION. THE FAMILIES ate dinner together and always talked about their issues and handled their problems at the table or on the front porch, and then they could go about their day. They seemed happy in their black-and-white selves, even if it was all made up by some screenwriter and a few actors. It was a false world that I wished I had. When David was alive, Mom would cook dinner, and Dad, David, and I would play catch or watch baseball on TV before we were called to eat. We would flock to the table like vultures, wait for Mom to sit down, and then dig into our meat, vegetables, bread, and dessert that we each took turns choosing. Dad and Mom would drink wine while David and I gulped down milk. I drank milk because David did, and he was strong, so I figured then I would be too.

Dad would always talk to David about the upcoming game in whatever sport the season offered. David excelled at them all, but baseball was his true gift. He would often just shrug off Dad's bragging.

"You are the best player in the conference," Dad would say. "There's nobody that can pitch to you." If it was football season, he would say, "You are the best in the conference. Nobody can tackle you." During wrestling season, it turned into, "Nobody can pin you," and so on. It was all true to a certain extent, but Dad bragged about David in front of his friends too. That was when David would get embarrassed. After he started his sophomore year, he and Dad argued more often. David used to just ignore Dad's bragging, but one day, Dad showed up in the locker room after a baseball practice and started telling David how good he was in front of the other players. David just stood there and stayed quiet until he came home.

"You're embarrassing me!" David had yelled. "I'm just one player. The others are good too."

"I'm trying to help you. I've always tried to help you. You would be nothing without me."

"Fuck you!" David shouted, and that was when Dad had lost it and hit him. David fell back onto his bed.

"You little shit! I have done nothing but support you," Dad snapped, looming over David. "Not so tough now, are we."

David had clutched the side of his face, then got up and ran from his room, rushing out the front door and fading away past the row of streetlights. He was faster than Dad and knew he could escape. I wasn't sure where he ran that night, but it was the beginning of David's fall from the pedestal that Dad had placed him on. It was the end of peaceful family time and picking dessert.

After the bus dropped me off after that first day at the new school, I slowly walked up the front steps and into the house. Mom was waiting by the front door.

"How was your day, honey?" It shocked me that she even asked.

I walked past her and shrugged. I appreciated her asking me, but she couldn't just ignore me for months and months and then expect me to start talking to her like nothing had happened. I get that it's devastating losing a child, but she had another one, me, and I needed her now more than ever. I was resentful. I did want to tell her about Mr. C and his crazy antics, and about the library, and about being a loner at lunch but still managing to protect my secret, but it was no use. Mom was not ready to hear me, and I'm not sure my words were ready to come out.

I walked down the hallway, past David's door, which had been closed since he died, and into my bedroom. As I lay on my bed thinking about how lonely I'd felt since David had died and how my mom had been emotionally abandoning me and how I was going back to school, my anxiety began to build. It was slow at first, and a slight chill spread over my skin. Then panic took over my brain and lungs.

I started breathing heavily, like a fist was squeezing my chest and suffocating me. I moved to the top of my bed against the wooden headboard, draped a pillow around my knees, and squeezed it tight, burying my head as deep as I could against the pillow. I sat and held my knees against my chest and shook. I had learned that putting my body in this upright fetal position and sinking myself into the pillow with all my might calmed me down. However, I kept shaking heavily, and my breathing wouldn't slow. This was it. This was the moment I slipped into craziness and never returned. They would put me away in some institution, and then my parents would lose two sons. I let the pillow go and threw it across the room and then reached into the drawer of the nightstand next to my bed. I pulled out a well-used baseball that once belonged to David. I gripped it tight and moved it in small circles within my hand. The feel and smell of the ball, knowing David's fingerprints were still on it, brought me comfort.

Eventually, my panic turned to exhaustion, my eyes became heavy, and I fell asleep.

Mom called Dad and me for dinner about an hour later, and I ignored her from the safety of my room. What was she doing? Turning over a new leaf? Trying to be a mother again? It was the first time that she had made dinner and wanted us all to eat at the table since David died. Maybe it was her way of working through the grieving process, but I wasn't having any of it. The forgotten boy could stay forgotten for all I cared.

A shaft of hallway light cut across my carpet as the door opened and Mom said, "I made your favorite meal." I didn't know what she was talking about. I forgot what my favorite meal even was.

"I'll get something later. I'm not hungry," I whispered. My throat felt weak. I wondered if my voice would ever work again.

"Did you have a bad day at school?"

I shook my head and turned my eyes away from her toward my book that was on my nightstand, then picked it up and pretended to read. Books were my other escape. I didn't want her conversation. I wasn't ready. I was angry and sad and wanted to scream at her at the top of my lungs, "You forgot about me, you bitch! Your only son!" I would probably blow up my vocal cords if I yelled as loud as the voice inside of me wanted to. Mom must have heard all of that through my expression alone, and she closed my door. She had tears in her eyes.

While Dad was obsessed with David and his talents, he always forgot about me. I was more of a sidekick, as he and David would go to baseball games and the park to practice hitting without me, so Mom spent more time with me to compensate.

Tonight, Mom went for a run and took a bath, Dad took his plate in front of whatever was on ESPN, and I stayed silent in my room. After her bath, Mom would often eat alone at the table. I would sneak in an hour or so later and find her still sitting there. She would stay at the table for hours, drinking coffee or red wine and looking over the photo album of our vacations. I would often hear her crying at the table, and then when my dad went to bed, she would go to the couch and fall asleep. This was our routine. My family was broken like a thousand pieces of shattered glass that couldn't be glued back together. They could only be swept into the trash.

The Woods is Where I Find My Voice

I WALKED THE WOODS TO REMEMBER WHO I WAS. IT WAS THE only place where I felt safe listening to my voice. I could express myself and tell the trees my thoughts with no one to judge me. The woods let me play and be little again. It begged me to be whoever I wanted to be and promised that as long as I respected it, I could find my serenity and peace. Sometimes, I wished I had someone to share it with. I never saw anyone else walking the woods; it seemed like people forgot about it, and that was okay with me. I didn't want intruders or anyone discovering the secret places where I hid for hours.

I'd been coming to the woods for years, since I was about six. Dad and David would leave on one of their outings, and I would walk out of the yard with my plastic Army canteen and jackknife and just walk. Sometimes I would whittle a stick to a sharp edge and stab at fake enemy soldiers, but I could never hurt anything on purpose. I did share the woods with David, though. He would come collect me when it was time for dinner. I would hide when I heard him crunching across the leaves, and he would act like he couldn't find me.

"Now, where is that kid?" David would say as I peered down from a tree I'd climbed. "I guess he'll miss out on Mom's meatloaf." He knew if he tempted me with Mom's food I would come running.

As we got older, David didn't come to the woods to find me as often. I figured he was struggling enough to find himself, so he stopped looking for me.

When David died, I spent two nights in the woods and came home early the third day because I knew his funeral was close. When I got home that morning, Dad was hunched over the table drinking coffee and Mom sat in the living room just staring at the blank television screen. I'd approached her and watched her for a second.

"Oh, honey, you scared me," Mom had said, sounding dazed. She wasn't even talking about me being gone, just me standing behind her and then touching her shoulder. My absence hadn't scared her because it went unnoticed. Neither she nor Dad knew I was even gone. That was the start of me becoming the invisible boy.

Looking at myself in the mirror, my clothes were disheveled and stained with mud and small fragments of leaves poked out from my hair. I looked skinny. More so than the two days prior it seemed because I hadn't brought that much food along except a bag of apples and a couple canteens of water. I stayed gone because I imagined that when I returned, it would have all been a dream and David would be back.

While I slept in my fox hole, I had dreamed that David stopped using drugs and that he and Dad and I played ball every day. We played catch until our hands were sore, and then David hit balls into the deep, snowy field where they would stay until spring and the weather warmed. In my dream, I could run and hit as well as David, and he noticed, smiling at me and giving me high fives. I ran across the snowy field after him, but I could never reach him. He was too far away, and the snow slowly piled over his head. David had stood there and smiled and I ran, slipping with every step and getting further away from him. Then, David's head was covered by snow, and he was gone.

I had jolted awake, covered in leaves, in a panic, trying to brush them off me. That's when I had run home to find that David's death was real and that my life would be changed forever.

When I Think About Talking

MONDAY ALWAYS CAME TOO FAST. I GRABBED TWO PIECES OF bread and spooned a scoop of peanut butter on each of them, then headed down the street to catch the bus across town. I almost didn't go. Staying home would have been so easy. I could have kept playing the game of skipping school and making excuses until they took me to truancy court. Then I could just tell the judge about David and how my parents had forgotten me. Maybe then I would get a new family. I could have skipped my classes without a second thought, like I had done in my previous school, but I was curious what would happen if I actually went. What crazy stuff would Mr. C have to say? Would I meet anyone else interesting? Nobody knew me or my secret yet, so I felt safe.

The bus dropped us off a block away from school, and I walked toward the building behind a group of boys that were all dressed in black and wearing eyeliner. A few were puffing on cigarettes, and they were listening to a boom box that one of them carried, which I thought was odd when everyone else had iPods. Punk music blasted out of the speakers as they walked, stuff I'd heard when I'd been curious who or what the Sex Pistols were. I'd found the band on the internet and had listened to their songs over and over, and that got me into the Ramones and Social Distortion and The Clash. It was good music, music that expressed my feelings of wanting to smash everything. I usually listened to my iPod while I walked the woods behind my house, singing to the trees while curling my lip like all the singers did, and took my anger out on rocks by battering them with big sticks, or I screamed out irrationally at the top of my lungs because I knew no one would be there to hear me. No one was ever in the woods it seemed.

These kids in front of me seemed cool though. I wondered if they were as angry as I was.

I guess I was walking too close to them because one of the kids swiveled around and said, "You want to just climb on my back? Give a little space!" He was tall and had jet-black hair along with painted black fingernails. Thick, black eyeliner circled his eyes, something I had never seen before on a guy except for in pictures of old rockers.

I shrugged my shoulders and didn't respond to him, which must have been the right thing to do because he just smirked and turned up the music, "London Calling" by The Clash. I continued to follow them because they seemed to be into their music and didn't talk that much. They might have looked threatening, but anyone that stayed quiet wasn't a threat to me.

Trailing them in silence, I wished I could tell someone why I didn't talk, but I think people felt too uncomfortable to ask me, so they just avoided me. Even Mom and Dad never really asked me. They'd just put me in therapy. I hadn't said much to the therapist and wound up on medication, which was the cure for everything, I guess. To me, the meds were just a Band-Aid for the real problems, and anyone who wanted me on them was just avoiding my problems, or convincing me to avoid them. They clouded my mind and let everyone else ignore my pain and my silence. I figured they made Mom and Dad feel like they were helping and assured the clinical therapist that they'd cured me.

Still, I didn't think meds were bad for everyone. I wished David would have taken antidepressants. Maybe he would still be alive. My best friend in fourth grade took meds a couple of times per day just to sit still and listen to the teacher for more than five minutes. He was always getting pulled out of class and taken to another room down the hall, the one all of us kids knew as "the special room," and they'd keep him there most of the day. I always hated it when they pulled him out of the classroom. It didn't seem to help, and it just made him look different. His name was Charlie. He died too, just like David did, except he hung himself by his belt in his closet. His death hadn't made me stop talking, but instead, I'd started talking more and louder than ever, interrupting the teacher several times per class period until I started getting pulled out of the classroom too. That's when I stopped sleeping.

David was the one who stuck up for me. He'd notice the change in me when I took the medication. I'd start telling him no or ignoring him entirely whenever he'd ask to play ball. I would never forget the day in December when he came into my room, gently laid my baseball glove in my lap, and told me, "You're not alone in this." I had looked up at David and saw tears in his eyes. "I'm your brother. Let me help." Then, David snatched my pills, and I'd followed him to the bathroom where he flushed the entire bottle down the toilet. "C'mon," he'd said with a nudge as I numbly watched the pills spiral away. "Let's play ball." I grabbed my glove and forced a smile on my face. We lost twelve balls in the snow that day. After running around and getting breathless from the cold, my head had started to clear. David gave me hope.

The kids in all black sauntered into the school building, still playing the music. Some of the jocks shot them dirty looks while a few of the popular girls just snickered and whispered. They didn't turn the music off until a teacher told them to. I continued to follow them closely until the tall kid who had talked to me on the sidewalk turned and smiled at me. "See you around, kid." He turned down the hallway where most of the senior classes were. He seemed like a nice guy, or at least didn't mind that I hadn't said anything to him.

I walked down the hall toward the library and peeked in from the outside window. The librarian was there behind her desk, standing guard. I wanted to see the old books again.

"Returning to the scene of the crime?" a voice said from behind me. It was Mr. C. "It's too risky now," he warned me in a hushed tone. "We would get caught for sure. She's on alert. Best to just slowly walk away and go to first hour." The librarian had turned toward us and glowered. Mr. C just grinned and gave her a little wave. She ignored his gesture.

I was glad to see Mr. C again. He did so much talking that I knew I wouldn't have to. As I walked with him to my first hour, he asked me the normal questions: "How was your weekend?" and "Did you do anything fun?" I just shrugged. "Silence is golden," he remarked. I looked at him strangely but had to smile. "Yeah, it's corny, but it's meaningful." I found myself wanting to talk to him, to tell him why I was silent and ask all the questions I had for him. But I was scared. It was safer to stay quiet. I could control who entered my world.

My second day was a lot like my first, and my secret stayed safe. I pretty much made myself invisible, so the kids and teachers more or less ignored me. Lunch sucked, again. I sat in a corner just outside the cafeteria where teachers walked by, students walked by, and nobody said a thing.

I saw the guys from that morning when getting on the bus to go home, and the tall one actually nodded his head at me before they started playing "Prison Bound" by Social Distortion as loud as their radio could muster. I knew every word. I'd listened to that song a hundred times. My whole world had become a prison since David died, both in my house and inside my head, and I desperately wanted to steal the key to my cell and escape.

Questions

SO MANY QUESTIONS SOUNDED OFF IN MY HEAD ALL THE TIME. They screamed at me over and over, as if I knew the answers.

Why did David have to die?
Will I want to talk again?
Why am I so scared all the time?
Will Mom and Dad ever love me again?
Will Mom and Dad ever love each other again?
Should I run away?
Should I hurt myself?
Will I ever be happy?
What will I do when I'm older?
Will I ever have friends?
Will I ever have a girlfriend?

I could only respond to my questions with a shrug, and the realization that I didn't have any idea where to start finding the answers made me sick with anger. After everything, I just wanted to be accepted and understood, to get over myself enough to go out of my head and do something important. My questions would never be answered as long as I would not and could not ask them. In the end, when the frustration buzzed through my head and the anger twisted my gut, I knew I had to calm myself down. I pulled the tiny razor from my pocket and pierced my skin, pulling the razor shallowly over my forearm. The blood bloomed from the little cut and trickled to my wrist, and it was warm, oddly soothing, dissipating my anger.

It was just one more secret to keep, hidden under my long sleeves from the rest of the world.

Keeping Fish Alive

I WAS LISTENING TO MY PARENTS TALK FROM MY ROOM. THEY were in the kitchen and must have thought I was asleep since my light was off. They started to blame each other for David's death.

"You enabled him and let him do whatever he wanted," my dad said sternly to my mom.

Mom yelled, "You!" and then lowered her voice, "You were too tough on him. He felt trapped."

Neither one of them said David's name while they were talking about him. I curled my knees to my chest tightly as my anxiety started to grow. David's death wasn't their fault. It was mine. I just couldn't tell them that.

Eventually, they stopped blaming one another and became silent. They went to David's room like they did every night. David's room was exactly as it was when he died. The bed was unmade, his video games were scattered around the floor, his baseball trophies still stood like monuments on the shelf, and his fish were alive and swimming. Mom and Dad obsessed over keeping those fish alive. It was the only thing that they agreed on anymore. They took turns cleaning the tank and feeding them. Mom did it in the morning, and Dad did it at night. They had a checklist next to the tank that they signed with the date and time when they finished. They'd even added a couple of new fish to the tank and a small white sailboat that lay on the blue rock at the bottom.

I heard Dad talk to the fish through my wall, saying, "You're the fastest little fish I've ever seen. I bet you're the fastest of all the fish." He talked to them, and then he cried.

I always felt like a witness. That's what happens when you stop speaking. I hated witnessing things because most things made me sad. Through the wall, I heard Mom start to talk to Dad, and then she said it. She used the dreaded "d" word, one of the worst words in the teenage vocabulary.

"I think we need to divorce. I'm not happy, and you're not happy." Dad was still crying. Mom continued, "We continue to blame each other, and we can't heal if we're together."

After she said that, I started crying too, but for perfectly selfish reasons. Suddenly, I had to worry about who I would live with and whether I would have to switch schools again. I didn't think for one second about their feelings and how they were losing their love. I just wasn't ready to think about that yet.

My anxiety kept climbing until I freaked out. I ran into David's room and stood, staring at them both. "I hate you! I fucking hate you!" Even as I spoke, I realized that I wasn't screaming at Mom or Dad, but at my dead brother who'd left me. I took David's baseball bat that he always had laying against the wall next to his bed and did the most hurtful thing I could think of. I smashed the fish tank. The fish came streaming out one by one. The boat fell to the floor, and all the blue pebbles tumbled over it. All I could do was sit on the floor, shaking, the bat still in my hand, as the fish flopped around. "I hate you!" I kept shouting over and over, then laughed as Mom and Dad struggled to catch the flopping fish. "Let them die! You let everything else die!" It was the first time they had heard my voice this loud in months. I didn't even realize that I'd let my guard down until Dad lifted me and threw me onto the bed. Then I went quiet again.

They only saved one fish, the blue neon guppy. I knew all of David's fish, and this one he'd actually named after me. He thought it was funny to call his pet fish Neil. I wondered if Mom saved that one on purpose. Did she think the fish represented me in some way? Was she trying to save another son? Who knew, but either way, that damn fish swam around in the Tupperware bowl like nothing had happened.

Dad couldn't look at me, but on his way out of the room, he said, "David would have never done this to you."

What he couldn't know was that I didn't do it to hurt David. I did it to hurt myself. I killed those fucking fish to hurt Mom and Dad the only way I knew how. Those very words almost came out of my mouth, but before they could, my throat froze and I was back to silence. Mom walked past me and went towards the kitchen. Dad left the house, and through David's bedroom window, I watched his car drive away. I'd failed. Killing the fish didn't convince them to worry about me or get them to understand how I felt. It was just one more thing that made me the weird kid who wouldn't talk and, now, who had killed his dead brother's fish. I was sure a psychological evaluation was next. They would want to numb my head with medication, and this time, David wouldn't be here to protect me.

The Shrink

I WAS RIGHT. THE NEXT DAY, MOM KEPT ME OUT OF SCHOOL and scheduled an appointment for me to see a psychologist. I knew all the questions that he was going to ask, so I thought I would mess with the shrink's mind. I let him hear my voice:

"Neil, did you want to hurt the fish?"

"Yes, they were yelling at me," I said with a straight face.

"The fish were yelling?" He scribbled notes on his yellow notepad, so I knew I had him going.

"Yes, they were saying awful things and making threats." I could hardly contain my laughter.

"What kind of threats?"

"They said they would smother me in my sleep." This was way too easy. "They said they would jump down my throat and suffocate me."

The psychologist paused, looking at the scars on my arms, and asked calmly, "Do you want to hurt yourself?"

"Not now that the fish are dead. I thought maybe hurting myself would stop them from hurting me." This was getting bizarre, and I almost regretted starting this conversation, but it was fun.

"Okay. I need to speak to your mom in private."

The shrink and Mom were in his office for about ten minutes before they called me back in.

"Neil, we are putting you in the hospital for further evaluation and more intense therapy." The shrink was still scribbling in his notepad, offering no eye contact. "You will also start a round of medication."

"Bullshit!" I yelled. "I was just kidding."

"Honey, it's what's best," Mom said soothingly, rubbing my back. "When you get out, you will feel better."

"No!" I insisted. "*You* will feel better. Dad will feel better. You'll have another son out of your lives and can do whatever you want."

With that, I abruptly stopped talking again. Part of me wished I could really let them have it, but as my heart pounded and the fear crept in, so did the silence. It was my only defense.

I had never been to the hospital to stay, and I didn't know what to expect. The car ride over was quiet except for the low static of the radio and the sounds of me fiddling anxiously with the strings on my hoodie. The hospital was in the middle of the city, close to the university campus. College students were walking around with their headphones and backpacks, looking content, like they knew they were headed someplace.

We pulled into patient parking, and from the car, I looked up at the tall building. As we walked toward the hospital, patients stood near the entrance smoking in their robes and gowns and doctors were talking on their cell phones. I didn't resist going in. Maybe the mental ward was where I belonged.

We walked through the automatic revolving door, and Mom said, "This is for your own good."

No. This is for your own good and Dad's own good, and you don't think about what's good for me at all. My mouth didn't say it, but my eyes did.

Maybe going away would be a good break from my life. I was sick of having a day-to- day routine that didn't involve David. Simply walking past his bedroom door was giving me panic attacks. Mom and Dad could figure things out without me and start to love each other again. My absence could make them face each other and solve their problems. The hospital might actually be the best place for me. I could just eat and read and stay away from people. As the elevator crept up to the ninth floor, I chuckled.

"This isn't funny, Neil," Mom said and shook her head. I wasn't laughing at the situation. I was laughing because they put a psychiatric unit, where patients are crazy or suicidal, on the ninth floor of the hospital. Why not just put them on the top of the building and tell them to jump?

The shrink met us just as the elevator opened to the psychiatric unit. His dedication to committing me to the hospital surprised me. He helped Mom check me in and then went to talk with another shrink and the nurses. Mom had my blue duffel bag with her. When she saw me staring at it, she said, "It's just a few pairs of jeans, a sweatshirt, and some underwear and t-shirts. I put a couple of your books in there too." What a bitch! She had my bag packed before I even went to my appointment. She knew that I would be coming here. It must have been her plan to get rid of me. I wondered if Dad had anything to do with it. The last time I saw him, he'd picked me up and thrown me on the bed. At that moment, I hated them both.

Mom handed me the bag and gave me a hug. "Be honest with them, sweetheart. Tell them how you feel. When you get home, things will be different." Without anything more than that, she disappeared into the elevator. I felt abandoned. Mom and Dad had already abandoned me emotionally after David died, but this time, I was left with strangers that wore a lot of blue and white and carried notepads and smiled too much.

"Hi, Neil. I'm Peter." When I looked behind me, a man wearing jeans and a flannel shirt was standing there. He was a few inches taller than me, with broad shoulders and a scruffy beard. He looked like he should be in the Northwoods cutting down trees. I shook his hand and didn't say anything. "That's cool. I heard you don't like to talk. We can keep things relaxed, but I will need you to talk to me if I am going to help you, whether that's spoken or in writing." I just shrugged my shoulders, which had become a habit whenever someone asked me questions or wanted to talk. A shrug meant nothing and everything at the same time, and people could interpret it however they wanted. "I bet you have strong shoulders with all that shrugging." Peter just winked and motioned for me to follow him.

He showed me the dayroom, where there was a television, a sofa, three cushioned chairs scattered around the room facing every direction, and five small, round tables with blue chairs around them. Then he took me to the nurses' desk and showed me where to pick up my meds each morning and the area where patients ate breakfast, lunch, and dinner. Everything was clean and white, except for the cheesy artwork of oceans that hung on the walls.

"This is where you'll meet for Group each morning," said Peter. He'd led me to a small room with beanbags and large pillows covering the floor. "We like to keep things on the floor," he laughed. "It gets everyone on the same level and helps people let their guard down."

That was all well and good, but it wouldn't work on me. My

guard sure wasn't coming down, and my silence would take a lot more than beanbag chairs and a cozy atmosphere to conquer. Whatever they wanted from me, my voice was only mine to hear.

We followed the long, shiny, narrow hallway past a row of closed doors and stopped at another room. "This will be your room. You will also have individual therapy in here." I just peeked my head in. I didn't want any therapy. "I will come and see you at ten o'clock every morning, and we'll meet for about forty-five minutes."

I just shrugged at first, but then my curiosity pried open that tight, anxious grip on my vocal cords. I had to ask, "You're a shrink?" At that, Peter just laughed. He sure didn't look like any kind of doctor. He wore jeans and didn't have a tie on. *What kind of hospital is this? How long will I be stuck here?* "That wasn't so hard, was it?" I just looked at him. "For you to talk to me," he said. Shit! I'd let my guard down. It wouldn't happen again.

"Neil, just one more thing. As part of our check-in, I need to take your shoelaces, belt, and the string from your hoodie," said Peter. I stood, unmoving, as I pondered his request. Then, it suddenly hit me that he was taking everything from me that I could hang myself with. I gasped. If I could have destroyed every rope, belt, shoelace, wire, and string in our house, maybe David would still be alive. I slowly took the belt, which was David's, from my pants and looked at the holes that I had cut into the leather in order for it to fit me. I was hesitant to hand it over.

I slowly gave the belt to Peter. He did not take it from me and instead placed his large hand in front of mine, palm up, for me to put the belt in it. Everything went in a plastic bin with my name on it. Peter paused, taking a long look at me. "I want to get you to a place in your life where no one will ever worry about you having a belt around your waist again."

Peter left me alone in my room, and the silence was dreary. The room was drab. There was a bed with a white blanket draped across its entirety and one white pillow. Another painting of an ocean, one that looked like a five-year-old could have painted, hung on the wall facing the bed. There was a small, wooden dresser with two drawers next to the bed and a desk that must have been donated from a local school. A big window broke up the white wall with a view of all the people below, scrambling around the surface, living their lives. I laughed as I looked at them and wondered what their secrets were. We all had them. They looked so peaceful way down below, even as they rushed to wherever they were going. I saw business people trying to rule the world and make money and college students with their hormones getting in the way of their studies. Did those students have dreams that someday they would have the perfect spouse, the perfect kid, and live in the perfect house in the suburbs? Did they realize that it could all turn in a heartbeat and their dreams would become memories? It takes a lot of patience and hard work to try to make dreams come true, and then it takes one moment, a whisper, to rip those dreams apart. I think it's God testing us. He wants to see what we're made of and if we can survive the turmoil that life makes us partake in. God must love us and put up with a lot of our shit, but He must be disappointed at the same time.

I went and lay on the bed and stared intently at the blue ocean of paint that hung forlornly across the room from me. I started thinking about the journey I've been on to be lying here, right now, in a bed on the psychiatric unit of the hospital. The painting must have done its job because I drifted off to sleep.

Suddenly, I woke up to a knock on my door and a voice saying, "Dinnertime." The light from the hallway came streaming into my room, disorienting me. Half-asleep, my first thought was, *This isn't my room* . . . and for a moment, I was sure the light must have been David ready to show himself to me. Was he in heaven? If anyone deserved to pass into heaven, it was David. I had chills as I looked out into the bright hallway, and then Peter stepped into the doorway. He was so big that he blocked the light from coming into my room.

"Let's go, Neil. You must be hungry," he said. "It's your first night with us, and some people want to meet you. I snuck in some pizza." Peter left the doorway, allowing the hall light to enter again, and walked toward the dayroom.

The last thing I wanted was to leave the confines of my room. The light from the streets and the cars below lit up my window, and I went and touched the cool glass. It was a long way down. It didn't look like it would take much to break the window and just jump. Mom and Dad would be free to live their lives then, and they could move on and be happy, maybe move to a different state and start over. I cried at the thought. Then, a shadow came through the doorway. When I turned around, a tall, thin kid was standing there. His brown, wavy hair was disheveled, and he wore jeans and a Nirvana t-shirt.

"Can I help you?" I whispered.

"You the new kid?" he asked.

"Yeah, came in today. My mo . . ." I began to tell him that I was dropped off by my mom when he turned and walked out. Shit! Again, I'd talked and let my guard down. Fuck my brain! I wasn't thinking right, and I hadn't even started the meds yet. But then again, what kind of kid just walks away in the middle of a conversation?

The smell of pizza was trickling in, and I decided to see what was going on in this place. Peter had made me curious, and so did the tall kid that disappeared from my door. I walked into the dayroom, and about fourteen other kids were gathered around the small tables that were pushed together. The kids were ignoring each other, scarfing down pizza and watching TV like being in the hospital was their home away from home. I looked around, and in one corner, the staff sat in a circle around a table. Everything was in a circle. There was no place to hide.

Peter looked over at me and motioned for me to come sit next to him. "Everyone, this is Neil. He joined us today." He dropped his heavily muscled arm over my shoulders. It felt like a tree branch, anchoring me down. "Neil has a lot to say, but not with words, so ask him what you want and accept what you get." A few of the kids ignored this, and the rest fixed their stares on me for a minute before turning back to their pizza. Peter glanced down at me and winked, then asked me quietly, "You okay, buddy?"

David used to call me that. I just nodded my head and reached for a slice of pizza. I looked around for the boy who had showed up in my room, but I didn't see him. Then, laughter erupted from where the staff sat in the corner, and I glanced over to see the boy sitting with them, talking and waving his hands like he was in the middle of a story. The staff was transfixed on him, and he must've been a good storyteller because they couldn't stifle their laughter. Then, as his story ended, he stood and walked out of the room without another word. From the way they kept laughing, the staff didn't seem to think anything of his abrupt exit.

I grabbed my piece of pizza and followed the boy. I knew why

I would've left the conversation, but I wondered why he would abandon being the center of attention without any hesitation or fanfare. I paced the entire psychiatric unit, peering in every room that I passed, until finally I came to a room with wall-to-wall books. There he was, reading. He flipped through the pages quickly and mouthed the words he read in silence. I couldn't believe that he was reading as fast as it looked; he had to be skimming over most of it.

Then, as abruptly as he'd stalked out of the room just before, he said aloud, "Do you believe Nietzsche when he said, 'To live is to suffer, to survive is to find some meaning in the suffering'?"

I was intrigued by what he was saying, especially how fast he was saying it. The words came out of his mouth at a speed faster than I've ever heard anyone talk. Actually, I had read that quote before, and the sentiment haunted me.

The boy continued, "Is that what we're doing here? Are we looking for meaning in our suffering? Can there possibly be any meaning in hurt?" I just shrugged, but he exclaimed, "Exactly!" He got to his feet and hurried toward me as I stood, frozen, and then he grabbed my shoulders. "Of course, a shrug is correct. Who the fuck knows anything? And the minute that someone thinks they do, a shrug can question them. A shrug makes them think more clearly, makes them question themselves." He continued, speaking with incredible velocity. "A shrug is everything! A shrug is the only thing that is truly real and honest, and honesty is the only thing that matters."

Then, without another word, he brushed past me out of the room, leaving the book on the chair. I picked it up and placed it back on the shelf. Books were sacred. They needed their homes. Ever since

I was little, I'd thought that a book by itself was lonely and needed to be next to other books. All of those words and titles and stories needed company. Once I put the book where it belonged, I headed back to the dayroom, wondering if the boy had gone there.

The other kids had the pizza eaten by the time I got there, and now that it was gone, the kids focused their attention on me. Some of them wore hospital clothes, blue pants and loose blue shirts, and others were in street clothes like me. A couple of kids had their wrists and arms bandaged. Some had no expressions whatsoever, looking numbed, like darkness had taken over them. It suddenly amused me, and I laughed aloud. No one really knew what to do with us, so all different kinds of crazy kids wound up lumped together.

"What the hell are you laughing at?" A girl ran up and stood in my face. Her arms were wrapped in white bandages. She had piercings in her eyebrows and nose, and about three more in her lip. I wondered how she could speak so clearly with those.

"You're the mute motherfucker that don't speak?"

I still had no response.

"Tiffany, lay off!" Peter called from across the dayroom. Tiffany walked away and gave me the finger. I guess I knew why she was here.

I went and sat down in one of the cushioned chairs. I didn't want Tiffany thinking that she intimidated me.

"Don't let her bother you." I looked up to see the boy from before standing above me. He'd changed his shirt from Nirvana to Alice In Chains and noticed me looking at it. "Cool band from the nineties," he remarked, then asked, "You know grunge?" I nodded. "Who's your favorite?"

I whispered, "Pearl Jam."

He grinned and told me the song "Jeremy" could have been written about him.

Well, shit. *Wait, this kid didn't actually kill a bunch of kids, right?* I wondered. *Or did he?* He must have seen the panic flash across my face because he said, "Don't worry, I didn't shoot anyone. I just went off on a bully and put him in the hospital. He's probably in this hospital as we speak." My eyes widened, and he continued, "I didn't really know what I did. He kept pushing me and then spit in my face. I just went off and wouldn't stop hitting him. His jock buddies jumped me, but the high school counselor pulled them off." Then, something happened that I didn't expect. Tears welled up in his eyes. "I hate it when I get that way. They tell me I was manic."

"How long are you here?" I stammered, hoping it would get him to stop crying.

"Been here a week so far. I have one more to go."

Suddenly, a burly shadow appeared next to the boy. It was Peter. "I see you've met Travis." Peter slung his arm around Travis's shoulder. They were close to the same height, but Travis was much thinner. "Travis knows the ropes around here," Peter commented as he looked down at me.

"This is my home away from home," Travis said, rubbing his eyes. "I come here to rest until I can calm down enough to go back to school. Not that I'm in any hurry to go back to that place. I can learn more from my books."

Peter laughed. "Yeah, but my brother would miss you." Travis didn't comment, but he cracked a smile. "You two should get some sleep. We'll meet for Group at seven in the morning." Peter cleaned up the pizza boxes and headed toward the front of the psych unit. I glimpsed at some new staff members coming in to change shifts, and when I looked back, Travis was gone. I thought about what Peter had said about Travis knowing the ropes. Would I know the ropes here someday? The thought horrified me.

Group

THE SMELLS OF EGGS, CITRUS, AND LATEX NUDGED ME AWAKE the next morning. As my eyes adjusted to the daylight, I noticed Travis staring at me through the open doorway.

"You know, I can talk for you at Group if you want. There really is no pressure. But you have a voice, and it should be heard." Before waiting to see if I would reply, he walked away, leaving the door open.

I just met this guy, and he wants to hear what I have to say? That's more meaningful than anything my parents have said to me since David's death. But I'm not sure if I'm ready to let him hear my thoughts yet.

I walked down the hall toward the cafeteria, following the smell of overcooked eggs and oatmeal. I wasn't sure if I could ever get used to the whiteness of the floor blending with the walls. My pale skin seemed to fuse with the wall and floor, making me feel invisible. I wasn't hungry, but I took a scoop full of eggs anyway. The medication that they gave me made my stomach upset without food. I sat down at a round table that was empty and within one minute I forced myself to eat the eggs and then got up and put my plate in the tub that held other dirty dishes.

Moving towards the dayroom, I noticed a sign at the entrance that said, "Be prepared to express yourself." Suddenly, I panicked, and I couldn't catch my breath. Everything started to move around me really fast, and I wanted to run, but I couldn't. Where would I go? My woods were out of reach. Would they try to make me speak? Would they find out about David? Would they ask about my mom and dad? The world was closing in on me.

"Don't worry." Travis was standing next to me. "Peter isn't the type that will make you speak. No one can make you speak. Your voice is yours. However, Peter may make you *want* to speak." He gave me a gentle nudge on my shoulder, and I followed him to the beanbags that lay in a circle and sat down next to him. He had a book in his hand called *The Painted Bird* by Jerzy Kosiński. I had never heard of it, or the author. Travis just smiled when he saw me looking at the cover. "It will change your life."

"How?" I whispered. It wasn't that I didn't believe books could change your life. I did. I just needed a life change, and I wanted to know how this book could make that happen.

"It's about a boy who gets abandoned by his parents and left on his own. It's about survival in a shit world. Need I say more?" Travis's wide grin showcased dimples and perfectly white teeth. He sunk into his beanbag even more and said, "I wonder where everyone else is?"

Peter showed up moments later with two other kids. They looked younger, probably in middle school. I guess being messed up has no age limit. As I studied the two boys and Travis, I wondered what in their lives made them the way they were. They didn't just start acting crazy one day. There had to be some significant event, like your brother hanging himself.

Peter was wearing the same jeans and red flannel shirt as the previous day, and his hair was disheveled, like he had stayed the night.

He sat on the floor with a cup of coffee in hand. "I would like to start with introductions," he said. "Travis, can you get us started?"

Travis sat up straight, glanced my way, and winked before clearing his throat. "I am Travis, reader of books and obsessive-compulsive smart-ass." I started laughing, which made Travis grin. "See, you do have something to say."

"He didn't say anything," countered one of the middle school kids.

"Laughter says everything," said Travis. He glanced back at me. "Today's youth. What will we do?"

I was beginning to like Travis. He was someone that I could share my woods with. In many ways, Travis reminded me of David with how he showed interest in me and who I was, and it felt like forever since that had happened. He had a sincerity in his words that made me want to share mine.

"Let's keep it rolling," said Peter, looking over at one of the younger boys and nodding.

"My name is Darius. I'm here because my parents are assholes." Darius had scars on his arms that resembled hashtags, long hair that fell to the middle of his back, and a tiny scar on his right cheek that was the shape of a small question mark.

"Thank you, Darius. We will talk about the assholes in your life in a moment," said Peter.

The next boy introduced himself. "I am Hell." Peter's attention slowly went to his clipboard.

"Do you mean you are the devil?" asked Travis. "Because I have some things to discuss with you."

Peter gave Travis a stare that said, "Knock it off," then he looked back down at his information and said, "Hal, nice to meet you." I guess Hal had trouble pronouncing words. Did they start putting you in mental institutions for not being able to talk right? Shit, I'll never get out of here.

"I'm here for jumping in front of a car on the highway." Except when Hal talked, it sounded like he said he was "humping an ant all the way." No one laughed after Peter repeated what Hal said.

"Since three of you are new here, Travis, maybe you could start us out by sharing your story." Peter put down his notepad, and his gaze went directly to Travis.

"You've heard it all, Peter," said Travis. "I'm not sure what else I have to say." He was rubbing the cover of his book with his thumbs like it gave him comfort. I just sat there, staring at Travis and waiting for a response.

"I am always happy to hear what's on your mind," said Peter.

"You sound like your brother," Travis replied. Peter just smiled and waited. "Well, I've been coming here for four years. It's my comfort place. The hospital gives me a special deal since my dad is in charge. I am an embarrassment to him, but I leave him alone and he leaves me alone." Travis smelled the cover of his book, and his right knee continuously shook.

"Tell us about your books," said Peter. "Tell us about how you cope."

"Cope? I cope by coming here and talking to you and not being judged. I cope by putting myself around people who are crazier than I am." Travis placed the book to his forehead as tears formed in his eyes. "I cope by reading stories about people who are like me. The words become me, and the characters are my friends."

"That's gay," said Darius.

"Look, you little fecal matter," said Travis in a calm, ominous voice.

Peter stepped in. "We do not do that crap here." He turned to Darius. "We respect each other or say nothing at all."

Group went on for about an hour. I didn't say anything, but Travis was right. Peter did make me want to talk. There was something about how relaxed and welcoming he was. He made me feel like I was normal for not wanting to talk, and Travis was normal for calling the book characters his friends, and Darius was normal for being a dick and cutting himself, and Hal was normal for jumping in front of the car on the highway. He didn't judge Darius for saying he wanted to kill his family or when Hal said that he wanted to run away to live in the Shire. Peter just accepted all of it without judgment.

Peter accepted me when he said, "Neil, good job today." I didn't say anything during the entire session. How could I have done anything good? "The world needs listeners, and I know the boys appreciated it."

I was a listener, but I didn't always listen close enough. Maybe David had said something that I didn't hear. There must have been something that would have warned me about his suicide. Perhaps he told me exactly what he was going to do and my ears betrayed me.

Coincidence

THE WORLD WAS TRULY STRANGE TO ME. I WAS UNSURE OF MY place in it, and I was scared as hell to find out. How could life get any worse? When I heard how Travis found friendship through characters from his books, I understood. When Darius said he wanted to kill his parents, I understood. I didn't actually want to kill my parents, but I sometimes wished they were out of my life because I knew they could never forgive me, or each other. It frightened me to think about Hal. I have thought about ending my life, but jumping in front of a car was stupid. Cars can swerve and miss, and two people died trying to avoid hitting Hal. That wasn't fair to their families or to Hal. Self-pity can also be damaging. I have never believed in feeling sorry for myself, but sometimes I wished things could be different. I wished that David were alive. I wished that my mom and dad loved each other. I wished that they loved me. I wished I could find the courage to talk again. I so desperately wanted friends and to communicate with people, but it honestly petrified me.

This was my second night at the hospital, and the medication was making my mind dull and my stomach turn. I found Travis with his friends, lost in a book and blocking out the world. I knocked on the open door.

Travis was reclining on two large pillows against the headboard of his bed and looked up. "Come in." I took a few steps into his room. His comforter was out of place compared to the normal hospital blankets. It was thick and dark red with two pillows with red cases. It felt warmer than the other rooms, and a few paintings decorated the walls, all of them initialed T.R. The six portraits were of a young man's face, thin with high cheekbones, and a dark blue background. The faces all had tints of orange and bright yellow, and the eyes were blindfolded. Gray tape was painted over the mouths. There wasn't any hair on the heads and no ears. The faces gave me chills because of the sadness they seemed to portray. A shelf of books and a recliner sat in the corner, and an antique lamp was perched on a table next to them.

"Nice room," I whispered. Sometimes when I talked, I was surprised that my voice even worked. "How come it's different?"

Travis shut his book and smiled. "Like I said earlier, my dad is in charge, and this is my second home. This is where I rest and escape. It's where my dad 'suggests' I go so he can have a break. Where do you escape?"

I was not sure I was ready to let Travis enter my world of silence. It seemed too risky. I just shrugged. Travis grinned and said, "Neil, it's okay if you don't want to talk. I just think that you probably have a lot to offer through words. If not aloud, at least be brave enough to put your words on paper."

Whenever I looked at Travis, I sometimes became stuck in thought. It was strange to me that this boy was considered nuts. He seemed like he was just a handsome, most likely popular boy who all the girls would like.

"Does your dad make you come here?" I asked.

"No. He knows that it helps me get back to the most normal self that I am capable of that meets his standards. The bastard is really abusing his position and privilege." Travis eased back further on his pillows. "When I graduate next year, I'll be on my own."

"Won't you still come here?" I asked.

"Nope. I'll be eighteen in May and can no longer come to the juvenile unit. I'll have to go with the old crazies." He laughed.

I thought of my own destiny. Would I be here when I turned eighteen? Would they send me to live with the adult crazies someday? I would do anything to prevent that from happening.

"Peter's brother is the one who got me connected with Peter. He's the counselor at my school."

"Where do you go?" I asked, my voice still a rough whisper, but clear enough.

"I go to Memorial."

My eyes must have shot from my head.

Travis smiled. "That's about as excited as I've seen you yet."

"I go there," I said. "Well, I just started."

"Cool! We can see each other again. I'll be here a couple more days. I'm feeling pretty good now, and my dad is ready for me to return home."

I nodded, then a moment of clarity washed over me. "Is Peter's brother Mr. C?" I asked.

"The one and only," said Travis.

Visitors

I WAS IN MY ROOM, LOOKING OUT MY WINDOW AT THE TINY, moving bodies below, when I heard them at my door.

"Hello, honey," said Mom. Peter told me they were coming. I had not heard anything from her since she dropped me off three days ago. Did she expect me to run to her in tears and have some Hallmark moment? I continued to look out the window without acknowledging them.

Tears were in her eyes as she looked around the room. Dad was different. His face seemed hardened like he despised being there, and he just glanced my way and nodded. I knew then that I had lost him. Those moments in life when a relationship, a love, vanishes have always baffled me. Was it a buildup of hurt, sadness, and anger over a long period of time that made someone say, "Enough is enough? It's time for me to let you go"?

"I heard that you're doing well and that you've made a friend," said Mom. "That's great, sweetheart."

She was trying to make being in a psychiatric unit a great thing, like it was where I belonged. I wanted to congratulate her for getting rid of me. The thought of her telling me that I was doing well made me want to kill more fish and scream out irrationally, really let them hear my voice. All of my emotions and aggression had built up to a near breaking point.

Then Travis came walking in. His smile was big, and his dimples sunk into his cheeks so much that you could probably stick the eraser end of a pencil inside them and it would hold the pencil in place. But it was Travis's eyes that stood out. They gleamed with a deep-blue confidence that begged you to look at them.

"Hello." He stuck his hand out to my dad, giving him a firm handshake. "You must be Neil's dad." His eyes twinkled as he turned towards Mom. "And this young lady must be your mother, Neil." Shaking Mom's hand, he invited them to the dayroom for coffee. Travis just winked at me as they followed him. Both Mom and Dad had the same mesmerized look that I had when I first met Travis.

The dayroom was empty since it was early morning. I wondered if my parents decided to visit me at seven thirty on a Saturday because they figured no one would see them. Having one son that killed himself and another in the psych hospital could be a dagger to their ego as parents.

Travis poured coffee for my mom and dad and started the conversation. "Please sit down," he said. My dad took the chair furthest away from me. Travis continued, "You have a great son. He's a gifted reader and thinker. He's always carrying a book around, and we have a lot of thought-provoking conversations about similar books that we've read."

"That's wonderful," said Mom. Dad stayed quiet and just stared at Travis.

"Neil has helped so much in Group and . . ."

Mom stopped Travis. "I'm sorry, but are you the counselor?"

Travis laughed, and I couldn't help my chuckle actually sounding out instead of being held in. "No, ma'am. I'm Neil's friend, Travis."

When he said "friend," I took a quick, deep breath. I didn't have any friends. Travis put his arm around my shoulder. "We've gotten to know each other pretty well in a short amount of time."

"How?" said my dad.

"What do you mean?" Travis asked.

Dad leaned forward. "How the hell can you get to know him when he won't speak?"

Travis leaned back to get some space, but he kept his arm around me. "Neil speaks volumes. He has a voice even if he doesn't speak all the time, but he talks to me."

The last time that someone stuck up for me was when David told my dad that he was skipping his baseball game to come to my game instead. The times conflicted, and David wanted to be there. I still remember Dad freaking out at David, telling him he would blow a scholarship just to come and watch me. David was at my game. I hardly played and was walked at my only at bat, but he cheered me on.

Back in the dayroom, Dad sat back and folded his arms. I could tell he felt uncomfortable being there. The other kids started to come out of their rooms and got their medications and breakfast. "Is it time for you to eat? We can leave," said Mom. I just shrugged, giving them their out. I knew they wanted to go.

"See?" said Travis. "Neil just said so much with a shrug." I laughed, Mom looked puzzled, and Dad just mumbled and stood to leave.

I wouldn't see them again until Mom picked me up a few days later. It was scary for me to wonder if I would be better off just staying at the hospital, but I had three days left here, and I knew I could get through it. Travis was leaving, but I hoped our friendship would continue when we got back to school.

"Well, that was interesting," said Travis. "I love parents. They have sex, produce a baby, think it's cute for a few years, and then completely abandon him when things get tough." I just shrugged. Travis grinned. "Exactly!"

The Funeral

PETER SET UP AN APPOINTMENT FOR JUST THE TWO OF US TO talk. I wanted to talk, and I felt I had a lot to say, but I had no idea how to say it.

We met in Peter's office, a place I hadn't visited yet. His office was lit by lamps, which gave a calmer feel than the bright lights of the dayroom. We sat at a round table that had several fidget spinners, stress balls, colored pencils, and blank, white paper.

Peter gave me a journal. "Write anything," he said. "Communication happens in more ways than just speaking. Put down whatever you want."

I took the journal and studied it. The edges of the plain, black cover were smooth as I traced my finger along them. As I flipped the pages, the scent of fallen leaves drifted to my nose, which reminded me of my woods. Would all my thoughts fill them? How many paper cuts would the journal give me? How many cuts did I deserve? Would my blood on the sharp edges heal me?

"I thought we could do a quick activity," said Peter. "Let's just communicate by taking turns writing in your journal." He pulled the journal toward him and opened it, then wrote, "How does that sound?"

"Good," I wrote back.

"Do you want to start, or should I?" asked Peter.

"You," I wrote.

Peter held the pencil against his cheek and tapped it. Then he brought the pencil back to the paper. "Do you have a girlfriend?"

"No."

"Do you want one?"

"Not sure."

"Do you miss your parents?"

"I miss the thought of them."

"What do you mean?"

"I miss them as they used to be."

"Before your brother died?"

"Yeah. It was different then. They loved each other and seemed happy. Now they just fight."

"Tell me about David. Tell me your memory of him."

I wasn't sure where to start. My memory of David was not what I wished it was. I wanted to tell Peter, but first, I had a question. "Your brother is the counselor at my school, right? Mr. C?"

"Yeah, tell him you like me better the next time you see him," wrote Peter. "He's my big brother."

"He's cool. Different!"

"Seriously, he is a great guy and a great counselor. I talked to him this week, and he's concerned about you."

"He hardly knows me," I wrote.

"That's what makes him who he is. He's concerned about everyone, and he wants to help everyone. It can be his downfall sometimes. Hell, mine too I guess."

"Downfall?" I asked. "How is helping someone a downfall?"

"He's just more concerned about everyone else than himself. That can lead to a rewarding but draining existence. He's all heart."

I looked up at Peter and nodded, then brought my eyes back down to the blank space in the journal. Taking a deep breath, I put the pencil to the paper. "I'm ready to tell you about David now. About my memory of him." Peter gave a nod and patiently waited for me to start. I continued to write, "I remember finding him in the basement with the rope around his neck." I took deep breaths and paused. I had to compose myself and make sure that I only told him what everyone else knew about how David killed himself. I wasn't ready to tell him what only I knew. "Veins stuck out from his forehead, and his hands were still warm when I touched them."

I paused and glanced at Peter. He was staring at the words on the page. He put his arm around my shoulders and squeezed with his large hands. The pressure was reassuring, so I went on. "David was laying there." Shit! He was supposed to be hanging, but maybe Peter wouldn't think anything of it. I continued, "I remember the paramedics taking his body out of the basement in a zipped-up bag. I remember thinking that I saw the bag move, and I rushed towards the paramedics screaming that David was still alive. My mom grabbed me and hugged me and I kept screaming that he was alive. This is where my silence began. Dad hung onto David's hand through the bag and followed him to the ambulance. I remember getting into David's bed that night and hugging his blanket and pillow against my body as tight as I could while I just looked out the window. The stars were out, and I watched Orion until I fell asleep. The next morning, my dad yelled at me to get the hell out of David's room. That was when I knew it was over."

I stopped writing and glanced at Peter. He had tears in his eyes. Why? Why would he be crying? This was my pain. Maybe he was thinking about his own brother.

"Do you want to stop?" he asked out loud, breaking the silence.

"No," I wrote, bringing our words back to the paper.

Peter wrote, "Go ahead, but stop when you want to. I'll just sit here quietly."

I continued with my next memory. "It's all a blur," I wrote. "I don't remember what happened the next few days until his funeral came." I stopped again. I hated having a memory. I wished it could be erased. If I had no memory, then I might be happy, and I might be talking and living my life. If I couldn't remember, I might have friends and a family. But for now, my memory was like the smell of burnt hair. It stayed with me no matter how many times I tried to forget. Maybe I shouldn't forget. I picked up the pencil again.

"I remember sitting in the back of my aunt and uncle's car wondering why I was with them and not my parents. The trees swayed by the window in slow motion and moved as if they were waving to me. My cousin, Darren, just stared at me but didn't say anything. We pulled into the parking lot where David went to high school. A line of people crying and wearing suits and ties and dresses and baseball jerseys flooded outside from the commons and into the gym. It was a sea of people. I didn't want to leave the safety of the car, but my uncle pulled on my arm until I got up. Was David in there? What would he look like? The thought drilled through my head like a nail. Was David really in the school? It all seemed like a bad dream. I hadn't seen him since the basement." I stopped when we were interrupted by a knock on the door from one of the nurses.

"Peter, Dr. Hendricks is waiting for you. He said you're late for your meeting."

"Tell him that I will be late or will have to reschedule," said Peter. The nurse looked at me, the journal, and then back at Peter and realized he must have been serious. I had a feeling it was not the first time that he made a doctor wait while he worked with a kid. I liked Peter even more at that moment. The nurse quickly exited the room. "Go ahead, Neil. Keep writing," said Peter.

I visualized myself back at David's funeral, walking outside the high school with all those people looking at me as I approached the school doors. It felt like everyone was glaring at me, accusing me of not saving David's life. I felt guilty.

I started to write again. "I remember not being able to walk in and running to the side of the building where I was alone and crying. I felt like people were judging me for not entering the building right away and being by my family. I stayed outside for several minutes until David's friend Darrel came to get me. 'Everyone's inside waiting for you, Neil. We're not letting anyone in the gym until you get there. Come on now, you can walk with me.' Darrel put his arm around me and guided me toward the doors. He was David's best friend. He was a good athlete, like David, and tried to help him so many times. I wondered if he felt guilty too."

My eyes filled to the brim with warm tears. Peter rubbed my upper back, and I fell into him. He hugged me. The comfort of knowing that someone cared about me meant so much right at that moment. I sat back up and whispered, "I'm sorry." Peter motioned for me to keep writing, so I placed the pencil back to the paper.

"I entered the gym and immediately felt everyone turn to me.

Darrel still clung onto my shoulders and walked me right past Mom and Dad and up to David. He lay there in a brown casket wearing his baseball jersey, with his hair parted to one side, which he never did, on display for everyone to see. It made me angry and scared, and my vision blurred as my breathing increased rapidly. I pulled away from Darrel and reached for David's hand, hanging onto him, pulling myself close to his right ear. I whispered over and over, 'I'm sorry!'"

Dropping the pencil, I stood up and moved slowly away from the journal as if it were something dangerous, then collapsed to my knees. I was numb. Everything came to life on the paper. My words, my apologies were scribbled on fine-lined sheets of cream-colored paper that told my truth. I had every reason to be sorry. David's death was my fault, and I could not be convinced otherwise.

Travis

I HUNG OUT WITH TRAVIS A LOT OVER THE NEXT COUPLE OF days. We went to Group together and asked Peter if we could meet just the three of us and skip the one-on-ones. He agreed, saying, "This is for you, so it's whatever you need." My respect for Peter grew to the point where I wasn't sure if I wanted to leave him at the end of the week. Was this admiration why Travis kept coming back?

While spending all of this time with Travis, I found out some truths about him. He cannot read as fast as I thought. His mind doesn't stay still, so he just skims every page. Even then, he can tell you about every book he's ever read.

"I just read the first and last part of each paragraph and get an idea of what's going on," said Travis. "I figured out one time that I'm usually seventy percent accurate with what the story or characters are about. That's passing, right?" He smiled.

I think we all know how our own minds work and how we learn best, but most of us are afraid to stand up and do something when we are told to learn some other way that isn't beneficial to us. Travis could not sit in his classes and just listen to the teacher. He needed to page through the readings during class as fast as possible and then process what he had just read.

"It's just a snippet of history, a slice of life," he said.

We became inseparable the two days before Travis had to leave. We read selections from books to each other, talked about our parents, and Travis told me about a girl he had been seeing for some time. He described her as "a pain in the ass, with the spirit and beauty to make you want to better yourself." I don't know a lot about girls, but she sounded like someone I would want to know. I needed to better myself.

Travis and I even went to receive our meds together. That was always a good time. The nurse gave me Fluoxetine, which I found out was basically Prozac. I hated how it made me feel. My head became fuzzy, and my mouth turned dry. I kept having bizarre dreams, which Travis loved talking about. He told me about a dream he had where he let a hundred goats into the school and no one could ever catch them, so the school just let them stay. He said the goats ate everyone's homework so teachers stopped giving it. Cool dream!

Travis never told me the name of his meds, but he said it helped for the short term. As we sat down ready to eat piss-yellow eggs and pieces of dry toast that you had to put butter and jelly on to be able to chew, Travis said, "They give me something for ADHD, even though I'm bipolar, but this supposedly helps for both." He downed his pills, then ate some food. "What did you dream last night?" he asked. "The only cool thing about taking meds is the dreams. Everything else sucks, especially not being horny all the time. What's the use of being a teenager if you can't be horny?" I didn't know what to think. I thought about girls constantly, but I never really talked to anyone about it. "So, tell me about the dream," Travis commanded as he shoveled the strange shade of yellow eggs into his mouth.

I opened my mouth to talk, but nothing came out. Travis started laughing, and I laughed along with him before clearing my throat. It felt good to laugh at myself with someone who didn't judge me. I wasn't sure how he did it, but Travis got me to talk to him. I guess I just wanted a friend, and friends talk, though Travis wouldn't have cared if I just listened and shrugged or wrote down my thoughts instead. He was like that. "I had a dream I was in a rowboat and my brother was on shore looking at me and waving. He was wearing a Bob Marley shirt."

"I love it already," said Travis. "Go on."

"He waved for me to come to shore, but I couldn't. I didn't have any oars in the boat, and the boat was too heavy for me to paddle with just my hands." I cleared my throat again and drank some water to bolster my weak voice. This was the most I had said at one time since David died.

"Did you have a life vest?" asked Travis.

"No. I was in a suit and tie. There was a flower in my hand, and I reached out to offer it to David, but he was still on shore."

"That's messed up," Travis declared. "I wonder what the flower means. Maybe it's a symbol of your virginity."

We both laughed. I couldn't eat any more of the pee-colored eggs, so I pushed my plate aside. "Then, David came into the water and started to swim toward me. He just kept swimming, but he never reached me. I woke up sweating."

Travis didn't make any other comments except, "Maybe you need a different dose." He continued to devour his eggs, spilling a few pieces onto his Alice In Chains t-shirt.

"What's with all the Seattle sound music?" I asked. "I'm not judging it, I just want to know."

"Seattle sound? I'm impressed," he said. "My dad used to listen to it before his possessions became more important to him than life." He stopped eating. "I found all of his old CDs, concert stubs, and t-shirts in a trunk in the basement. I figured he kept them to remind himself of what he used to be. That is, until he met my mother. She has her needs."

I pulled a fidget spinner from my pocket that Peter had given me from his office and began twirling it on my index finger. "Why are you here?" I regretted the question as soon as I asked. I wanted Travis as my friend so badly, and I wanted him to still like me when we went back to school. I was afraid I just blew it.

"Can't you tell?" he asked. "That's why I like you so much, Neil. You see so much more than the rest of these idiots. Except for Peter, they all think I'm nuts."

I cleared my throat. "We're all a little nuts."

"If we're lucky," said Travis. "I would hate to be boring. It would suck to be like everyone else, conforming to their friends' standards. It makes me sick."

"Conforming?"

"Yeah, you see it. I know you do. Everyone tries to be like everyone else. Well, it's good to have a screw loose. I like being an individual. This is who I am. Like me for everything or nothing at all." Travis was so confident in himself. He truly did not care if anyone knew he was in the hospital or that he was bipolar. I wish I could have his ability to be comfortable in my own skin.

Travis checked out two days later. He left everything in his room for his next visit, then went around in his Soundgarden shirt and torn jeans and shook the staff's hands and hugged Peter. I hoped that I would see him when I got back to school and that he would still want to have our talks. I needed someone to tell my dreams to. He didn't say goodbye to me, but when I went back to my room, a note and a faded Pearl Jam t-shirt and CD sat on my bed. The note read, "Don't conform!" On the CD was a post-it that said, "Listen to this CD starting with 'Release' and then we'll talk later." That was all I needed.

Release

THE PSYCHIATRIC UNIT WAS A STRANGE PLACE. THE KIDS looked like "normal" teenagers: they watched a lot of television, lounged around, ate snacks, flirted, and slept through the day. I guess they all just needed somewhere to go. Maybe they needed a break from life, and nine floors up from civilization was the place to take that break. I didn't really get to know any of the other kids. They called me "Mute" when I walked by, and sometimes they would just shrug at me because that was what I did if they asked me any questions. Shrugging at me was apparently funny. Even in a mental hospital, teenagers all acted alike.

Now that Travis was gone, the only one that I cared to talk to was Peter. He understood me, and when he gave me the journal, it had this weird effect. I didn't want to use it to communicate with him. I actually wanted him to hear my voice.

I did use my voice and told Peter my dream about David. He didn't try to analyze it, which I appreciated. He just listened as I recounted every detail, then asked, "Are you glad you see him in your dreams?" I stared back at him, thinking. His eyes stayed fixed on mine, patiently waiting for me to process my thoughts. "Yes." I thought for a moment longer. "I see his face every time I close my eyes, but it's either his pale face in the basement with a rope tight around his neck or his body stiff in the casket. I guess my dreams are the only time I can picture him alive."

There were times when I looked forward to sleeping because it was the only time I had hope of seeing David alive, but there were also times when it backfired and I would wake up more depressed because I would lose him all over again.

"Then dream away," said Peter as he leaned back in his chair with a slanted grin, placing his hands behind his head. "You're leaving tomorrow. Are you ready?"

I shrugged, then pictured Travis in one of his manic states yelling, "EXACTLY!"

"You will be in good hands," Peter assured me. "My brother is one of a kind. He's a pain in the ass, but he's a one-of-a-kind pain in the ass."

"I can go back to my school?" I said. "I didn't know if Mom and Dad would let me."

"I talked to them about it. I recommended that you not change schools again since you met Travis. Your dad doesn't seem crazy about Travis, but your mom appears to like him."

"My dad isn't crazy about anything. He only cared about David."

Peter placed one hand on my shoulder and stared at me until I made eye contact with him. "Parents often favor one child over the other, even if they don't like to admit it. They see themselves in the kid and want to relive their youth."

"They should have the parents committed to a different psych unit the same day their kids are." Peter laughed at that, but I was serious. Parents usually had a big role in why their kids were so messed up in the first place. Travis's dad was ashamed of him to the point where he broke hospital rules and used his power to secure Travis a room whenever he wanted to escape from home. Hunter, a kid from Group the other day, had burn marks up and down his neck. He tried to kill himself because he couldn't take being burned anymore.

Peter asked Hunter, "Why don't you stop burning yourself?"

"Nobody can stop the dragon," he replied.

It turned out that Hunter's stepdad would sneak into his room at night and burn him on the side of his neck with a cigarette. When Hunter screamed, his stepdad would whisper, "It's just the dragon." Peter was pissed, and he wasn't a guy you wanted to piss off. I think Hunter's stepdad got a visit from the police that day.

After Group time, I decided to go to the small library where Travis went to read. There was a red, imitation leather chair next to the bookshelf and another identical chair against the wall along with a small, wooden table. I felt comfortable there among the books. Starting a new book was like starting a new journey or walking in my woods. I never knew what I would find, and it excited me. Before Travis left, he told me to go to the shelf and start reading Jerzy Kosiński's *The Painted Bird*. "It's raw, chaotic, and void of sentimentality," he said. I had never heard anyone describe a book that way before, so I pulled it from the shelf. A folded, white piece of paper stuck out of the middle of the book. Tugging the paper free, I slowly opened it. "Let it begin. See you at school. Travis."

I fell asleep in the chair next to the books and had another dream about David. This time, David walked my woods like he used to when we were little. He pulled back downed branches and scattered piles of leaves looking for me. I used to go to the woods and hide, knowing David would come looking for me. In the dream, David walked and walked and couldn't find me. Then he started running. Three wolves were happily following him, almost as if they knew him, and they leapt over logs and dodged trees in their pursuit. David seemed happy. When I woke up, I tried going back to sleep so I could watch him run with the wolves, but sleep wouldn't come. I lost him again.

The day of my release finally came, and while I waited for my mom to pick me up, I went to the library to page through some books. The red chair closest to the bookshelf had become my favorite place to sit. My stay at the hospital wasn't quite what I had expected. I met Peter, who showed me that men could be sensitive and caring, something that I wasn't used to seeing with my dad. I also met Travis and now had the hope of being his friend at school. He would be my first friend in a long time, and I would be lying if I said I wasn't nervous. Travis made me feel cool for being a reader and getting lost in my thoughts, and his craziness and bipolar ways made me feel normal. He validated my feelings about everything. He made it okay that I didn't always feel good. He told me before he left that I would understand when I got back to school.

"Understand what?" I had asked him. He just shrugged and smiled. "Smart-ass," I said. Part of me hated that Travis got me to trust him so easily, but the other part of me needed to trust someone.

I also finally felt okay taking my medication. It was something that I had hated before because my thoughts were not always clear and my brain felt like cotton balls had been stuffed in it every morning, but I slept well at night and my dreams were awesome, though often haunting. The rest of my stay at the hospital was a blur. I had only been in contact with my parents twice, once when they visited and one phone call from Mom.

The doorway filled, and the bookshelf went dark from a shadow. I looked up to find a large boy standing there. He was wearing a tight t-shirt and jeans with no belt, and his ink-black hair was plastered to his head with gel.

I nodded his way and returned to my book, watching him out of the corner of my eye. "Are you the fucking mute kid?" I didn't respond. He moved closer, hovering over me. "I asked you a question." This guy must have been dense because my silence should have answered his question. He was huge, Peter-type huge. His body was the size of an adult's, but his face was like a twelve-year-old's. "I knew your brother," he scoffed, which made me sit up in my chair. "I'm glad he's dead." The boy sounded like he was commenting on a good meal.

What happened next was a blur. All of a sudden, I was on top of the boy, rapidly beating his face with *The Painted Bird*. He didn't see it coming. Within moments, Peter ripped me off and held me, hugging me and asking me to calm down. The boy's nose was clearly broken. I had never seen so much blood before.

"It's over," said Peter. "It's okay." He ushered me down to my room and sat with me as the nurses tended to the boy.

"I'm sorry," I whispered. "I didn't realize what I was doing. I didn't know I was hitting him."

Peter's arm wrapped around my shoulders. "It's okay. He's been here before, and he's always starting trouble. We shouldn't have trusted him alone. He probably got what was coming to him."

"I really didn't want to hurt him," I said. As I sat with Peter and thought back to what happened, I remembered the boy saying that he was glad that David was dead. Suddenly, my only regret was getting blood on my book. Something told me that Kosiński wouldn't have cared.

"You must pack a pretty good punch for a little dude," Peter chuckled. He stayed in my room while I got ready to leave. I was surprised they were letting me go after the fight, and I kept waiting for my consequence, but it never came. All that came was Mom waiting to take me home. Home. I wasn't sure what that meant for me anymore.

The Conversation

PETER TOLD ME THAT IT WOULD TAKE A COUPLE OF DAYS TO adjust to home before returning to school, which was why they sent me home on a Friday. Dad was at work, so it was just Mom and I for lunch. She made meatloaf, with a heaping bowl of mashed potatoes. The refreshing smell reminded me of how life used to be at our house.

"This is usually for dinner," I wrote in my notebook before showing it to Mom.

Mom had dark circles under her eyes that seemed to protrude from her head, and her dyed blond hair was pulled back into a ponytail and was losing its color, turning rusty brown. She slowly followed what I wrote with her eyes. "Your father and I will be home a little later, so this is dinner too."

I couldn't believe it. My first day back, and they had made plans. I took the meatloaf to my room and listened to Travis's Pearl Jam CD over and over until I started to remember some of the lyrics, though I didn't always understand what Eddie Vedder was saying. I had to look them up on the internet in order to sing along to the entire song. After a while, I turned the music off and read. These were my escapes, but it still wasn't enough.

A few hours later, I woke up to a dark room. One thing I learned from being in the hospital was how to rest again. It was expected that kids would take naps during the day, or at least read and relax. There were absolutely no video games played. "They distract thought," Peter warned me. I wasn't sure about that, but it didn't bother me. I hardly played video games anyway. David was the gamer.

I wandered into the kitchen, then the living room looking for Mom before I remembered that they were gone. How could they leave me on my first day back home? I left the lights off in the house and walked down the hall to David's bedroom door. The moon and streetlights that trickled through the windows and open doors into the hallway were my only guide, and the light seemed to carry me right to his doorway.

Standing on heavy legs outside David's closed door, I had this strange, sudden rush of anxiety thinking that he was in his room. I actually caught myself right before I knocked. Peter said it was a part of the grieving process, that I would sometimes think, or wish, that David was here and that I might even go as far as seeing him or talking to him. I turned the knob, but it didn't open. Pushing the door with my shoulder didn't budge it. I flicked the hall light on and noticed that the doorknob was changed so it was locked from the outside going in. I needed a key.

"This is horseshit!" I screamed to no one, punching my fist against the door.

I searched for the key all through the house. I checked my dad's office and went through his desk. I ran down the hall to the kitchen and looked in the bowls where Mom and Dad kept their car keys. Nothing! I stopped myself, thought for a moment, breathing heavily, and ran back to my parents' bedroom. I threw my dad's socks around and looked under their mattress. I felt like I was about to go crazy

needing to see David's room. I needed to smell his clothes and lay
in his bed. He was my brother. I ran back to the living room and
collapsed to my knees.

"You selfish, fucking prick!"

I tried to breathe from my stomach the way Peter taught me
when I became upset, but being locked out of David's room felt like
betrayal, like Mom and Dad were the only ones that had a right to
grieve. They never even asked me how I was doing. "Breathe!" I said
aloud to the living room furniture. Eventually at the point of calming
down, I looked up towards the mantel and studied David's line of
baseball trophies. The trophies were Dad's prized possessions, and
only his to touch. I started to look under them one at a time. A gold
key that I didn't recognize sat under David's *Most Valuable Player*
trophy. Holding the trophy, I remembered the night that he received
it. It was his last year of playing baseball, and he gave a speech that
wrecked my dad.

David had stood at the podium getting ready to deliver his most
valuable player speech at the end of the year banquet and surveyed
the crowd. The gym was filled with the baseball team, coaches, and
the players' families. Each player had also invited a teacher that they
wanted as a guest, and the principal was there too. David had their
attention. "This seems a little odd to me to be accepting something
that says, 'Most Valuable.' I do not think there is anyone more
valuable than the next." The crowd cheered. "I have been playing
baseball all of my life, like most of the other players. I've been
groomed into a winner, whether I wanted to be or not." Some of
the players nodded their heads, and the parents looked around at
each other, but Dad stared straight at David. "Baseball is only one

piece of who I am. It's not all of me, just a small slice. There has to be more."

The gym was dead quiet as everyone stared at him. Mom nervously shifted in her chair. David cleared his throat. "There is one person above all that I would like to thank. He has chased a million balls around a field for years, and even caught them with his frozen glove in knee-deep snow. He taught me how to walk quietly in the woods and appreciate more than just a tiny, white ball and bat." David was looking directly at me, his eyes bright and his smile wide. I could tell he was truly proud to be my brother. I became nervous because I knew he was talking about me. He was talking about my woods. "My brother, Neil. Please come up here and accept this trophy." The audience applauded as I slowly stood. I hesitantly looked down at Dad because I knew he wouldn't approve. He stared straight ahead, but Mom clapped, tears pouring from her eyes. I walked up to David, slightly embarrassed, but as his team cheered me on, I graciously accepted the trophy. It was one of the last times I was truly happy. David stayed with his friends after the ceremony, so I went home with Mom and Dad. When we got home, I sat down on the couch and held the trophy in my hands, just staring at it.

That night, my dad said, "That goes on the mantel," and held his hand out. I cradled it a moment longer before giving it to him. It was the most defiant thing that I could get away with. Then I heard him mumble, "Who pitched to him all these years? I spent my life making him better. I don't see other fathers doing that." Dad placed the trophy on the mantel next to the rest of David's trophies from when he was six years old all the way through high school. When I woke up the next morning, the trophy was lying next to me on my pillow. That was when things started to change.

Now with David gone and with my week away in the hospital, the trophy is back where my dad wanted it. I took the key and went to David's room, trying it in the lock. It worked. I pushed the door open and took one small step into the bedroom. It was exactly the same. The mess I had made was cleaned up, and a new fish tank sat on the desk. I stuck my face close to the tank. The fish, the rocks at the bottom, everything was the same. My eyes spilled tears, but this time my cry wasn't from rage. I cried out of sadness. A sadness that hurt so deep that I felt weak. I collapsed on David's bed. My guts and my heart were being torn from my body, and I had to hug my stomach tight to keep everything in.

I woke up on David's pillow, wet with my tears. It was still dark outside, so I had no idea what time it was, but I felt rested. I once read in an article that crying was supposed to release toxins and purify your system, and to my surprise, a good cry and a short nap did make me feel good. But I was in David's room. I shouldn't feel good in David's room.

Getting off the bed, I turned to leave but heard voices in another part of the house. Mom and Dad. I couldn't leave the room now. Dad would kill me. Keeping the door shut, I listened to their conversation.

"Neil must be gone," said Mom. I was surprised she even noticed.

"He could have left some lights on for us." Dad sounded like his usual self.

"I wanted us to be together tonight." Mom's footsteps echoed down the hall and passed David's door. "He did just get back."

"Yeah, from the nuthouse."

"Don't say that. He is doing the best he can. They told us that we need to support him and let him grieve." Peter must have said that. "Besides, we're all he has, us and my dad. I don't think he has any friends."

"That's because he's just . . . so strange." Dad was not one to hold back. "And your dad is a nut bag too. That's why they get along so well."

I wanted to burst out of the door and defend my grandpa, but I kept listening. This was good stuff. How often do your parents say what they really think about you?

"I think we need to tell him that we've been to counseling," said Mom.

"No. Then he'll think we're as nuts as he is. Besides, it was your idea." They always blamed each other. It was funny to me how adults could tell you to take responsibility, but they couldn't do it themselves. It was like there were two sets of rules, one for kids and one for adults.

Then, it came. The two words that over half the children in this country hear: separate and divorce. The words that form a pit in your stomach because even though you know your situation is not the best at home, this divorce will turn your world upside down. I had heard them talk about divorce before, but none of it seemed real until now. Who would I live with? Where would I sleep at night? Would I spend weekends with my dad, alone? What would we do or say to each other? Where would I go to school? What about Travis? Would I ever see him again? What about my woods? David's room? His fish? Strangely, I didn't want anything to change. I wasn't happy. My mom and dad weren't happy. I could tell they didn't love each other anymore. But I still didn't want anything to change.

Suddenly, I regretted eavesdropping on my parents. My head was spinning, and I wanted to grab the baseball bat and take out the fish tank again, but the last time that happened, I ended up in a shrink's office and then the hospital. Besides, I regretted hurting the fish. David would not have liked that.

Before I knew it, I threw open David's door, stormed into the living room where my parents sat facing each other, and screamed, "Do me a favor and get a fucking divorce!" Mom and Dad just looked at me like they knew I had been listening. They hardly reacted. Maybe it was shock. "Do it!" I screamed, burning my throat. "Get out of my life. Both of you! I know you don't want me in yours." Mom and Dad looked at each other without saying anything. "You're both fucked up." I walked out the front door and ran to the woods.

I walked deep into the trees and then stopped and built a shelter. The sloping roof was made from downed branches and leaves, and the entry was high enough for me to crawl into. No one would find me here. I crawled inside and quickly fell asleep on a pile of leaves.

When I woke up the next morning, raindrops trickled through the branches built over me. Today was Saturday, which gave me two days to figure out a way to stay in my school where I could see Travis and Mr. C. How would I face my parents after what I said? Hell, maybe they should be the ones figuring out how to face me.

I crawled out of my shelter to find Mom sitting on a toppled tree, waiting for me. She looked strong, confident, and determined. With a slight smile, she moved straight in front of me and held me tight. I resisted at first, but I needed her hug. It gave me hope.

"Honey." She held my face gently, making sure I was looking at her. "Life can be complicated. It's full of everything that makes us feel. Good, bad, and everything in between. It's what makes life interesting. It's also what makes life hard, but we can survive it together."

The Separation

I WALKED OUT OF THE WOODS WITH MOM, NOT SAYING anything, and her arm stayed snug around me. When we came into the house, I realized that Dad was gone. He had not been gone on a Saturday since David died. I think it was part of his grieving, not wanting to be too far from David's things. His material items and our memories were all we had left of him.

After taking a shower and changing into clean clothes, I walked into the kitchen to the smell of eggs and bacon. The table was set, and Mom was waiting by the stove, ready to scoop me some food.

After filling my plate, she said, "Sit down, honey."

I took my eggs and bacon and sat on the opposite side of the table. Mom sipped her coffee and glanced at me. Suddenly, she looked old for her forty-five years. Her hair was a mess, dark circles sat under her eyes, and her shoulders slouched. I was so used to seeing her young, before David had died. She still ran every morning, and after David's death, she started yoga. I even went with her to yoga a couple of times. She was trying to move forward with her life, and I guess that was why I felt betrayed when she dropped me off at the hospital. Moving on should have meant being there for me. I knew she wanted what was best for me. She always did. She tried to compensate for what my dad didn't offer, and I loved her for that. But I felt like maybe she lost the battle she was fighting.

Mom sat down across the table from me. Her hands were visibly shaking, and she tried to hold them still by placing them under her legs. "As you heard last night, your father and I are separating."

I don't know why, but I started crying. Maybe I was just relieved. I never really loved my dad, and now I felt guilty. It was hard to love someone that didn't love you back. After a while, I think you just forget how to love them.

I didn't know what to say as my mom moved closer and hugged me. "What will happen to me?" I whispered. I knew it was selfish to ask, but I was scared.

"Well, we can't afford to live here anymore. I told your dad to keep his money and I will keep mine."

"You don't have any money," I said.

"Yeah, well, I have a little."

I took a deep breath. "Where did he go?"

"He's taking a job in Chicago. He said that he couldn't stay here anymore. In this town."

This was all a shock to me even though I suspected they might not stay together. They barely talked anymore, and I didn't know much about relationships, but I knew enough to know that you need to talk. Marriage can be like flipping a coin. With that chance, I never want to fall in love.

"He's such a selfish bastard." He didn't even want to be in the same town as me.

"He said he's coming back later today to talk to you."

"He can go to hell. I don't want to talk to him." I didn't even want to see him. My dad wasn't there for me when I was blaming myself for David's death, when I was reenacting every conversation that I had with David before he killed himself just to see if there was anything I could have done to save him, or when I was in utter turmoil about my role in it all. The bastard was never there for me.

Mom grabbed my hand and held it tightly. "We're putting the house up for sale. Dad told me to keep the money we make from it."

"Where will we live?" My hands were shaking. I felt displaced. Would I need to get a job and help Mom? I had to grow up. Grow up way too fast.

"Grandpa is coming to get you tomorrow. He's excited to have us."

Living with Grandpa meant I could still go to school with Travis. A smile erupted on my face, which pleased Mom.

"I knew that would make you happy," she said, her eyes welling with tears.

I ate my food and let Mom have some time to herself. It must have been hard for her to tell me all of that. She got up from the table and went to her room, then came out about twenty minutes later with her running clothes on. I was happy that she was exercising. Mom was a pretty woman and took care of herself as much as she could while taking care of all of us. I used to hate how David's friends would gawk at her when she cheered at his baseball games. A bunch of horny teenage boys making comments about my mom while they sat on the bench. "Your mom is hot, David." David would just laugh it off unless they got carried away, and then he would give them his look. I liked to call it his "action hero" look, where he was about to give them a reason to stop if they didn't. They always stopped.

I finished eating, Mom ran, Dad was gone, and I wondered what could possibly happen next. My life was a carnival ride that made me want to vomit.

Pictures

I WOKE UP A COUPLE OF HOURS LATER ON MY BED. I NOTICED that I'd been sleeping a lot since I went to the hospital, a side effect of the medication I guess, but not the worst one for a teenage boy. I went to get something to eat and see if Mom was home yet. There was a note on the kitchen counter that said, "Went to the store. I love you!" The house was so quiet and calm, and I felt relaxed here for the first time in months. I made some coffee, extra bold, dark roast. I'd started drinking coffee about a year ago, although I don't really know why. Maybe it was a way for me to feel like an adult, and coffee wasn't as bad as smoking or drinking, although I did like sneaking one of my dad's beers now and then. I would hide the beer in my coat pocket, head out to the woods, and drink it while I walked through the trees. I've never had more than one and had a feeling I wouldn't do very well with more. It was probably thanks to seeing my dad drunk. It's amazing how we try to avoid becoming our parents.

I walked into the living room with the warm coffee mug in my hands, and for the first time in a long while, I started looking at the family pictures that hung on the walls and sat on the entertainment center. It's odd how photos can be placed all around a house, the hallways, bedrooms, even bathrooms, and people so rarely look at them. The photos become ghosts, images of our pasts nagging us and saying, "Look at me! Look how much happier you were then!" I felt like the photos mocked me sometimes, like my own face from years ago was laughing at who I'd become.

As I paced around the room, going from frame to frame and dissecting the images, I noticed something. There were pictures of me and Mom, me and David, David and Mom, David and Dad, but there were none of just my dad and me. The pictures of our vacation to South Dakota were arranged on a shelf, of my dad and David standing with Mount Rushmore behind them. There were a few in sleek silver frames of David in his baseball jersey and Dad with his arm around him, a proud fatherly smile curving his lips. There were a couple of Mom and Dad holding David when he was a baby, and one of Mom and me fishing off a pier, with my cane pole and stupid hat that was too big for my head. I checked every picture in the living room and then went to the hallway, decorated with a sequence of black-and-white photos of David and me as little kids with our arms wrapped around each other. It had been Halloween, and they'd had me in a firefighter outfit and David dressed as a police officer.

The pictures made my heart sink. I looked into David's childlike eyes and couldn't help but wonder if he had any idea back then that he would take his own life one day. Anxiety welled up in my chest, and I hastily continued on with my photographic journey through the house. Our bathroom was filled with pictures of Washington, D.C. when David was in a baseball tournament there. I'd stayed with my grandpa during that trip, so I wasn't in any of those pictures. Above the dresser in Mom and Dad's bedroom were two pictures of them, when they first met and at their wedding, set in matching white frames. They looked so happy. Did they forget how they felt about each other then? Would they have made it if they'd just looked at those pictures every once in a while and reminded themselves that they were once in love?

I walked to my Dad's study, where the pictures lined up across his desk were all of David and his baseball games. They showed him in action, hitting, catching, running, and sliding. A few of the pictures I thought were David, and when I examined them further, I realized they were of my dad. They looked a lot alike. They had the same running stride and swing. Their faces had the same relaxed, confident look as they threw the ball. Did my dad see his face in David's, and when David started throwing it all away, did he see himself doing the same?

I needed more! I knew the rest of the photos were in the basement, where I hadn't been since I found David hanging. As soon as I flung open the door to the stairwell, I involuntarily froze. It scared the hell out of me to take that first step, and my foot hovered for a moment over the stair before I took a deep breath and forced myself onward. As I descended, the air turned cold and musty, and I found myself ducking and batting away cobwebs as they hit my face. I'd never asked Mom why she always took the laundry to the laundromat, but now I realized that I wasn't the only one who couldn't go down into the basement. At the bottom of the stairs, I paused before I turned the corner. A vision of that night came rushing into my head. I remembered turning the corner, and there he was, his face blue and his body dangling. David's bony fingers were limp, and his strong legs looked like salamis hanging off a shelf.

As I forced myself to round the corner tonight, I felt all the air being sucked from my lungs. Suddenly, I was dizzy and shivering, my teeth chattering. My heart started pounding out of my chest, and I felt it beating against my shirt. This time, I knew what was happening. Peter had identified it in the hospital as a panic attack. I'd had three during the week I stayed there. He said it was from stress and trauma. "Just breathe slowly from your belly and accept that it's happening," Peter would say. "It will go away." Part of me knew that it would, but the rest of me felt like I was dying, and even knowing the attack would stop soon, I couldn't help being scared. I made my legs move to the blue plastic crate that held a lifetime full of pictures. So many vivid memories that now lived in the corner of a damp basement where a son and brother decided to kill himself and leave the rest of us behind. As I shuffled my feet over to the crate, I saw a box with David's name written on it in large, black letters. His Handwriting. The box held his antique toy tractors. "Fuck you, David," I whispered. "You selfish asshole. You left me." I heaved the box up, and my skinny arms struggled to carry the memories that filled it.

I had only seen inside the blue crate once before. Four years ago, my mom had been looking through the photos on her birthday. I remember sneaking down to see what she was doing and sitting on the bottom step, watching her smile as she paged through photo after photo. She cried at the sight of her mom, who'd passed away a year earlier from cancer. Then I went and sat next to her, and we looked at the pictures together. It was like a personal history lesson on our existence as a family. Some of the photos were fading, and some were stuck together. All of them told a story, one that was constantly changing.

I was excited to open the lid of the crate and look at the photos again, my past, our past and memories. I wanted to see if the photos would look different to me. Could pictures change over time? Maybe just our interpretations of them and the way they make us feel. I needed a place to look at them where no one would come home and find me. Not that Mom would care, but I didn't want to be interrupted and I didn't want to upset her. Then I realized that I was in the only place in the house where I would not be bothered. No one would come down, and no one would expect me to be here. I was surprised Dad didn't seal off the basement. I pulled the thick plastic lid off the box and began my journey.

I grabbed a handful of loose pictures and pulled them from the box, laying them out on the blue lid. There were a few pictures of my mom's parents, some of them from when they were young and some just before Grandma died. One of the pictures showed Grandpa kissing Grandma, holding her tight. They were desperately in love. I could hardly remember a time when I didn't see them together or holding hands. There were pictures from vacations and more pictures of David playing baseball. I even found some older shots of Dad when he was in the Army. He never talked about his time in the Army, but he'd spent six years in the military police. I remember Mom mentioning once that Dad was in Operation Desert Storm and spent six months in the Middle East, and David had told me that Dad used to be in charge of prisoners. The photos showed him surrounded by miles and miles of sand.

Underneath those were several pictures of Mom pregnant, probably with David. She looked tired, but happy. Farther down in the bin, I found a black-and-white photo of a couple that I didn't recognize, dressed up and sitting stoically in front of a white Christmas tree. The little boy next to them seemed familiar; his eyes looked like David's. These people had to be Dad's parents. I'd only heard a couple of stories about them. My grandma was kind and did her best to raise my dad. She didn't have a job but volunteered to help people in need. My grandpa had been a businessman, owned a bunch of land, and seemed like a pretty straight-laced guy. He looked the complete opposite of my mom's dad. This man had a suit and tie on and was tall with styled hair, looking indifferent, and my mom's dad wore jeans and t-shirts and had a buzz cut. His photo showed him as average height and muscular with a big smile on his face.

The next picture nearly took my breath away. David and I were walking together when he was about nine and I was around seven, and David had one of his arms around me and a baseball bat slung over the other shoulder. I missed him so much. I missed being loved like that. I hugged the picture against my chest and glanced around the basement, feeling like maybe he was near me. I felt a sudden chill, and the bumps on my arms rose to the point I thought they might pop off.

I put the picture in my back pocket, and as I looked up with a deep breath, I noticed a rack full of wine next to the crate of pictures. My parents used to open a bottle about once per week for dinner. The corkscrew hung from a hook on the rack. "What the hell," I said to no one. I went over and looked through the six bottles, wiping off the dust and cobwebs to read the labels. I didn't know anything about wine, but two bottles said "Merlot," another two read "Cuvée, from Italy," and the other two bottles were in a foreign language. I figured that since I'd never had wine and couldn't understand the rest of the labels anyway that one of those looked like a good start. It was warm on my throat as I drank from the bottle. It tasted like sweet cherries mixed with cinnamon. I took little sips, and the droplets that spilled from the bottle onto my t-shirt looked like specks of blood.

Retreating back to the bin of photos with the wine bottle, I pulled up a stool from the dusty corner. As I drank, I pulled out a photo album to page through. On the front was the quote "A happy family is but an earlier heaven" from some dude named George Bernard Shaw. I figured my mom had to have put that quote there. She loved quotes, but it wasn't because she was being pretentious. I'd always felt like my mom was searching for something that she read in a quote, for some big insight that would put her life in perspective. Maybe it was because her life didn't turn out the way she wanted it to, and platitudes from famous people gave her a certain optimism for what her life could still be. I hoped she would find what she was looking for now that my dad was gone.

On the next page was a picture of Mom and Grandpa playing chess. I assumed Grandma took the picture. Their chess games were legendary. They'd played once from Friday night until Saturday evening. I remember watching them trying to outmaneuver each other. I was always quiet, even before I stopped talking, and Grandma would just read a book while they made their moves. The only sound in the house that night was Grandpa farting every so often. He would laugh when my mom scowled and then look at me and say, "Strategy."

The wine was starting to have its effect. I wasn't sure what it would do. I'd seen my dad drunk, and even David a few times, but I was still unsure how it would make me feel. The pictures were getting blurry, and I started mumbling aloud when I would come across one that needed commentary, like a picture of my dad holding up one of David's baseball trophies with a huge smile on his face. I felt like I was standing over my own shoulder, listening to myself slur the words, "Get a life, you bastard."

There was one more mouthful of wine in the bottle and one more picture that I looked at before I passed out. My eyes were watery and hardly open. The room spun, and I fell off the stool that I was sitting on. I'd thought that getting drunk might help me stop feeling, but instead it just made me more depressed.

I held the picture and sobbed. It was what I was searching for when I began my photographic journey through the house. It had taken me a few hours and a bottle of wine to find it, and I just shook and cried because I never really thought I would see it again. It was a simple picture, one that was taken a few years ago, of my entire family—Mom, Dad, David, and even me—next to a sign that read *Rocky Mountain National Park*. David and I have stupid-looking moose hats on, and we're all smiling.

I lay on the cold cement floor, drunkenly clutching the picture against me. It was my family, whole and happy. It was proof that it once existed.

One More Goodbye

I ROLLED OVER IN MY BED, NOT SURE HOW I GOT THERE. I didn't remember walking up from the basement. My head was killing me, and I felt like I could puke. The sun was going down, and just a trickle of light was coming through the end of the blinds on my window. Thank God that full sunshine wasn't coming through; I don't think my head could have taken it. My bed felt like it was spinning, and suddenly drinking wine didn't seem like it had been such a good idea. I felt my back pocket, and the picture was still there. My vision was blurred like I was looking through a glass of water, and when I looked over to the chair next to my desk, I thought I was seeing things. Someone that looked like my dad was staring back at me. The person was an outline of a body, broad shoulders and a thick head. Through squinted eyes, I reached my hand out.

"Looks like you tied one on," the familiar voice said. I abruptly sat up and planted one foot on the floor in hopes of stopping the bed from spiraling out of control. I didn't realize being drunk would be like a bad carnival ride.

"David," I said, reaching my hand further. "I knew you'd come back."

The lamp on my desk suddenly flicked on, and the light blurred my glassy eyes even more. A hundred knives were stabbing my brain.

I fell back on the bed and just lay there, waiting for the image to say something else. Then, it stood and stepped toward me. It was a silhouette of a man in jeans and a hat. My bed shook as he sat next to me.

"Your first time?" It was Dad, and he had a strange smile on his face, a smile that I'd seen him wear only when he was with David. I nodded my head. "I remember my first time getting drunk. I was about your age. It was my dad's Scotch. Shit! I was sick as hell, and when your grandfather found out, he wasn't mad that I was drunk. He was mad that I drank a three-hundred-dollar bottle of Scotch. Man, he could give a beating."

Dad placed his hand on my leg. "Head hurt?" he asked. I nodded again and held my temples where it hurt the most. "It will go away. You're just dehydrated. Drink some water, and then let's go get you a cheeseburger and milkshake. The perfect hangover food."

I hadn't spoken to my dad for this long in what seemed like years, if ever, and he actually seemed proud of me. He was angry when I started a fire on the side of the house two years ago. He hated it when I had stopped talking. He said he wanted to kill me when I took his car for a drive last year and crashed it into our neighbor's mailbox. He had me committed when I broke David's fish tank. But now, here he was, seemingly proud of me for drinking a bottle of wine in the basement where his son had killed himself. My life had become even more bizarre, and the fine line between right and wrong had thinned.

I left the house with Dad. We drove a couple of miles down the road and took a right on Highway 16, which went into the country. It was my first time alone with him in a few years. The last time was when Mom was sick and he had to take me to school. I remember that drive as being silent, different from this one.

The back seat of the car had two suitcases and a green, Army duffel bag. Was he still leaving, or coming back? For a moment, I thought it was the latter because he was being so nice to me. Nicer than he had ever been. I didn't ask where we were going, and he didn't tell me.

The movement of the car made my head spin, and Dad cracked the window from his side of the car. "Hang your head out the window if you're going to get sick," he said with a smirk across his face, and then I felt something I had not felt since I was nine. My dad stroked the back of my shoulder and neck with his hand and patted the back of my head. Dad never showed me affection, and his gentle touch felt unusual. It was what fathers should do with their sons, but it didn't happen with me. I wished I could take this for granted, but there was a time when realities overtook ideologies and you just had to accept your fate.

We drove another ten minutes and pulled into a gravel parking lot with a beer sign out front that read *Pabst Blue Ribbon.* Inside, the bar smelled like stale beer and peanuts. For a moment, I thought my dad brought me here to torture me and teach me a lesson because the smell of alcohol made me gag, but he put his arm around me and said to the old man behind the bar, "Hey, Bill, my boy had his first drink today. Hell, he had his first thirty drinks. Damn, son, a whole bottle of wine? You could have started with beer." Dad laughed with affection as we sat at the bar. Bill brought us two menus, Dad a beer, and me a glass of water, a glass of orange juice, and a glass of vegetable juice.

"Drink that up, kid," said Bill. "I'll get you a cheeseburger started." The man had a gruff voice and an anchor tattoo on his fat, hairy forearm. He seemed like a guy I wouldn't want to tangle with.

"They have the best cheeseburgers here," said Dad. "We'll get you fixed up, Neil. Drink all that up. The salt and sugar will do you good."

Dad's demeanor abruptly changed. He sighed and started tapping his fork against the counter.

"Let's talk about this not-talking shit."

I didn't know what to say, so I shrugged.

"Enough!" he snapped with a different tone, a tone that I recognized. "I'm not going to be around as much anymore, Neil."

"Yeah, you won't be around at all if you're in Chicago." I regretted it as soon as I said it.

"You need to start speaking, helping your mom more, and getting some friends." He was actually trying to give me advice. I almost felt sorry for him that I was the replacement child to David. I was now his only son. I was the mute who didn't like to play sports and talked to himself alone in the woods. I felt bad for him and his shitty last-ditch effort as a dad, so I did my best to have a conversation.

"I have a friend," I whispered.

"Speak up, Neil. Be confident. Be a man."

"I said, I have friends." This time, my voice crackled a little but was louder. The bartender looked over. "Well, a friend."

Dad didn't ask me who my friend was. He'd never cared about my friends. "I don't want to hear about you going back to the hospital either," said Dad. "That place is for crazies who can't handle life. You can handle it, Neil. You just need to start accepting responsibility."

My armpits were sweating, and the back of my neck was getting warm. "They're not all crazy. They're just kids that need some help."

"Yeah, shithouse crazy kids. Not my son," he said.

I stopped talking. I was scared of my dad but wanted to tear his eyes out at the same time. I wished I could stick up for Travis, because I knew who "shithouse crazy kids" was directed at.

"See, now you're quiet again. You need to stand up and speak your mind. If you can't even have a conversation with someone, you'll get walked on." He was trying to teach me how to be a man while sitting in a bar while I had a hangover and we ate cheeseburgers. One part of me felt like clinging to this time because it was the only time he tried to teach me anything about life, and the other part of me wanted to scream, "Fuck off!" and run out the door.

"I'm sorry," I said, my voice strong. It was all that I could come up with.

"What?"

I cleared my throat. "I'm sorry that you are stuck with me for a son. I'm sorry that David is dead. I'm sorry that I couldn't save him. I'm sorry that I don't play sports."

"Keep your voice down, Neil." He was probably sorry that he'd asked me to speak up.

"I know you blame me," I went on. "I know you think I could have saved him, but I couldn't."

The bartender brought our cheeseburgers over, looked at my dad, and asked, "Everything okay?" Dad nodded.

I continued, "It's not my fault that you and Mom fell out of love."

Dad slammed his hand down on the bar. "Enough!" He didn't look at me. He picked up his beer, took a few gulps, and started eating. I didn't want to stop. I didn't know when I would see him again, and he needed to hear me.

"I went to get help," I said. "He was still alive, and I tried to get help." I started crying. "I couldn't carry him up the stairs. I had to leave him there while I went to call 911. He was breathing, and he noticed me." Dad wouldn't look up from his beer glass. "I know you blame me, but I didn't kill David."

Dad stood up and dropped some money on the bar, then walked out the door without saying another word. I watched through the window as he drove away. He didn't turn back toward town or our home. I watched the car and the outline of the back of his head as the drowning sun reflected off the windshield. My eyes still hurt from the wine and the tears that filled them.

The Night Before

DAD MUST HAVE THOUGHT THE LONG WALK HOME WOULD continue his teaching me about being a man. Little did he know, I'd walked this far before and then some. I loved to walk! As I made my way along the side of the road, I wondered if I would ever hear from him again. I was old enough that I didn't have to go see him, and I knew that Mom would understand.

Just after nine thirty, I walked in the door and found Mom asleep on the couch with the television on. Boxes were packed and stacked by the kitchen door, ready to be moved. I looked around for David's trophies, but they were all gone, obviously tokens that Dad had taken to Chicago.

I watched Mom sleep as I drank some water and ate a peanut butter sandwich. I still had a headache from the wine, and the walk home had made me even more dehydrated. I covered Mom up and realized that it was now just us and Grandpa. We had to take care of each other.

I found the box with David's clothes and took one of his flannel shirts to wear on my first day back to school. I was anxious to see Travis and Mr. C. I wanted to start my new life, and I figured it would be better now that Dad had driven away to a new life of his own. I laid my clothes out on my chair and set my alarm clock. The anticipation of starting school was keeping me up, so I just lay in my bed, staring at the ceiling. I inspected the tiny cracks and small spider carcasses that I have killed over the years and never cleaned. I've looked at the ceiling of dead spiders so many times before; being a daydreamer and a professional insomniac had brought me to know my house well. As I stared around my room with the moonlight trickling through the half-open blinds, I wondered how many nights I would have left to do this. Mom seemed frantic to move in with Grandpa. She probably felt the same as I did when Dad left, a sense of abandonment and relief all at once. I leaned over and picked up the journal that Peter had given me in the hospital. "Write down your thoughts," he'd said. "I know you have a lot to say."

So I wrote:

Dear Journal, I am scared and excited at the same time. I stare at my bedroom walls and realize that for fourteen years, they have been my sanctuary. This house has felt so much happiness and so much pain. It has been a witness to love lost and a brother that used it to kill himself. I cannot wait to see Travis tomorrow at school. I would like to make this a new experience. Maybe I'll be brave enough to find my voice and show people who I really am. Though I am not sure who that is. I feel displaced. Perhaps I can be brave enough to use my voice and forget about this journal. Sometimes what is written is more dangerous than thoughts, since it's all out there for the world to see. I'm scared!

New Beginnings

MOM DROPPED ME OFF AT SCHOOL. SHE'D FILLED THE BACK seat with clothes from our house and was moving them to Grandpa's.

"I will be going back and forth today, and then I'll get you at three thirty," she said.

"Are we staying at Grandpa's tonight?"

"That's up to you, honey." She brushed the hair from my eyes. "I'll need your help moving some things, and you need to decide what you want to keep. Grandpa is bringing his truck over to the house later. Why don't you just walk to his house after school and go with him?"

I nodded, giving her a slanted grin. It had been about a month since I last saw Grandpa. He was out West someplace, hiking for the past three weeks, and recently returned. As far as what I wanted to keep? Maybe it would be good to get rid of some stuff and the memories that went with them. Even my Spiderman lamp and old pairs of shoes had memories. I wore down plenty of shoes chasing baseballs for David.

While Mom drove out of the horseshoe driveway of the school, I watched her intently, like a sunset losing life, until she was all the way down the street. I felt bad that I'd left her alone to go back to the house. I knew she would be sad there, but I also knew that she would be with Grandpa and he would take care of her. After turning around, I immediately heard laughter and saw the circle of students around Mr. C outside of the entrance. When I woke up this morning, I wondered if I had just imagined this place and Mr. C and the library. It felt like my first day at Memorial again, and in many ways, it was.

As I started to walk toward the doors, I took a closer look at the kids that surrounded Mr. C. It was the same ones that were there over a week ago, sort of a strange mix of them. The tall goth boy stood off to the side, but still with the group. A girl with several piercings was trying not to laugh, looking tough instead. There was a boy that stood with a black case that carried a band instrument and glanced at the ground. Then there was this girl with short, blond hair. Her eyes were sad but beautiful, and even from this distance, they looked like they could tell an entire story. Worryingly, I didn't see Travis. I didn't want to assume that he would still want to be friends, so I hoped he would find me before I found him.

I had to check into the office since I had been gone awhile, and I needed a new schedule because I forgot mine. School used to be important to me when I was in elementary school and part of middle school, but I'd lost interest since David died. I didn't see the point. It bored me. There were too many lectures, too many dull books to read, and too much drama. I hated it all. I could do the work, that wasn't the problem. It was actually easy for me. But I didn't want to do it. I had no motivation. David lost his motivation for school when he quit baseball. I lost my motivation when David quit me.

After the secretary handed me a new schedule, I looked down to examine it:

1st hour: American History
2nd hour: Study Hall
3rd hour: Physical Education
4th hour: Geometry
5th hour: Creative Writing
Lunch
6th hour: Biology
7th hour: English 9
8th hour: PB Club

As I walked out of the student services office, I took a second look at my eighth hour class. "What the hell is PB Club?" I mumbled out loud. That wasn't on my schedule before I went to the hospital. I almost turned around to go back to the office and tell them that I didn't sign up for a club, but I had made a pact with myself on my long walk home from the bar the other night. I decided that I wanted to take more risks, meet more people, try to talk more, and never disappoint my mom. I figured that those four things were a good place to start, but clubs were supposed to be after school. I was confused.

History was okay for first hour. We learned about World War I. The only thing I hated about textbooks was that they never really showed the true horrors of war. Teachers should make us read *The Things They Carried* by Tim O'Brien if they want to show students what it was really like. At least, that was the book Grandpa gave to me when I wanted to read about war.

Toward the last five minutes of class, the phone rang, and after picking it up, the teacher looked over at me. He nodded his head like the person on the other end could see him. He wrote something on a slip of paper and then hung up. He handed me the note while he finished his lesson. "Go see Mr. C after class." It was exciting to get to see him again, and especially to not have to approach him on my own. I also couldn't help but be a little nervous. Sometimes people disappoint you and don't live up to their first impressions.

I walked down the long hallway to the office's front desk, then to Mr. C's office, quietly laughing to myself remembering how his office was stuck in the back away from everything. The first time I'd gone back there, I felt like I was going into the custodians' closet.

I knocked. "Enter if you dare," called Mr. C. I walked in and sat down in the chair next to his desk. He was typing something using only two fingers. Typing obviously was not his strength. "Neil. Welcome back. I missed you!" He sounded sincere, but how could he miss me when he'd only met me once? "I thought we could spend second hour together and get caught up."

I liked this idea. All I would do in study hall is read, which I was looking forward to, but I could get into my book later.

His office hadn't changed in the week and a half that I was away, and neither did Mr. C. It was silent for a moment, and then he broke the silence. "I heard you met my brother?" I nodded. "He's a good guy," said Mr. C. "He sees a lot of kids come through each week. Some get better, and some don't. Some kids don't make it at all." Mr. C shifted in his seat. "Sorry," he said. I couldn't remember the last time an adult said they were sorry to me for anything. I didn't mind him talking straight with me, and I wanted him to know that, but all I could manage was a shrug. "I don't know how Peter does it. I can't see him lasting forever at the hospital. It's kind of like here, it's sort of a burnout."

"What do you mean?" My throat was raspy.

"Well, I try to help as many kids as I can, but sometimes I feel like I don't make an impact. You know, the progress I make with them gets all fuc . . . um . . . messed up at home." I loved that he almost dropped an f-bomb. "Sorry," he said again. "Sometimes I'm not sure I'm making any difference at all. It makes me want to go work in the woods somewhere."

I really didn't know how to respond to him. I wanted to tell him that, with just our two meetings, he had helped me, that he'd made me want to come back to school for the first time in a long time. I wanted to tell him that from meeting him one time, I knew he actually cared about kids. Except, nothing came out. I sometimes hated that I hid my voice, but I'd hidden within myself for so long that I was worried I might not ever open up again. I was suffocating in silence.

"Peter said he gave you a journal. You been writing?"

I shrugged. Shit! Wait! I wanted to talk, so no shrugs. I sat up in my chair. "Yes," I said. "I write every day. I've been trying to write about my brother and Mom and Dad."

Mr. C didn't respond right away to make sure I was done talking. I could tell he was a good listener, that a main part of his job was to listen. "Good. Journaling can lead to other types of writing. It's a great form of communication. Some people struggle to be open with their words aloud, so writing can help with that." He leaned back with a crooked grin on his face. "I would have given you a journal when you got back here, but that brother of mine beat me to it. We can get competitive."

I recognized that kind of grin and competitiveness. I used to have that with David. I could never compete with him in sports or anything athletic, but we used to see who could read a certain book the fastest or who could find the strangest quote and dare to paste it to our bedroom door. The challenge was to have your quote survive the longest on the door before Dad finally tore it down. David won the last *battle of the quotes* by posting, "Go to heaven for the climate, hell for the company," by Mark Twain. I heard my dad rip that one down, and when he did, David slung open the door and said in the calmest voice I had ever heard him speak, "It's my door. Please leave it alone." My dad didn't like that and mumbled something about who pays the bills, and then he walked away. David saw me peeking from my door and winked at me. That was two days before he died.

I pulled my schedule out of my folder. "Can you tell me what this is?" I pointed to eighth hour.

"It will be in here," said Mr. C. "I think you will be an excellent addition to our little club. You know, it's very exclusive." He grinned.

"What does PB stand for?"

"Polar Bear," he replied, beaming. "The kids named it last year about a month into the school year."

"Why Polar Bear?"

"Sounds a little elementary, doesn't it? Well, many of the kids that first started coming to see me were bipolar." He paused. "Are you familiar with that?" I remembered Travis telling me about it in the hospital. I nodded. "So, we didn't have a name, and then kids with other problems like depression, drugs, you name it started to come. Then, last June, we went to the zoo for a picnic, and the polar bears were pacing back and forth like they were manic, and one was sleeping and looked sad, so one of the kids said, 'It's like our club,' and henceforth we named it the Polar Bear Club. Cool kids. All of them," he said.

I could tell Mr. C genuinely loved the students he worked with because he grinned every time he brought them up. I smiled at the story. "Do I need to bring anything?" I asked.

"Nope. Just yourself. If you want to bring a notebook to write in so you don't feel the pressure to talk, you can do that. It's pretty laid back. We basically just check in, talk about any issues at home and school, and try to plan some outings in the community. Sometimes we work with the kids at the elementary and middle school."

"Sounds cool!" I said, a little too excited. Cool was not a word that I used very often because I was not considered cool, but I felt good saying it.

"It is cool," said Mr. C. "Especially if you like being around people that could be manic one day and depressed the next, or hate their parents, or self-medicate through smoking pot, or just don't fit in anywhere else." He smiled. "It is pretty cool anytime you find like-minded people that don't judge. Especially at this age."

After my meeting with Mr. C, I went through my morning listening to teachers talk and getting strange stares from students. When I got to creative writing, the first thing that caught my attention was the teacher. I guess I didn't pay any attention to him the last time I saw him. He was tall and hairy with an obvious comb-over, and he had a thick, gray beard and gray chest hairs flowing out of the top of his striped sweater. His eyebrows swung upward at the ends and hung off his forehead. When I entered his room, I had to shake his hand, and instead of saying, "Hello," I just nodded. Three stacks of the same book were lined up on a table in the back of the room. When I looked closer at them, I noticed his name on the front cover. "Miles Strombul," it read in large, red letters. From what I could tell by the book cover, it was a mystery. *The Disappearance of Mr. Jolly* was the title. Mr. Strombul motioned for me to sit in the desk that was in the front and center of the room. I hated having people sit behind me where I couldn't see what they were doing.

One book was propped up with the back cover showing a picture of Mr. Strombul, but a much younger version of him, still with a comb-over. I was not introduced to the class, which felt slightly awkward. Mr. Strombul started the class with a poem by William Butler Yeats called, "A Crazed Girl." He read it in a deep voice and paused often for effect:

> *THAT crazed girl improvising her music.*
> *Her poetry, dancing upon the shore,*
>
> *Her soul in division from itself*
> *Climbing, falling She knew not where,*
> *Hiding amid the cargo of a steamship,*
> *Her knee-cap broken, that girl I declare*
> *A beautiful lofty thing, or a thing*
> *Heroically lost, heroically found.*
>
> *No matter what disaster occurred*
> *She stood in desperate music wound,*
> *Wound, wound, and she made in her triumph*
> *Where the bales and the baskets lay*
> *No common intelligible sound*
> *But sang, 'O sea-starved, hungry sea.'*

Mr. Strombul's voice was loud and demanded to be heard. You could tell by their body language which students liked poetry and which didn't. However, everyone listened. With that trombone voice of Mr. Strombul's, how could you not?

I felt like clapping because Mr. Strombul had put so much effort into the reading, but was glad I didn't. In this crowd, clapping would have been the kiss of death.

A girl leaned over and said to me, "He starts every class with a poem. Get used to it." She was pretty in the sense that her teeth were very white and her hair was clean. I know it's weird, but that's what I noticed. I wasn't used to girls talking to me, ever.

Then, from the back of the room, a familiar voice said, "Isn't Yeats being shallow by reducing the girl in the poem to 'a beautiful lofty thing?'" I looked back, and there was Travis. He gave me a quick nod and a sly grin that I recognized from the hospital. I had been looking for him all morning, and here he was in my creative writing class.

"You dare to call Yeats shallow?" Mr. Strombul's voice roared out from the front of the room.

"He calls her 'crazed,' which again is shallow in his thought. She is no more crazed than you or I, but instead she is searching."

"What does she search for?" asked Mr. Strombul.

"Love and life and maybe some security."

"Travis, you have just proven my point for reading the poem in the first place. The girl is searching, yes, and she is crazed for living in a fantasy world."

"Then, I would argue that we are all crazed," said Travis. "Our lives are not real but always fantasy."

The other kids started to laugh at Travis, making remarks about him being a "crazed boy." Travis ignored them, and Mr. Strombul shook his head. "Moving on." Then he continued into the lesson, which was writing a research paper on someone we admired and why. We were required to use APA style to format our papers. "I am preparing you for college," Mr. Strombul said. He seemed proud of that statement when the kids shuffled and whined.

The class ended, and it was time for lunch. I was afraid to look back at where Travis had been sitting because I didn't want to be disappointed if he just got up and left without acknowledging me.

Before I could stand, I felt a hand on my shoulder. I looked up, hoping it was Travis, and it was. He said in his best impersonation of Mr. Strombul, "Dear crazed boy, would you care for a bite of lunch?" A smile erupted across my face, and I nodded. "You can meet some of 'The Kids,'" he said. "They can see who I spent a week at the hospital with. I told them about you."

I was surprised. I didn't think anyone would find me interesting enough to tell their friends.

The cafeteria was like any other school lunchroom. It smelled of strange meat, seemingly irritated women passed out the food, and a crowd of kids scrambled around and acted like this was their last meal ever. The one cool thing about this lunchroom were the round tables; however, they would make it hard to hide when everyone was facing each other. There's no escape, but I didn't want to escape. I kept thinking about my goal of speaking again. I didn't want to be a freak.

"I think that was once meat," said Travis, peering at my tray. We walked through the cafeteria and the sea of tables and kids.

"Where's yours?" I asked.

"Oh, I bring my own." He held up a steel lunch box that was painted light blue with blotches of yellow and had a large, white peace sign. "They don't cater to vegetarians here."

I followed Travis's broad shoulders and black Soundgarden shirt over to a round table where four other kids were sitting, two boys and two girls. One of the girls was talking really fast, and everyone else at the table just kept eating while she talked. She had red hair and pale skin with tiny freckles on her cheeks. Her hair was pulled back, which made her pale forehead look huge. Her green eyes were pretty, but they were overshadowed by the blotch of loud red lipstick that it seemed like so many high school girls wore. Maybe it was just me, but that look was a little unsettling. Their moms should teach them how to put on makeup.

"Everyone," Travis spoke up and placed a hand on my shoulder. "This is Neil." The girl with the red hair kept talking, but not in a rude sort of way. It just seemed like she couldn't stop. "He will be eating with us every day." Those words lifted a weight off my chest. Every day! I needed something the same every day, a routine, and now on my first day of school, I already had that. Nothing sucked like being the new kid with nobody to sit with.

A boy with a black-and-gray, striped dress shirt and a thin, white tie stood and shook my hand. "I'm Devo." He moved over so I could sit next to him.

"Devo is stuck in the eighties," said Travis. "He says it's his generation."

"It's my dad's generation, asshole. I just honor it." Devo continued, "Look at the music that came from the eighties: The Cure,

Adam and the Ants, Depeche Mode, Siouxsie and the Banshees, The Human League, Joy Division, The Smiths."

"And fucking Devo," Travis interrupted, cackling.

"And fucking Devo," said Devo. "That shit you listen to doesn't compare."

"Oh, I think you're just mad because Nirvana killed all of that shit you listen to. Killed it with true lyrics that actually mean something."

Devo didn't say anything. He just flipped his Walkman on.

Travis saw me looking at the Walkman. "That's his dad's. Devo found it after his dad died, along with a bunch of cassettes. His backpack is full of that stuff."

There was another boy at the table that didn't say much, but he smiled at me and waved his hand. He wore jeans and a plain white t-shirt and had a case that I assumed carried a band instrument. He just listened and every so often nodded when the red-haired girl talked. It seemed like he wasn't really listening to her, but was just being nice and giving her the impression that someone was.

The girl that sat next to Travis was pretty. Her blond hair was short in the back and longer in the front, and she wore an old, black jacket that looked like it used to be a man's suit coat with a pink t-shirt underneath. Her outfit went well with the faded jeans she had on. Bracelets stacked on top of each other on both her wrists. I had seen a lot of pretty girls, but they mostly looked alike. You know, the same kind of prettiness that eventually makes them look ordinary. This girl was beautiful but in her own unique way.

She reached her hand out. "Hello, Neil. I'm Lux." I shook her hand and could feel the coolness of the silver rings that covered most of her fingers. "Thanks for helping Travis get through last week."

I was taken back and looked at Travis. I wasn't as surprised that they knew he was in the hospital, but that I was also there. I suddenly felt insecure.

"Oh, I don't hide the fact that I'm nuts with these guys," said Travis. "Especially Lux." He kissed her softly on the cheek. I took the kiss to mean that they were dating. "You won't be judged at this table. We're all nuts."

The red-haired girl paused. It was the first time she had stopped and acknowledged my presence. "Who's fucking judging who?" Her voice was loud, and she was looking directly at me. "We don't do that here. Be who you want to—"

"Point in hand," said Travis as he interrupted her. The red-haired girl looked at Travis like she was about to go up in flames. "You just made our point." She exhaled angrily and, without missing a beat, went back to telling some story about the college course that she was taking and how her professor was a pervert.

Travis was perfectly calm today, the calmest that I had seen him. The red-haired girl kept talking, and Devo put on his headphones and did some strange dance in his seat, swaying back and forth. The quiet kid with the band instrument just watched and laughed at Devo and acted like he was listening to the red-haired girl. I ate my lunch and enjoyed being a part of their group.

As it got closer to the end of the day, my anticipation for the Polar Bear Club grew. I wasn't sure how I felt about being placed in a club where everyone was screwed up in some way. Wouldn't the other kids find out, and then I would be labeled for the rest of high school? Mr. C assured me that it was a confidential club. There were times when other kids wanted to join, but after talking to them for a while, he turned them away. They wanted to join because they wanted out of class, not because they needed help.

"It's not seen as a bad club, Neil, because no one knows what the hell it is," Mr. C had said this morning. I'd never heard a teacher say "hell" before. I liked how open Mr. C was. He didn't try to act above everyone else. He was real.

I made it through art without being inspired, and in biology, I sat with two kids at a lab table with a dead rat between us ready to be cut open. I liked animals too much, so I just sat there and let the other two kids do the dissecting. They were talking about rats' small and large intestines and appeared to love this gross display of a rat autopsy. Science geeks. I guess I labeled people too sometimes.

After biology, I walked down the hall to Mr. C's office. I had not seen Travis, Lux, Devo, the quiet band kid, or the red-haired girl all afternoon. I guess that made sense. They were seniors, and I was a freshman. The only class that I had with seniors was creative writing, so at least I would get to see Travis then and again for lunch. It had been a long time since I had friends, and while I relished it, I was scared to lose them. It scared me to lose anything these days.

I heard a lot of talking and music as I walked toward Mr. C's office, and my stomach started to tighten. I froze, and my legs stiffened with adrenaline. Then, I felt a familiar arm around me and found myself walking again. It was Travis with a crooked grin on his face. I smiled and then felt another hand on my arm.

"Welcome to your education," said Lux.

Polar Bear Club

"THE CRAZIEST ONE IS HERE, SO LET THE FESTIVITIES BEGIN," said Travis with his arm still around me. I wondered if he meant him or me, but I smiled anyway. "This is Neil, our newest and youngest member."

Mr. C was pouring coffee and laying out some snacks of chocolate and fruit in the middle of the coffee table. The kids, the same ones that stood around Mr. C outside the doors every morning, started to applaud, and then I heard another voice from the corner of the office.

"Great, another crazy kid. We're running out of room." Then she started to laugh. It was the red-haired girl. "I'm totally kidding. You are more than welcome here," she went on. "Just keep your mouth shut, and everything will be okay." She smiled and added, "Someone tell him the rules." Man, she loved talking.

Travis's arm around me had a familiar comfort to it. It almost made me emotional, but I caught myself because crying would not be cool or make a good first impression. However, something told me that these kids might be okay with it.

"Let's get some food," Travis said to me, and I realized that I'd frozen where I stood.

"Okay. Everyone have a seat," Lux announced. "We want to welcome our new member and tell him what we're about."

Mr. C sat in his swivel, gray chair facing the center of the room, and the rest of the kids followed suit. I sat on a small couch with Travis and Lux.

"Who's leading today?" said Lux.

"Go ahead." It was the quiet kid from lunch. "You're good at it."

"Let's introduce ourselves first," Lux said. "Though, you know most of us."

I looked around the room a little more slowly. When I first walked in, everything was a whirlwind and sort of blurry. I knew Travis and Lux, recognized the red-haired girl and the quiet kid, and then there was Devo. Then, I looked over and spotted a tall kid wearing black, with jet-black hair and piercings. It was the goth kid from the bus on my first day of school. He still looked pissed off, and his big radio sat on the floor next to him.

Travis leaned forward, holding a small, plastic white bear. It was the kind of plastic bear that you buy from a machine at the zoo. "I'll start us off. I am Travis. Manic depressive, bipolar, grunge music lover, and part-time smart-ass." Travis laughed and passed the white bear he held to Lux.

Lux rolled her eyes at Travis, then said, "I'm Lux, and I have depression. It's like my little dark friend. I also love to read and listen to music. I want to go to college next year, but I'm not sure if I'll have the money." She passed the bear to the goth kid, who wordlessly passed it on to Devo.

"I'm Devo. Paranoid schizophrenic. I like eighties music and eating Blow Pops." Lux giggled.

"You and your fucking Blow Pops," said the goth kid.

"Hey. None of that," interjected Mr. C. It was the first time he had spoken. Devo flipped the goth kid off, and they both laughed. It was friendly bantering.

The quiet kid spoke up and said, "I'm Eric. I really don't have any depression or other psychological disorder. I guess I'm just lonely, and you are my only friends." Eric smiled. "It's the only club that would take me." Everyone laughed.

Eric passed the bear to the red-haired girl, who snatched it eagerly. "I'm Melanie, but everyone calls me Mel. I am addicted to pills and sex, and I've been told that I'm a narcissist because I won't let anyone else talk. That's total bullshit because I just let all of you talk about your depressed, crappy lives, and I didn't say a word." Travis looked at me and pretended his hand held a Muppet and imitated Mel's talking. "I'm also a bit of an obsessive compulsive." The bear went to Mr. C. I was surprised he was going to share.

"I'm Mr. C, counselor extraordinaire and young adult whisperer. I'm an avid traveler, and I also have depression." He and Lux pounded fists and laughed. Mr. C passed the plastic bear to me. He winked at me and said, "Go for it."

I hesitated, and everyone waited patiently. Strangely, the silence wasn't awkward. They just chilled out and waited. I cleared my throat, unsure if my voice would be strong, raspy, squeaky, or just a whisper. I started to speak, and thankfully, it was my normal voice. The one I remembered, but a little deeper.

I held the bear in my hand and started nervously twirling it. "I'm Neil."

"Don't fondle the bear," the goth kid said. Travis shot him a look, and he just shrugged.

"I guess I have depression." I tried hard to remember what Peter told me at the hospital. "I have some anger issues too. I killed some fish." That last part just slipped out, and I regretted saying something so stupid. Everyone erupted in laughter, but it didn't make me feel stupid. They weren't making fun of me. Hesitantly, I laughed with them. It felt good to laugh at myself. "I stopped talking a couple of years ago, and then I met Travis and wanted to talk again, and now everyone thinks I'm nuts."

"We don't," said Lux.

"Screw everyone else," said Travis.

"They're the ones who are nuts," said Devo. "However, stay away from my fish."

The goth kid made a fist with his hand, which was covered with a large, black glove that had the fingers cut off, and slammed it into his other hand. "That's what I think of everyone else and their opinions."

"Here's the thing," said Lux. "We decided a long time ago that we would just be open about who we are, and all of the mental health stuff you just heard is a part of who we are. Instead of hiding it and acting like it's bad, like we're broken or something is wrong with us, Mr. C taught us to control it and not let it control us. My depression is a part of me." Lux looked over at Mr. C, who smiled warmly at Lux and nodded his head in agreement.

"Yeah. This is a club for people who accept who they are. It gives us a place to go where we can feel normal and be ourselves because, frankly, these are the only people who accept me when I'm manic." Travis reached for Lux's hand.

"Knowing who you truly are is one of the greatest gifts that you can give to yourself. To find that is like seeing an old friend again," said Mr. C. "All I ever ask of you guys is to be true to yourself, respectful to each other, and to let your guard down while in this room. It's hard enough everywhere else. This is a safe place to be who you are." Mr. C leaned forward and looked at each one of us. "I didn't create this club. You did. I am just here to guide you and help you become the best people that you can be. This life is full of wonder, hope, loss, and plenty of misguided material thoughts."

With the introductions over, the conversation turned to the club's official business. The club, or "small gathering of misfits" as Travis liked to call it, was planning a field trip to the art museum in Chicago. I had never been there before. Everyone had input into what we would do in Chicago and when we would go. Even the goth kid spoke up and asked if we could stop at a music store that he'd found on the internet. They all talked about food that we would bring and about maybe taking a walk to Navy Pier if the weather cooperated. I just listened and didn't add to the conversation, but everyone seemed to accept that and reminded me that I was part of the club and could speak up whenever I felt like it. Mr. C took notes and guided the conversation, but didn't try to take over like so many teachers or adults did. As a group, we had a voice. I didn't want the day to end. I wanted to stay there with my new friends, and for the first time in a long time, I felt like I was part of something. It was a new beginning. I had been getting too used to endings.

I've Got Your Back

I WALKED TOWARD MY GRANDPA'S HOUSE AFTER SCHOOL. IT was about a half-mile walk from school down uneven, cracked sidewalks. It was considered one of the older parts of town, and Grandpa had been there for over thirty years. On my way there, I heard someone honk a horn and yell, "Neil, you want a ride?" I looked over, and it was Travis and Lux, driving slowly as they pulled closer to the curb. Travis drove an old, brown station wagon that looked like it could hold ten people. It smelled of exhaust, and the tires were nearly bald. When they screeched to a stop, I walked up to the window on the passenger side and leaned over to look at Travis.

"Come for a ride in the Brown Bomber," said Travis.

"Brown turd, more like it." It was Devo from the back of the car. He was sunk down so far in his seat that I could hardly see him.

"You can walk," Travis shot back.

I got into the back seat with Devo. It was the first time that I had been in a car with another teenager driving. My mom probably wouldn't like it.

"Where are you going?" asked Lux.

"I just moved in with my grandpa," I said. "Actually, I'm not sure if I'm moved in or not, but I know I'm not going home again."

"Displaced soul," said Travis. "We need to adopt this young man." He ran his hand through Lux's hair. "He needs us."

I just smiled. Travis was right. I did need them. They had helped me find my voice, and now I had hopes that they might help me find myself.

"You want to go with us to Simon Says?" asked Lux, twisting around in the front seat to look back at me. She could tell by the look on my face that I had no idea what she was talking about. "It's a diner we like to go to after school."

I nodded, then immediately regretted that I didn't take the opportunity to speak. I didn't want my newfound friends to think I was a freak, but in a way, we all were.

Devo handed Travis a cassette tape. I'd seen cassettes in my dad's office, and had even played a few in his stereo. My dad had similar tastes to what Travis listened to, grunge music like Pearl Jam, Soundgarden, and Nirvana. The cassette started playing something with a great beat to it, and Travis turned the silver radio knobs of the Brown Bomber all the way up. For an old car, it had a great stereo. Devo was bobbing up and down to the music; it was this weird song about a Jenny, and it kept repeating her number, 867-5309. Sitting right next to him, I could see that Devo was skinny, so skinny that I could probably put my hand around his entire arm and two hands around his leg.

"Hey!" yelled Lux. She reached over and turned down the radio, then grabbed Travis's cell phone from the holder on the dashboard. "Let's call the number and ask for Jenny."

In the eighties, that was probably done thousands of times, but she seemed so excited. I already loved to watch her eyes light up. No one else answered her, and she was looking at me, so I said, "Yeah. Then start singing to them." Lux laughed and started dialing.

I liked making her laugh. A moment later, her smile turned to a frown. "It's not a number," she said. "Guess too many people called it."

"Lux, can I use your phone to call my grandpa?" I asked. "I need to let him know that I won't be home right away." I didn't want to sound lame, but I also didn't want Grandpa or Mom worrying about me. Lux handed me the phone, and when I called my grandpa's house, Mom answered. "Mom, I'm going with some . . ." I paused, not knowing if I wanted to take the risk of calling them my friends yet. "Um. My friends from school, to a diner."

She paused for a moment. "That's great, Neil." Her voice shook on the other end. "Go have fun. I would like to meet them sometime."

"Should I come to Grandpa's?" I asked, worried from how she sounded.

"Yes, we're all moved in."

"I wanted to help," I said. "I can come and help now if you need me to." I knew I should ask, but secretly I hoped she'd say no.

"You go have fun! Try to come home by six, and then you can help Grandpa get the two dressers out of the truck." She told me she loved me, and I just said thanks back to her, which seemed like a strange response but I wasn't ready for *that* in front of my new friends.

The diner stood sandwiched between two brick buildings, and it had this funky, lime-green roof, and the white paint was chipping off the outer walls. Blue neon lights that read "Simon Says" shone in the windows. The door creaked as we opened it, and music filtered out onto the sidewalk. I almost expected it to be a thunderous beat that you hear out of so many cars as they pass by—music that didn't make any sense to me, that seemed like it was made for compact cars and insecure boys. But this singer was talking about being a creep. It was good.

We sat at a booth with red benches, one of only about twelve benches throughout the room and six round stools at the counter. A waitress with a crew cut, black eye makeup, and three piercings in one nostril came over to take our order. She seemed to be about twenty-five if I had to guess, and her name tag said "Marlene."

"How are you guys today?" she asked.

"Fabulous!" Lux chirped. "Meet our newest misfit, Neil." Lux motioned over to me.

"Nice to meet you," I said.

"Isn't he a polite one," said the waitress. "Unlike this little shit." She gave a gentle slap on the back of Devo's head. "Can't even say hello to his big sister. The usual?" she asked. Everyone nodded. Then, she walked away. All of a sudden, I panicked. I didn't have any money. Plus, I didn't have a "usual," so I had no idea what I would be eating.

We heard the door creak open, and the tiny gold bell rang. A group of boys came in, two of them wearing football jerseys and the other two wearing preppy, collared shirts under their jackets and looking like they were trying to model for Abercrombie.

"What the fuck are they doing here?" Travis was staring them down.

"Shit!" said Lux. "It's Derek. Just keep your cool, Travis."

I sat in the booth wide-eyed as the boys walked over. "Saw your brown piece of shit out there."

"Piss off, Derek," Lux said as she peered at the muscular kid that stood in front of the pack of boys. The boy looked around the table and shook his head at Devo like he was disgusted, but Devo didn't pay any attention to him, lost in his music. Then Derek looked over at me. "Who's the new freak?"

"Go fuck yourself," snapped Travis.

"I thought you guys were too cool to come to Simon's," Lux said.

"We thought we would see how the freaks live." Derek's friends started laughing. Suddenly, I was glad to be a freak. I wouldn't want to be like these dipshits, whatever category they were in. David was a jock, but he'd never been a bully like these guys. I wanted to defend myself when he called me a freak, but I just stayed quiet to see who these guys were and what they wanted. Plus, getting my ass kicked was not in my plans today.

Marlene came over and delivered "the usual," which turned out to be a platter of thin cheeseburgers and a huge basket of French fries with Cokes for all of us. The food smelled great. I hadn't eaten since lunch, so I was starving. If we could just get rid of these assholes, it might be a great evening.

"Nice piercings," Derek said to Marlene.

"Screw you, punk ass," she fired back. That's when Devo clicked off his music and looked up. "Get out if you came here to be a little prick. There's an alley out back for you and your little friends to go play with each other." I liked Devo's sister. Lux was laughing pretty hysterically by now.

"You little bitch." Derek was looking at Lux.

Travis stood up, getting right in Derek's face. "Let's go and see that alley."

"I would love to." Derek turned to his friends. "Ready?" They all started slapping each other on their backs and shoulders like they were the kings of the world. One of them said, "Dude, this will be fun."

I glanced around the diner to see if anyone was watching, if they were going to let this happen. Unfortunately, there was just one cook in the back who looked so old that he'd probably worked here since the opening, Marlene, and a lady at the counter carrying three bags with her and sipping on tea. Her gray hair sat past her shoulders, and she wore layered clothes that looked like she had slept in them for a month. Unless Marlene called the police, this was going to happen.

"Just take it to the alley, boys," Marlene said, and then I knew that there was no hope of the police or anyone else intervening. I sure wasn't going to call them. I needed to back up my friends. Travis started walking outside, and Derek and his friends followed. Lux hurriedly jumped up and grabbed Travis's arm. "Listen, he's an asshole, but if this is some weird courtship where you want to defend my honor, you don't have to. I'm already yours."

"Look, his girlfriend is trying to save him," Derek sneered, putting his arm around one of his friend's necks.

"These dickheads need their asses kicked," Travis said to Lux. "I'm sick of this shit. I've had enough." When Travis said that, I realized that this wasn't the first time this had happened.

Lux sat back down. Devo didn't move. He looked freaked out, his skinny arms shaking, and he kept his eyes to the floor. He sure wouldn't be any help to Travis. I followed Derek out and sized the other boys up to see which one I might be able to take, but I hoped this fight was between Travis and Derek and the rest of Derek's friends would just stay out of it. When I looked back through the window, Lux's head was buried in her hands.

The alley was narrow between the diner and the brick business next door. I couldn't see Travis or Derek through the wall of Derek's friends in front of me, and I wasn't sure if they even knew I was there. They all smelled of cologne, and from the back, their hair looked perfectly cut and their clothes like new.

We came to the end of the alley, and right when Travis turned around, Derek swung at him. He missed as Travis leaned back. Travis put his hands up, his fists covering his face, looking like he might know what he was doing. Derek took another swing at him with his arms wide, his friends cheering, and Travis darted for the opening to punch him twice in the nose. The cheers stopped when the rest of the group saw Derek's nose run red, then they all lunged for Travis.

That's when I tackled the one closest to me and started throwing punches as fast as I could. He wrestled me off him easily, and two of the boys held Travis while the other two pinned me. Derek loomed in front of Travis and went to punch him, but Travis kicked him in the balls. While Derek yelped in pain, the two boys holding Travis took turns hitting him, blows raining on his stomach and chest. The other two threw me against the brick wall. My forehead hit it hard, and I fell.

Things were a little blurry after that. I smelled sweat and blood and heard the thump of punches landing. Then, all of a sudden, the boys that threw me were flying up against the wall and grunting. All I could see was someone in black moving fast and Derek's friends slamming against the wall or falling to the ground. When I staggered back to my feet, I saw the goth kid beating the shit out of all of them.

Kicking them when they were on the ground, hitting them in the head, shoving them against the brick wall. Then, as abruptly as the fight started, it ended, with Derek and his friends scrambling to their feet and running away.

Derek turned back and shouted, "We'll get you, freaks!" The goth boy took a couple of steps their way, and Derek yelled, "Go!" to his friends.

A little dazed, we made our way back into the diner. Travis held his ribs and tried not to laugh. My head was bruised, but I would survive. It was my first real fight, and my adrenaline surged. The goth kid just sat down and started eating French fries like nothing had happened. Then he looked up at the group and said, "Sorry I was late." The tension broke as we all burst into laughter. Devo turned on his music again. It was like it never happened, except for Lux, who had her arms crossed tightly over her chest and her jaw set in a frown. Travis put his arm around her.

"I know how you get," said Lux. "I just don't want you getting into any more trouble."

Travis smiled and said, "I was in control. I was just going to hit him in the face a few times and then go."

The cheeseburgers and French fries tasted great, like victory with a side of the blood that ran from the inside of my lip, and then I realized that Mom and Grandpa were waiting for me and had probably made dinner. Travis must have seen my expression and said, "I think it's time to go meet your mom and grandpa."

Fighting Monsters

GRANDPA WAS WORKING UNDER THE HOOD OF HIS TRUCK when we arrived. I was unsure what to expect from my new friends since the only adults I'd seen them around were the teachers at school. I wasn't worried about Grandpa keeping an open mind if people looked or acted a little strange though. Grandpa was strange too, but in a good way. He was a Vietnam veteran. He never talked about it much, but my mom told me that he'd been in a search and rescue unit in the Air Force from 1965-69. She said she could remember when he came home; he'd stayed in his room for a month or so and would either wake up screaming or wouldn't sleep for days at a time. She said that sometimes he would drive away and disappear for a couple of weeks and no one knew where he was. I guess Grandma would just wait patiently for him to come home and explain to my mom when she asked where he was, "He's fighting monsters, honey. He'll be back soon." Mom said she grew up telling her friends that her dad was a monster hunter.

"She loved that man," Mom would say with tears in her eyes when she would think back to Grandma and Grandpa's time together. Grandma died a few years ago, and Grandpa never really recovered. He left for the mountains for a few weeks shortly after she died, and when I asked where he was, Mom had said, "He's out fighting monsters, honey." I didn't really know what that meant until David died. Now, I go to my woods to fight monsters.

Travis parked in the street, and we all got out. Lux bounced right up to my grandpa and stuck out her hand. "Hello, I'm Lux. I'm friends with Neil." That still surprised me, to be called a friend.

"It's a pleasure, young lady," said Grandpa. He peeled off his work gloves and shook her hand.

Travis came next to my side, "I'm Travis." Grandpa had the same look that I had when I first met Travis; the difference was that Grandpa pointed it out.

"You're a good-looking son of a bitch." Most people might be embarrassed at Grandpa's bluntness, but I wasn't. Grandpa was the best man that I'd ever known.

Travis went over to Devo, who was still sitting in the car, lost in his music, and then biffed him on the head through the open window. "What the fuck?" Devo said as he looked up at Travis, then he noticed my grandpa. "Oh, sorry, sir." I don't think Devo even realized that the car was parked. He turned his music off, clambered out of the car, and shook Grandpa's hand. "Just listening to my music. It's the best music in the world, you know, from the eighties."

"Shit, son." Grandpa grinned, and the lines around his eyes creased. "That's not music." He walked over to the open garage to the stereo that he'd found in a pawnshop and turned up the volume. From the speakers, Jim Morrison and the Doors roared out "L.A. Woman." I knew all of Grandpa's music.

"That's classic," said Devo. He walked into the garage and admired Grandpa's 1970s stereo.

Lux and Travis had already started to pull some of our things from my old house out of Grandpa's truck. "Where should we take these?" asked Travis, a big plastic bin in his hands. Grandpa showed him where everything went inside the house. We didn't have much except clothes, pictures, dressers, and a few keepsakes. We all started moving everything, and what would have taken Grandpa and me at least a couple of hours took us about forty-five minutes. I was proud of my friends. That might seem like a weird thing to say, but that's how I felt.

"Where's Mom?" I asked Grandpa.

"She had to get some papers filed over at the bank. Sounds like the house sold pretty fast, a young couple waiting to get into the school system," he said.

I wanted Mom to meet everyone, but sometimes I wasn't sure about her being sad and not able to handle it. Though she had been happier since Dad left. We all sat on Grandpa's front porch. Lux, Travis, and I settled onto the porch swing, and Devo decided to stay in the garage and flip through Grandpa's record collection. Grandpa brought out some hot chocolate for us. It was a little chilly out, but it had been one of those autumns where October days were sometimes sunny and in the fifties. That hardly ever happened in the Midwest. Most years, today would have been bitterly cold with snow. Grandpa liked staying outside anyway. He did even more so after Grandma passed away. I remember him telling me once, "Every corner I turn, every place in this house, brings up a memory of her."

"So, how did you guys meet?" asked Grandpa, sitting in a rocking chair across from us.

"The two of us met at school," said Lux. "Neil just came into our lives from nowhere, and here we are."

Grandpa smiled. "Neil is one to show up out of the blue." He winked at me. "He once walked here from his old house, which had to take a few hours, and his grandma and I found him sleeping on the couch the next morning. He was only about eight then. Don't know how the hell he remembered how to get here." Everyone chuckled, and I stared down into my hot chocolate. Grandpa continued, "There was another time when he was ten where no one could find him for two days, but he was up in the attic playing with all of my old military stuff. I finally heard him rustling through my trunk. He dropped my helmet."

"What'd you do?" asked Lux.

"Well, I just let him keep playing because I knew his dad would tear him up, or at least want to, so I went up when I knew he was sleeping and brought him downstairs. He woke up downstairs the next morning not knowing how he got there."

"Did your dad tear you up?" asked Lux. I just shook my head.

"No. His dad and I had an understanding." Grandpa's crooked grin filled his face.

"Which was?" asked Lux.

"Well, we agreed that he would never touch my daughter or grandkids out of anger, and I would do the same for him."

"Maybe I should have you meet my dad," Travis remarked.

Grandpa said to Travis. "You seem like a strong kid. Why are you letting anyone bother you?"

"It's amazing what you get used to," said Travis.

"Yeah. You're right about that." Grandpa suddenly got that distant look that I'd seen before. It was usually when he thought of the war or Grandma. Pain was hard to hold within. It eventually showed on your face. "Where did you meet Neil?"

"In the hospital," said Travis. I was surprised to hear Travis say it so casually, but one of the reasons that I liked Travis was because he was never ashamed of who he was. "Neil helped me make it through the week."

"Well, sometimes the only way to make it through things is with a good friend by your side," Grandpa mused. "It's too bad you kids have to put up with some of the bullshit that you do. You should be able to enjoy your childhood. Hell, high school should be some of your best years before you have to start worrying about other shit."

Lux and Travis listened intently to Grandpa. I'd heard him talk like this before, but it never got old. He was my greatest teacher.

Grandpa leaned further back in the rocking chair and then held it steady. "Life is a gift. You need to hang onto every bit of joy, pain, loss, and love that you can. It's the experiences that count. Good or bad, they are what make us who we are." Grandpa didn't look at anyone as he talked. He just drank the warm chocolate from his mug and stared out into the sky. The evening sun was just about to sink below the treetops, and it offered a glow of orange and red that lit up the porch. "I never understood why adults feel like it's their place to run the world. Hell, kids are better than us. They aren't as corrupt. They're not as stained by life. We all have something to offer." Grandpa looked back at me. "Like Neil. I don't think that I could have made it through his grandma's passing if he didn't stay with me every night for that first month. Every time I looked at him, I saw what I still had to live for." He stopped and stared at Travis, who sat up, anticipating what was coming next. "Like you, Travis." Grandpa looked back out to the stars. "I haven't seen Neil's face so relaxed or happy in two years. He always talked to me, even when he stopped talking to everyone else, but it's been awhile since he's had true friends. I think you both helped each other in that hospital."

Lux rubbed my back, and when I glanced over to her, she had tears in her eyes.

"Grandpa," said Travis, which took me a little off guard since Travis just met him. But Grandpa didn't mind, and he smiled to acknowledge Travis. "Can we talk for a moment?" They both got up and walked down the sidewalk side by side.

I sat with Lux, and we didn't say much, just stared at the last glimpse of sunset as it dipped below the trees. About ten minutes later, Grandpa and Travis came back. None of this seemed strange to me. Teenagers always loved being around Grandpa. David's friends were constantly stopping by to listen to his stories.

"Your grandpa would make a good member of the Polar Bear Club," said Travis as he reached the porch.

I had no idea what they'd talked about on their walk, and part of me didn't want to know. Shortly after Travis and Grandpa came back, Travis, Lux, and Devo started walking down the driveway, ready to go home. Before he got into the car, Travis hugged me, which I didn't find strange. I think I needed it. It wasn't a typical "man hug" with a slap on the back. He really held me tight. Lux must have wanted in on it too because she came up and started hugging the both of us. Then the three of them drove away.

As the Brown Bomber disappeared down the road, I felt a rush of fear. I was scared of getting close to someone when losing people was so difficult. It was a risky business to start to love someone again, to start a friendship, and in that car, there were at least two people that I thought I'd started to love. I felt vulnerable knowing I had opened up and let them hear my voice, and my anxiety grew as I wondered if I would see them again at school. Would they be there and still be my friends? Was Travis's hug sincere? Was he trying to tell me something, and maybe that something was goodbye? Over the past two years, it'd been hard for me to be friendly to anyone.

Suddenly, I felt a warm hand on my shoulder. "Those are keepers," said Grandpa. "I think they would go to the ends of the world with you, Neil."

"But I just met them," I said.

"Yeah, those are the best kind, the ones that see you right away for who you are. The kind of people that spending a day with makes you feel like you have known them for years. It's comfortable."

I smiled and felt a tear fall down my cheek. "I would go to the end of the world with them too." Maybe true friendship was similar to true love, and maybe friendship at first sight was as real as love at first sight. I'd never had either one until now, and now I had both.

Mom pulled into the driveway. She was crying as she just stared at us from the car, then smiled as she saw us wave to her. Grandpa's arm was still around me. Mom got out of the car with a folder full of papers. Her tears turned to laughter, and none of us needed to say anything. We walked up the driveway to the house, *our* house, with our arms around each other and our feet stumbling because it's hard to coordinate three people walking. Grandpa held us tight and steady like he always did, and we made it. We would fight monsters together.

Spring

THE WINTER WAS A BLUR. IT WAS HARD TO CELEBRATE Christmas with David not being there. Maybe it would always be like that. January was filled with taking tests at school and feeling depressed. My doctor said I had seasonal affective disorder. I didn't know about that, but I do know I felt like sleeping for a month. In February, I watched my mom cry. February 15th is David's birthday. I have a feeling winter will send a chill through my body for the rest of my life. One of my fears is that when I get older, there won't be any months left that do not have some significant event that affects my life, and the entire year will be filled with past memories that bring sorrow.

I hated March because I got anxious about the anticipation of April. April is when baseball starts, and it was the month when David killed himself, so March sucked knowing what I had to look forward to. I hadn't told the Polar Bear Club about David's suicide. I hadn't even mentioned David. I just wasn't ready. All I talked about was feeling depressed and angry with my dad, which was kind of a high school cliché. Everybody in the club was pissed at their parents. Even Mr. C mentioned how much of an asshole his dad was.

Mom had taken a job as a paraeducator at the nearby elementary school, her first job in over seventeen years. She stopped working when David was born, and then she took care of the house and our family. I guess she figured that since it was just Grandpa and I now that she should take care of herself. I was glad. She loved the little kids. It seemed like they gave her hope, like all little kids who haven't been tainted by everything awful in the world yet.

We went for a walk, Grandpa, Mom, and I, every night before bed. I usually didn't say much, and Mom told us funny stories about the kids she worked with. It'd become our routine, and routine was good for now.

Tonight, we came back from a walk in the crisp air. Mom gave me a hug before I went upstairs to my room. I lay down in my bed and watched the sun as it slowly disappeared through the window. As I lay there, my anxiety started to grow as I thought about what had been happening two years ago, a month before David died. David was using a lot of drugs by then, and drinking too. I knew it, but I didn't say anything because he would have gotten into trouble. I'd just hoped that it was a phase and he would stop. I was only in middle school then and not equipped to deal with that kind of shit.

I remember David cut his hair to a buzz cut, which freaked my mom out because he'd had beautiful blond hair that he loved. He liked the way it stuck out from underneath his baseball cap. David would say, "It drives the girls wild," and then give me a grin. March was also the month that he came home with a tattoo that he cut into his arm. It had the look of a baseball, and was almost as large as one, with the word "Why" in the middle. He bled for two days and wouldn't go see a doctor. Mom had to sneak into his room at night while he was asleep and dab peroxide on the wound so it wouldn't get infected. David would wake up screaming, and Mom would vanish before he knew it was her that was stinging him.

March was also when Mom and Dad had started getting calls from school on a daily basis that David was skipping class. I think the teachers ignored his behavior for a while because everyone loved him so much. We all thought that he was going through a phase and just hoped he would get out of it. So the month of March could fuck off.

April came, and I sat silent in Polar Bear Club.

"You okay?" asked Lux. I nodded.

I trusted the people in the room more than anyone, but I wasn't ready to tell them yet. What if they thought different of me, or thought that maybe I was even crazier than I appeared and the truth would come out? Silence was always my weapon. I wanted to say something, I really did, but April was a month when I felt like I was holding my breath for thirty days. David killed himself on April 28th, so I waited all month for the day to come.

I wondered if it would be like this for the rest of my life. Always obsessing about the months and how David had been feeling. It was like a movie reel in my head. Play by play, scene after scene spinning through my mind, trying to figure out if he already had a plan, then holding on through April, realizing that it was a matter of days before he would take his life. The weird thing is that David had seemed like he was becoming himself again a couple of weeks before he died. I remembered when I was reading on my bed and a baseball glove landed on my stomach. "Let's go," was all he said. We played catch that night for three hours. We could only see the ball in the moonlight right before it hit the glove. It was a challenge not to get hit in the face. My glove hand was sore for the next three days. That had been two weeks before.

Three days before, David joined me for a walk in the woods. I'd always remember our conversation.

"Neil, promise me that you'll keep doing well in school and go to college someday."

"We could go to college together," I had said.

"I might have blown my chance," David told me. "I messed up this year. My GPA is screwed."

"You could play baseball again. You already had that college in Michigan looking at you. Maybe you could get a scholarship."

David had just smiled. "Thanks for always believing in me, Neil."

I'd analyzed every word of that conversation every day for two years. Was he losing hope or gaining hope? Was he telling me to do well because he wouldn't be there for me anymore, or was he just being David and giving me good advice? Perhaps he was just having a conversation with me because we were both in a safe place among the woods? I had so many questions, and it terrified me that I would never find out the answers. It also terrified me that maybe I would. So the month of April could fuck off too.

April 28th

MOM STAYED HOME TODAY. SHE WAS SITTING ON THE PORCH drinking coffee when I left, her eyes red, and I could tell she hadn't slept. She would probably never sleep on April 28th ever again. Grandpa was in the garage tinkering around with an old '67 Army Jeep that he had bought at a military auction for $200. He always said that it was good to keep some bad memories.

Grandpa saw my hesitation to leave. "You go on to school, Neil. I'll be here with her," he urged me. "Go on now. Be with your friends."

School was a blur all day long. I really had no idea what any of my teachers taught. Mr. C was out of the building at training, and Travis and Lux had a fight so they didn't eat together at lunch. I sat with Devo, but his headphones limited his conversational ability. The goth kid was there, whom I finally learned through Travis was named Henry. That made me laugh. I would not have thought of a Henry as being tough, or wearing makeup and having piercings. I hated stereotypes, but we all faltered. Travis told me to never call him Henry, said I would get pounded if I did. Henry liked to be called H. Even the teachers called him H. However, the teachers hardly ever called him anything because H didn't say much and he did his work. This tough-looking kid who freaked people out never actually caused any problems. He took care of a few though. Two days ago, those idiots had come back to the diner and tried to jump Travis and me again right before we got into the Brown Bomber. H had walked up right as Travis was getting thrown to the ground. Just like last time, we didn't hear him, just the sound of him throwing kids around before walking into the diner without saying a word. It seemed like it was just a natural act, like taking out the garbage. But the strangest thing was being around this kid for a couple of months and only now knowing his name.

"Today's the day, isn't it?" said H as he ate French fries, staring at me from across the cafeteria table.

I was taken aback. He talked even less than me. "What do you mean?" I asked.

"Your brother," H said. "David."

My heart started beating fast, and tears slowly welled up in my eyes. "How . . . ?" I could hardly speak. "How do you know?"

"I knew David. We played baseball in summer league for three years together." H, a baseball player? I loved watching David play summer league, but I didn't recognize H. "He was one of the best players I've ever seen. The cool thing about your brother was that he always tried to make everyone else better. It wasn't about him. That's a true player."

I cleared my throat, which had suddenly become tight. "How did you find out?"

"I read the paper and watch the news," said H. "I stayed in touch with him online, and we would meet every so often."

I couldn't believe this. I thought David had stopped hanging around with anyone except the people who gave him drugs. How should I react to H? My arms and shoulders tensed; he'd known this entire time and didn't say anything. I did understand not wanting to talk to anyone and remaining silent, but he *knew*. Standing up from the table, I gripped my tray, and before I knew it, the tray was flying through the air. It hit the white brick wall, and the remainders of my hot dog and fruit salad painted the floor. I ran out into the courtyard that sat in the middle of the school, barely knowing where I was running to, and glimpsed at two teachers running after me, calling for help on their radios. When I reached the gazebo, I felt two arms wrap around me. I couldn't move; the arms held me tight, and they were strong. When I turned my head, it was H.

"Get back!" H yelled at the teachers. "I've got him. He's fine."

I couldn't get loose from H's grip. He was strong, but there was also this strange comfort in his arms. Then, as I started to relax, I noticed H's forearms full of cuts. Razor cuts. I recognized them because I had cut myself a few times after David died to see if I could alter my pain. It never worked for me. With the amount of cuts that H had, it must be working for him.

H hugged me. "Just relax, buddy." Some kids were laughing through the window, and a few looked freaked out. The teachers all stood around and watched, ready to intervene. There was no need for that. All of a sudden, I had more arms hugging me. It was Travis and Lux, along with Mr. C.

Everyone let me go but H. He walked along my right side as he held me around my shoulders. We followed Mr. C back to his office. As we walked through the cafeteria, I told the custodian who was cleaning up my mess that I was sorry. He just smiled and said, "Gives me something to do." I felt humiliated. Kids were talking about me and either giggled or looked freaked out. I heard H tell a couple of boys, "Say anything, and you're dead." Those boys stopped laughing.

I sat in Mr. C's room with him, H, Lux, and Travis. He had just returned from wherever he was and heard my name on the radio that he carried on his side. They just sat around me and didn't say anything. Lux took my hand, and I couldn't help noticing how soft it felt. Her nails were painted light blue and looked like candy. I loved the feel of her fingers caressing mine. No one said anything, but the silence wasn't uncomfortable. Instead, it felt right for the moment. The silence was supportive and calming.

I broke it by saying, "I'm sorry." I looked over at H.

"No worries," he said. "I think your reaction was right on. Those hot dogs suck ass." Everyone laughed except H; I think he was serious.

"Am I in trouble? The teachers looked pissed." I'd never been in trouble at school before.

"No," said Mr. C. "No harm done. Like H said, those hot dogs suck." He continued, "We're just going to hang out here for the rest of the day. Polar Bear Club can start early."

Travis leaned in, his blue Nirvana shirt matching his eyes, "You don't have to talk, Neil, but it might help to tell us your story." He smiled at me, then said, "Don't get used to my girl rubbing your hands either."

Travis and Lux and Mr. C had been my respite from myself the past four months. They were a break from my reality, but it was April 28th, and reality bites. I just nodded my head and took a deep breath. The Pearl Jam shirt that I was wearing, the one that Travis had given me, was stained with ketchup. Could I finally tell them my story? Could I tell them why David's death was my fault? What would they think of me after? I dug my fingernails into my palms until they left a mark.

After a couple more minutes of silence of me contemplating and Mr. C drinking more coffee, I started to talk. "Two years ago, I found a letter from David on my dresser. It said, 'You are the only truth I have ever known. I will always be there with you. Go and make something of your life. Stay in school, make friends, find love, and take care of Mom. She will need you now more than ever, but I think with me gone she might find freedom. Please help Grandpa fight his monsters.'"

As I recited, Lux gripped my hand harder. I continued, "I immediately went to his room, and his bed was made. David had stacked his baseball trophies in the middle of his room, and his baseball cards were scattered on the floor among them. I ran into the living room, checked the garage and the backyard. I couldn't find him anywhere. Then, I heard a thump in the basement. I opened the basement door and turned the light on. I heard gurgling and gasping, and I jumped down the stairs and saw David hanging by the wood beam. The rope was tight, and his face had turned blue. There was a stool kicked out from under him. All I remember is running over to his dangling body and screaming. Then I lifted him as high as I could and grabbed the rope so it came off the wood beam. David and I fell to the ground with him on top of me. He was so heavy. He was barely conscious. I'll never forget how blue and cold his lips looked."

I stopped my story. Tears were filling my eyes, and I could feel my rage coming, but Lux kept hanging onto my hand. Then Travis came over and sat next to me. H had tears in his eyes, which I think surprised everyone. Mr. C was calm, our rock, and just let what was about to happen unfold naturally. I continued because now that I'd started, I wanted to say it. I wanted to tell them how I killed my brother.

"Then, David started to whisper to me. I tried pulling the rope from his neck, but all I could do was loosen it. He whispered again, so I placed my ear next to his mouth. He said, 'You should have left me, buddy.' I freaked out because his eyes started to roll and I could tell he was struggling to breathe." My words were becoming shaky and grew louder. "I wanted to carry him, but I couldn't. His hands were freezing when I pulled him toward the stairs. I screamed for Mom and Dad to help, but then I realized they were out with Dad's work friends. I had to leave him. I had to fucking leave him, and I was afraid!" My voice rose until I was screaming, and H leaned forward, ready to grab me again.

I forced myself to take a deep breath, and with the others silent, I could hear my teeth rattling in my head. I went on more quietly, my voice shaking. "I ran upstairs and called 911 and told them to get to my house. They started asking me too many questions. I didn't have time for questions. I needed to get back to David, but I told them everything. I slammed the phone down and . . ." I stopped because I was gasping. The class bell rang but no one moved. It seemed like they didn't even hear the bell because there was no reaction. They were completely focused on me. It occurred to me that Travis, Lux, and H were sacrificing their time for me. They were here for me, and they deserved to hear what I'd done. They deserved to find out. I held my head in my hands, and Lux ran her fingers through my hair. I loved her right at that moment. I think I'd loved her from the first moment I met her.

"I ran down the fucking stairs, but he wasn't on the floor anymore. I was afraid to look up. I knew right then. I ran to his body hanging from the beam. I lifted him up again, and he fell on top of me. This time, he didn't look at me. He didn't whisper. There wasn't any breath. He was so strong. He was strong enough to hang himself again."

Mr. C was wiping his eyes. "This isn't your fault, Neil," he said.

"Fuck him!" I screamed. "He fucked my life up! He left me. Selfish bastard! I should have stayed with him. I should have never left him in the basement. I killed him!"

"He left *you* in that basement." H sounded mad. "He's the one that left you."

H was right. David did leave me lying on a cold basement floor in a house that I will never walk into again. He left me to live with Mom and Grandpa and go to a new school. He left me to go through this high school on my own. He left me to discover girls, go to college, get married, have kids, work, and travel, but never share any of that with him. He just left me. I hated him for it.

Travis leaned in closer to me, and with a gentle arm around me, he said, "He brought you to us, Neil."

Trying to Move On

THERE WAS ONE MONTH LEFT IN THE SCHOOL YEAR. MY grades were okay for my first year of high school, three A's and four B's so far. Grandpa had told me earlier in the year, "Neil, don't let this thing control your life. Don't let it decide your future. Keep focused on school." That's what I did, to the best of my ability.

Grandpa was a lover of words. He read relentlessly and tried to find meaning in everything, a lot like my mom did. I often found quotes in my sock drawer that he had written out. They were usually meant to inspire me, or they were related to something that I was going through. On April 28th, I found a poem by William Ernest Henley, "Invictus", set on top of my dresser in a wood frame. It read:

Out of the night that covers me,
Black as the Pit from pole to pole,
I thank whatever gods may be
For my unconquerable soul.

In the fell clutch of circumstance
I have not winced nor cried aloud.
Under the bludgeonings of chance
My head is bloody, but unbowed.

Beyond this place of wrath and tears
Looms but the Horror of the shade,
And yet the menace of the years
Finds, and shall find, me unafraid.

It matters not how strait the gate,
How charged with punishments the scroll.
I am the master of my fate:
I am the captain of my soul.

I was the master of my own fate. I knew it, and I wanted to act on it, but all of these intersecting tragedies and surprises interrupted my life. Sometimes I thought I was going crazy. Would I truly go nuts and not come back someday? Would the people I loved keep coming and going? Would I lose them? I read the poem over and over and realized that no matter our circumstances, we could either lie down and die or keep moving forward. I hoped I'd have the strength to move forward, that I could create my own path and live a life worth writing about.

The Polar Bear Club was planning their trip to Chicago for the last week of May. Travis had spent a couple of days in the hospital shortly after I told him about David. I felt like maybe my story pushed him into a manic state, but when I visited him, he said, "I just needed the break." He would be back to school at the end of the week. I spent a lot of time with Lux during that time.

Lux and I were eating at the diner the Thursday before Travis got out. She leaned in across the nearly empty plate of French fries and asked, "You want to sneak into the zoo tonight?"

To my own surprise, I nodded my head. I didn't ask her why or how, just, "Can we see the chimps?" I'd never done anything that bad before, breaking and entering. I never did anything that was too far from the rules, but Lux had me transfixed. Sometimes I just found myself staring at her, and then felt like a stalker whenever she caught me.

"I will pick you up at nine thirty," she said. "Wear dark clothes." Then she darted out of the diner faster than I've ever seen her move, and the Brown Bomber drove away.

There were two hours until I would meet Lux. I had to laugh because she'd forgotten to take me home, and Grandpa's house was a long walk.

"Your date leave you?" I looked up. Derek. The smell of his aftershave made it hard to breathe. "I heard your boyfriend is in the fucking crazy ward again."

"Fuck off!" I didn't have much else to say, and those two words seemed appropriate.

"How about we go to the alley, just you and me, and settle this? My boys aren't here, and your crazy friend isn't either." Derek leaned over me. "Unless you are too much of a pansy-ass like your big brother."

I tightly gripped my fork in my hand and fought the impulse to stab Derek in the leg. His flowing hair that was parted to the side and his brand-name shirt made me angry, so I decided to take the mustard and squirt the bottle all over the both of them. It whizzed out of the bottle, messing up his designer shirt and jeans, and as he tried to wipe the mustard off, it smeared into his clothes even more. Marlene was laughing by the counter and yelled over, "Get out of here, you little shit!" I didn't know if she meant me because I made the mess, but she was looking right at Derek.

"You asshole!" Derek grabbed my shirt collar and yanked me out of the seat. "In the alley. You're crazy, just like your crazy friend and your dead brother."

He walked out ahead of me, and I followed. I figured Derek was about to kick my ass, but I didn't care. The mustard in his hair and his reaction were worth a few bruises. Devo's sister shouted from behind me, "Careful, Neil. Maybe you should just stay in here." I didn't listen. Derek disrespected my best friend and my brother, and I just wanted to get in one good punch to break his nose and make his pretty-boy face crooked. One punch was all I wanted.

The walk seemed longer than it was. I'd learned that when you were about to do something where the outcome wouldn't be that great, the journey there became a blur. It was a narrow tunnel with no end in sight. I'd had my share of long walks: the hospital to the teen psych ward, the walk into David's funeral. They were just hazy moments in time. This time, I was going to feel a different kind of pain, physical instead of emotional, and I calmed knowing what was about to happen because, on some level, I wanted the pain. Maybe it would mask everything else. When two of Derek's friends grabbed me from behind, I knew I would get my wish.

My arms got twisted behind my back, and one of the kids whispered, "No one to protect you now, asshole." Derek stood in front of me with a strange smile. Then he started to put on his fingerless weight-lifting gloves. As he took his time to do this, less than two feet in front of me, I decided it was time to get my shot at him. I kicked him in the balls as hard as I could. He dropped to the ground in agony. I just laughed, even though I knew what was coming next. His friends started punching me in the ribs and head and knocked me to the ground. All I remember is lying next to Derek, getting kicked in my back, watching him writhe and hold his balls. I smirked as I took my beating.

All I could do was cover my head and hope for the best. Then, in a blur, the blows stopped and the other two boys were lying next to Derek holding their heads. One of the boys looked up and gasped, "What the fuck, old man!"

"Just stay down, kid." It was Grandpa's voice. How did he know that I was in the alley? Derek and his friends stayed put. It must have been something in Grandpa's eyes that told them this wasn't an old man they should mess with. I'd seen that look when Grandpa and Dad had their "talks."

Grandpa pulled me to my feet, and we walked out of the alley to his truck. My ribs and entire face hurt, but I still grinned. Marlene waved from the window, and the cook smiled and lifted his spatula. Grandpa didn't say anything. He just drove off like it was any other day. He and H were like souls in many ways.

"How did you know where I was?" I asked.

"Lux called me," he said. "She's a good girl."

"But . . ."

"She felt bad for leaving you there. She said she spaced it out because she was excited about the school project you guys are doing tonight. I guess she forgot you didn't drive." Grandpa looked at me holding my ribs and frowned. "You need to see a doctor?"

"No. I think they're just bruised."

"You can take a beating," Grandpa noted with a slanted grin.

"Yeah, I guess I can."

Hospital Visits

I SAT WITH MOM AND GRANDPA AND PICKED AT MY DINNER. Mom talked about her day and asked me about school, but didn't say anything about the bruise above my eye. Grandpa didn't explain what happened and redirected the conversation to fixing up the Jeep and the problems it was causing. I guess we both figured Mom didn't need anything else to worry about. Lux would be there in an hour to pick me up in the Brown Bomber.

"You guys are getting a late start on this project, aren't you?" asked Mom. She looked at Grandpa and smiled.

"Oh, leave the boy alone," said Grandpa. "I remember my first crush. You never forget the first."

I wanted to speak up and say it wasn't a crush, but I didn't want to lie either. I felt bad because I did have a crush on Lux and Travis was in the hospital. In truth, I just liked being with her. She was smart, fun, and beautiful, never trying to fit in with perfect makeup and brand-name clothes. While it seemed like half the girls at my school dressed and acted like they were copying whatever they saw on TV or in music videos, Lux remained beautiful just being Lux. She always looked out for me and the rest of our group and was always true to herself no matter what others thought of her, and I fell in love with her for that.

I slept for about a half hour after dinner. I didn't know what Lux had in mind for the zoo, and we had school tomorrow. I wasn't used to staying out that late. I think Mom liked that I had friends, so she offered me some liberties with my curfew.

As I showered, I felt my ribs. The right side was bruised and had a mark from one of Derek's friend's shoe treads. As much as I hated violence, I did have a sense of pride about my bruises. I laughed at the memory of Derek holding his balls and the boys flying to the ground, holding their heads and yelling, "What the fuck, old man?" They didn't know my grandpa. He could have killed them if he wanted to. The only other time I'd seen Grandpa get physical with someone was years ago, when two drunks at a Fourth of July festival wouldn't stop swearing in front of my mom, David, and me. Grandpa had asked them calmly if they would mind stopping. The drunks both told him to fuck off and then commented on my mother. Grandpa told Mom to take us to the snow cone stand and gave her a few dollars. She didn't react to the situation because she must have known what was about to happen. She knew her dad well. David was excited about the snow cones, but I turned around just in time to see Grandpa punch one of the drunks in the middle of his forehead and grab the other one behind the ear until the man sunk to his knees. The men were not there when we got back. Grandpa silently watched the fireworks, holding me like nothing had happened.

I heard Lux come into the house. I quickly sprayed some body spray and tried to do something with my messy hair, but it was no use. My hair did its own thing; I could brush it to the right, and it would slowly migrate left. I shoved some of Grandpa's old camouflage clothes into my backpack because I didn't want Mom seeing them and headed downstairs to find Grandpa showing Lux a picture of David and me that hung on the wall in the hallway.

Still out of sight, I heard him ask her, "Does Neil talk about David much?"

"Just recently," said Lux. "I think he keeps a lot of his feelings inside." I stood on the steps, up against the wall, listening.

"David's death took a lot out of that boy. I've only seen him come back to life in the past couple of months thanks to you and your friends."

"We love him," said Lux. "He's a misfit like the rest of us."

"We're all a little bit of a misfit. I feel sorry for the people who aren't," said Grandpa. "It must be boring to live perfectly happy lives. Though, you show me someone who thinks they are flawless, and I'll show you someone who's full of shit."

I walked out into the living room and kissed Mom goodbye. She was on the couch already falling asleep. She had slept a lot since we'd moved to Grandpa's house. Grandpa said she finally felt comfortable enough to rest. I wasn't quite sure what he meant, but I had an idea.

When I went over to the front door, Lux gave me a quick hug like she always did and then walked out ahead of me, but Grandpa held my arm and asked me to stay back with him for a moment.

"You have any money?" he asked. I nodded, but he pulled out his wallet and gave me forty dollars. "Neil, remember that Lux is Travis's girl. I know you like her, and that's okay, but Travis is a loyal friend to you."

"I won't do anything to stop that," I said. "I love them both."

"I know," Grandpa replied. "I just don't want anyone getting hurt. It needed to be said, so have fun, but not too much." His mouth turned upright.

We walked out and got into the Brown Bomber. Just being in the car made me miss Travis. I couldn't wait until he got out of the hospital. Lux started the car, which took two tries, then looked over at me. "You ready for the zoo?" she asked me with a grin. I nodded. "First, we have a quick pit stop to make."

The pit stop turned out to be the hospital. "I called Mr. C, and he said he would meet us there and his brother would let us in," said Lux.

"Peter," I said happily. "I haven't seen him since I was at the hospital."

"Travis said he was cool."

"He's a lot like Mr. C."

Mr. C was waiting at the entrance of the hospital, and when we walked inside, Peter waved us over to the staff elevators. I had forgotten how big Peter was. He practically filled up the elevator door. Mr. C looked small in comparison. He must have noticed what I was thinking because he said, "How do you like my baby brother?"

Peter smiled at me. "Neil, how have you been? I heard school is going well."

"Pretty good. I've met a lot of great people," I said. Suddenly, I remembered that I hadn't been talking much when I was in the hospital, and now I felt insecure with my voice, as weird as that was around people I trusted. It's strange how something that becomes a defense, like not talking, stays a part of you. I fought it and said, "How about you, Peter?"

"Oh, you know, just taking it a day at a time. Travis will be glad to see you. He's doing well. His old man is busting his balls to get him out of here," Peter replied.

"Is that a technical term?" Mr. C gave Peter a playful tug on his large bicep. It was clear that even though Peter was huge, he would always be Mr. C's little brother. That brotherly playfulness was familiar to me, and seeing them together made me wish I had it back.

We walked down the hall to where Travis was staying, and Lux held my hand. "You okay?" I asked.

She gripped my hand a little tighter. "I've never been here, and it scares me."

"Why?" I caressed my index finger against hers and regretted it immediately. It felt too sexual, too flirtatious. "There's nothing to be scared about. Travis is just getting some rest."

"I'm afraid because my dad always threatens to have me committed when I'm not feeling so hot."

"It'll be okay," I said. I pulled my hand away before we entered the room. I didn't want Travis seeing Lux and me holding hands, even though Lux was always holding my arm or hand when we were all together. She was just like that.

The unit had the same smell and same noises that I remembered. There were a few kids playing board games and watching television. I recognized one kid from one of my group sessions when I was here for the week. His wrists were bandaged, and his hair was now purple. I remembered he'd cut his wrists the last time too.

The hospital was just a Band-Aid for the extremely depressed. The program here was not to "fix" anyone or make kids better. It was basically set up to get kids through their roughest spots so that maybe they wouldn't hurt themselves, and then it would send them back out into the world with the same shit and wait for them to return. Hell, Travis had his own room and left a dresser full of clothes here. It was no fault of Peter's. Peter was great. He just had his hands tied by insurance companies only letting kids stay for a week, or parents that didn't want to do the hard work of parenting themselves. I was still angry at the system and at my mom for letting me come to this place. My body tensed.

"Are you okay?" Lux rubbed my back.

I looked into her eyes. The bright blue was beautiful and stood out against her bare skin. I liked it when girls didn't wear makeup; I knew they had plenty of reasons to, but I admired the confidence it took to walk out with dark circles, red spots, and all. As I felt her hand on my back and walked toward the mini library where I knew Travis would be sitting, I realized that one good thing came out of my parents putting me in this place. Without being committed, I would have never met Travis or Lux. Sometimes our paths are altered to give us a new one to follow. Destiny isn't for the blind or weary. You have to look for it.

Travis was sitting in the chair he always sat in, engrossed in a book, when we walked into the small room. He jumped up when he heard us come in and grabbed Lux, hugging her. He acted like he hadn't seen her in months when it was just a few days. He did the same to me and then hugged Mr. C. We all sat down and let Travis tell us about the book he was reading. It was called *On the Road*, by Jack Kerouac.

"I started it this morning," he said. "I figure if the author can write it in two weeks, I can read it in less than a day."

There was something different about Travis. He seemed calm, too calm to still be there. It was a demeanor I didn't expect, and it worried me. He looked at peace, holding Lux's hand and touching my shoulder as he spoke. He asked about Devo and H and wanted to know how the plans for the Polar Bear Club trip to Chicago were coming along.

"You guys are slacking without me, aren't you?" He glanced at Mr. C.

"We need you back, buddy," said Mr. C. "It's not the same without you."

"I want to finish my book," was all he said. Then he added, "I'm doing this when I graduate." Travis held up *On the Road*. "I think I'll get in the Brown Bomber and go west and stop in Denver and just roam."

My heart sank a little when Travis talked about leaving. I was a freshman, and there was no way I could leave with him. As Travis talked about the road trip he wanted to take and the adventures that he wanted to stumble upon, he reminded me of Grandpa. They were one and the same in many ways, except the manic part, and maybe that was why I admired Travis so much. Grandpa had his demons too. His just came in a different form. I guess we all have demons, the things that keep us up at night or wake us at two in the morning with intense clarity that makes our minds race. Maybe I could go with Travis for a few weeks this summer. Mom liked him, and I would be sixteen, but I doubted it would happen.

We hugged Travis and left the hospital with Mr. C and Peter, who were meeting some friends. Lux and I went to the Brown Bomber. Before getting in, I looked up to the window where Travis's room was and saw his silhouette standing there. He looked down at us, his hand raised against the light in the background. I waved back, and Lux blew him a kiss. The Brown Bomber started on the first try, and we drove off down the road with Travis still standing in the window. This time, both hands were raised.

The Zoo

THE ZOO WAS WITHIN A MILE OF THE HOSPITAL. LAST YEAR, A patient escaped from the adult psychiatric unit and ran the entire mile to the zoo in a hospital gown and slippers. He climbed over the fence, then made his way to where they housed the polar bear, climbed over its steel gate, and was mauled and killed. The bear was shot, and the man's body was found half-eaten. I was sad to read about it in the newspaper. The man had made the mistake, not the bear.

On the way to the zoo, we were silent for a few minutes, and then Lux said, "He seemed good to me." She stared straight ahead, like she was trying to convince herself that Travis was fine.

"Yeah," I said, trying to reassure her. "He seemed relaxed and into that book. You think he'll really go on a road trip west after graduation?"

"I think he will. When Travis gets something in his head, he usually does it."

"Will you go too?" I asked, then for some reason, I reached over and held her hand. After I did it, I regretted it. I had no business holding her hand like that, even though Lux had held mine a hundred times. The difference was that she was always touching people. It was just her way, and it wasn't mine. She pulled her hand away, and I muttered, "I'm sorry."

"It's okay." She drove down a road behind the zoo, pulled off into a dirt drive, and parked the car. "The zoo is through the woods. Take that path, and we end up next to the giraffes."

Suddenly hesitant to break into the zoo, I asked, "What are we doing, Lux?"

"I want to see the animals sleep." She must have seen my reservation, and then she reached over and took my hand. "Neil, have you ever kissed a girl?"

I froze, startled, but mostly embarrassed. "No." I was fifteen and had never even attempted to ask a girl out, let alone kiss her. "Never had a chance to."

"Let me show you what to do," said Lux. She leaned over, and I remembered what Grandpa had said about Lux being Travis's girl and loyalty. I wished he would've never said it. As she turned her head in towards me, my gaze dropped from her eyes, staring straight at mine, to her lips. I ignored Grandpa's advice and leaned into her and kissed her. I couldn't help it. As wrong as it was, I wanted Lux for my first kiss.

"Close your mouth a little more," she said. "Move your lips slow." I'd thought about kissing Lux since the moment I saw her, but I loved Travis like a brother, and I would have never done something like this to David. As we kissed, the fragment of my brain that could still think straight tried to justify it by saying that Travis wouldn't *really* mind, because after all, Lux was just teaching me how to do something I'd never done before. She pulled away slightly. "Move your tongue slow with mine," she said softly.

We kissed for a few minutes, which I think qualified as making out. Then, Lux abruptly stopped and reached into the back seat, grabbing a black backpack.

"Okay. Now you've had your first kiss, so let's go."

She got out of the car, and, still a bit dazed, I did too. We pulled on our camouflage clothes, and Lux started walking toward the path that led to the giraffes. I followed her into the woods and the darkness. It felt good to be in the woods even if they weren't *my* woods, which I hadn't walked since we moved in with Grandpa. The taste of Lux's lips was still on my tongue, and I had this craving for something sweet.

A few minutes later, we were at the fence. Lux was like a spider monkey. She scaled it in a few seconds and jumped over to the other side. Her face was directly across from mine, and I hated to think it, but I was hoping she wouldn't kiss me again because I didn't want to try to climb the fence with a hard-on. Her eyes were bright with the moonlight, and I grabbed the fence and climbed as fast as I could. When I got to the top, I threw one leg over, but the other leg was caught on the metal spear of the fence. I fell and hung there, dangling upside down. Lux started laughing. I loved it when she laughed really hard, even at me. It almost sounded like a cry as it went up and down in different octaves. As I dangled, the thought of David hanging in the basement flashed nauseatingly in my mind, and I wondered how he must have felt, although this was just my leg and not my neck. I quickly let go of that thought because David would probably be laughing too if he saw me now. I pulled my pant leg from the top of the fence and landed hard against the ground. Lux tried to help me up, but in the process, she slipped on the uneven ground and fell on top of me. The feeling of her body against mine gave me a sudden sense of security, among other things.

We walked around the corner and stopped by the giraffes. Two adult giraffes stood above their sleeping baby, which was on the ground, curled up with his head on his back. I'd never seen a giraffe lie down before.

After admiring them for a minute, I finally asked the question.

"Lux, what are we doing here at night?"

"Seeing the animals," she replied, as if I were crazy for asking the question. "I told you, I want to see them sleep."

"Yeah, but why not come during the day?"

"Because there are no little kids being pulled on leashes and getting yelled at every second by their parents. This way we can have it to ourselves."

I was hesitant to ask another question because I didn't want her thinking that I was a coward, but I said anyway, "There must be security."

She turned to me and placed a finger on my lips. "Then keep it down," she whispered with a grin.

Lux waved goodbye to the giraffes, and then we went to the exhibit where the otters swam. There were four of them floating on the surface of the water. Lux stared at them intently, but I couldn't take my eyes off her.

I really did love her, and as much as I knew I shouldn't, I wanted to kiss her again, or at least know if I had been any good at it. I kept remembering what Grandpa had said and decided that I couldn't go against his advice twice, but I did want to know how I'd done. I wanted a girlfriend someday and didn't want to suck at kissing her once it came to that.

"Lux," I whispered. "Can I ask you a question?"

She turned her full attention to me like I was about to ask her the most important thing in the world. That's one thing I loved about her: if you were talking, she made you feel like you were the only person in the world and that everything you said was astonishing words of wisdom. Her eyes would fix onto you, consume you, to a point that was overwhelming.

"Was I any good?" I felt myself blush right after I asked, and I was glad it was too dark for her to see my embarrassment.

"At?" she asked with a smile. "Because if you mean climbing a fence, then hell no."

"Kissing," I said. "Was I any good?"

I knew Lux had a lot of experience with kissing. She and Travis had been dating for two years, but I'd heard her talk about other boys that she dated before him.

Suddenly, she twirled around in slow circles with her hands raised high in the air and smiled and laughed. "It was beautiful, Neil. Very gentle, and it made my toes tingle."

I knew she was kidding with that last statement, but I really wanted a straight answer.

"I just want to know, in case I ever get a girlfriend."

She stopped twirling and stood directly in front of me, her face turned serious and her eyes soft and sincere. "Neil, it was a great kiss. Someday you will be the best boyfriend to some lucky girl."

"Really?" I asked. "I didn't know kissing was that important."

"It's not the kissing," she insisted. "It's the kindness and gentleness and vulnerability that you put into the kiss." She paused, searching for words, then went on. "It's how you care about people for who they truly are. Just like how you love Travis and accept him when he disappears for days without any word, or how you love your mom and grandpa, or how you're true to yourself and don't try to be like everyone else. You're natural and real and raw. You can hurt and feel pain without self-pity, and you're willing to break into a zoo at night knowing that we could get arrested." She smiled at that last statement.

"Man, all I was looking for was, 'You're a great kisser, Neil.'"

Lux laughed, and then we saw a light coming at us, bouncing in full speed. The security guard must have heard us, and he was sprinting toward us with his flashlight. We ran and tried to hide behind a tree, but he kept coming. The monkeys in the exhibit across from us started jumping and gave our position away. We ran down further and passed the polar bears. One of them was swimming in the water, and one was sleeping next to the edge of the pool. Lux gasped with delight and gave them a wave.

Running from the guard was exhilarating. Adrenaline surged through my legs. Lux started to get ahead of me, and I considered sacrificing myself so she wouldn't get caught. She must have known because she slowed down and grabbed my hand. "No!" she yelled. The guard heard her and started blowing a whistle. The touch of her hand gave me the motivation to keep running.

The guard yelled, "I know it's you, young lady!"

"To the woods," I said, then pulled Lux to the right. The woods were thick with trees and would be the perfect place to hide.

"We need to reach the car," Lux whispered.

"We won't make it. There are two of them now." Lux glanced back quickly. I looked up and saw the roof of the hospital over the tops of the trees and wished that Travis were here with us. He would love this. I wondered if he was looking out his window at the tiny lights bouncing up and down as we were chased.

We made it to the fence, and I let Lux climb first, making sure she got over. Silly me, I forgot she climbed like a monkey. I climbed up and jumped over, not getting caught this time, and as I landed like a cat on my feet, I felt redeemed from my failed earlier attempt. The lights gained on us since the climb slowed us down.

"Those fat asses won't be able to climb," said Lux.

To our surprise, the guards climbed the fence faster than we did and they both kept pursuing us.

"Jesus, they take their job seriously," I gasped as we ran.

We fled further into the woods, which would eventually come out to the road where the Brown Bomber was parked. We almost fell into a small hole when I grabbed Lux's hand and pulled her into the hole with me.

"Lie down," I whispered.

Lux lay down, and I covered her with branches and leaves. I moved under the concealment with her, and we lay together under the smells of leaves and dirt.

"Are you sure this will work?" she asked.

"I used to hide in my woods at home all the time. We'll be okay."

I held her with my arm around her waist and our bodies forming the same shape. My lips were near the back of her head, and even among the dirt and leaves, she smelled wonderful. Moments later, we heard the guards pass by us. We waited a few minutes until we heard one of them yell, "You little sons of bitches, we'll get you next time!"

"They always say that," said Lux. I guess she had done this plenty of times before. This was my time though, and I relished it.

We drove away with the headlights off in the Brown Bomber. "So," said Lux. "We found out a lot tonight."

"Like what?"

"That you are a hell of a kisser, you can't climb or run worth shit, and you know how to hide in the woods."

Lux looked at her phone. There were five missed calls and one voicemail from Mr. C. She played it aloud, and his voice shook as he said, "Lux, call me as soon as you get this."

Mr. C answered on the first ring. I heard him on the other end. "Lux, it's Travis. He tried to kill himself tonight."

The phone dropped, and the Brown Bomber veered sharply toward the curb. I grabbed the wheel and steered us back onto the road as Lux gasped for breath, her blue eyes suddenly blank. My lips didn't taste her anymore. I just tasted guilt.

Can't Handle It Twice

AFTER LUX CALMED DOWN, SHE DROVE THE BROWN BOMBER to the hospital. On the way, I kept thinking about what Mr. C had said. Travis "tried" to kill himself. That had to mean that he wasn't dead. My mind flew back to that night in April with David. With him, I wasn't allowed to go to the emergency room, but I already knew he was dead at the house.

Mr. C met us outside of the automatic doors and held Lux on the walk to the emergency room. I wondered if she hated me now for kissing her. Maybe Mr. C sensed something between us and Travis somehow knew what had happened. I would be responsible for another death. I couldn't take it. I started to shake and felt that feeling again, like I was hovering over myself and my body and mind weren't mine anymore. Lux was standing with Mr. C across from me in the waiting room. I nervously swayed back and forth. Lux must have realized what was happening because she walked over to me. It seemed like she was moving in slow motion, and I braced myself, waiting for her to slap me across the face for betraying Travis.

"Neil." Lux fell into my arms. "Can you stay with me?" I hugged her tightly, which told her my answer. Holding Lux helped me calm down because I realized that I had a good friend in my arms. Then, a familiar hand gripped my shoulder. I looked over and it was

Grandpa, with Mom right beside him. We all stood in the waiting room, hugging, and it was the first time in a long time that I felt like I had a family. Devo and H showed up right after Mom and Grandpa, and then Eric and Melanie came in.

Mel was in tears and wouldn't stop swearing. "What the fuck happened?" Her temper matched her fiery red hair.

The entire Polar Bear Club was sitting in the waiting room. Only Travis could bring together such a hodgepodge group.

Mr. C stood at the nurses' station, trying to find out more information. The nurse kept shaking her head, and Mr. C slammed his fist down on the counter. I figured they wouldn't tell him anything, but then Peter emerged from the double doors that led to where Travis was. He grabbed Mr. C and escorted him toward us. As they came closer, I saw the tears in Peter's eyes, and I stopped breathing. Lux let go of my waist, but Grandpa kept holding me. Whenever he was with me, I knew that everything would be okay. Maybe it was because he survived Vietnam or that he always kept my dad in check and never let him go too far with my mom, but I knew I could get through this with his guidance.

My heart stopped as Peter started to speak. "He's okay."

I started breathing again. Everyone hugged in relief.

"What happened?" asked Grandpa. "Why did he do it? Any idea?"

Peter continued, "I will tell you as much as I can, and a little more than I should." He slowly looked around the room. "I can see that you are Travis's family, so I will throw a bit of confidentiality out the window."

We all nodded our heads.

"He checked himself in earlier in the week and told me he just needed rest. We have always taken Travis ever since he was twelve and his dad started running this place. I figured that all he needed was some sleep and someone to talk to, so I met with him every day, and we would talk, and sometimes he would join the group sessions. He seemed calmer than normal, like he wasn't actually manic or depressed. He read a lot and spent most of his time in his room. I noticed that he was trying to hide a limp, and he said that he hurt his leg playing football."

Lux and I looked at each other. Travis hated football, and besides, who would he play with? Everyone he knew was here.

Peter continued, "He didn't want the docs examining his leg and said it was okay. Anyhow, his mom left for Europe on Wednesday. Travis made a comment that she would never be back and that he was stuck. I couldn't get much more out of him. He helped a couple of our troubled kids through a bad week. You know Travis." Peter paused as a tear ran down his cheek. "He's just one of those people that others listen to and want to be around."

We all nodded our heads. We knew firsthand what it was like to want to be with him.

"Anyhow," said Peter as he wiped his eyes. "I found him in the chair in his room. His head was tilted back, and he was barely breathing. Travis had moved the chair so it faced the window, and he had a copy of a road atlas and *On the Road* in his hands. We rushed him down to the emergency room, and they pumped his stomach. It was full of pills. He had to have been stashing them for weeks. Man, with all the pills he took, I'm surprised . . ." Peter didn't say it, but we all knew why he was surprised. Then, Peter's voice and posture changed. "They found bruises all over that kid's body. His leg was beaten with a bat or something. It was blue all along his thigh."

We didn't know what to think. H was gripping his large fist and slamming it into his palm. He was always there when any of us needed him, but he hadn't been there for this. Was it Derek? Did he and his asshole friends finally get the best of Travis? I started to plot revenge in my head.

"They're lucky they arrested that bastard before I could get to him," said Peter.

"Who?" asked H. He looked like he was plotting revenge too.

"Travis's dad," growled Peter. "That son of a bitch beat that boy all over his body. I would be willing to bet he's been doing it for years, but this time, he got out of control. That's why Travis limped and groaned every time he sat in a chair at Group. It wasn't a fucking football game. It was that asshole beating him."

"When did they arrest him?" Mr. C asked.

"About an hour ago at his home. I bet those rich fuckers he lives by won't want this getting into the papers. Too late for that! The board is going to fire him."

"Will Travis be okay?" asked Lux. "Will his mind be okay?"

"Yeah, they said he'll be alright. There was no permanent damage, just bruises. He's actually awake but extremely tired. Tough kid," said Peter.

"Where will he live?" I asked. His mom was gone, and his dad would be in jail for a while. "He'll need someplace to go where he feels safe."

Grandpa placed an arm around my back. "Don't worry about that, Neil. He's got a place."

Tears welled up in my eyes. I didn't think I could love Grandpa any more than I did in that moment.

We waited at the hospital until the next morning. Nobody said much throughout the night. We just waited and supported each other by being together. Peter finally came out and took us back to see Travis two at a time: Mr. C and Lux went first, and then H and Devo, followed by Mel and Eric. I went in with my mom, and Grandpa said he would see Travis by himself.

I was frightened to see him. I was angry at him too. I couldn't lose another brother.

Travis lay in his bed, hair disheveled and eyes red. He apologized for what he did. He said he knew it must have hurt me the most because of David, and he promised to never try to kill himself again. I wanted to believe him, but reality and pain and darkness sometimes don't allow you to create your own destiny. All I could do was be there for him and convince him that this life was worth living. I loved Travis, and I didn't want to be angry with him for trying to leave this world like David did. It just made me feel sad and helpless.

I didn't tell Travis anything about living with us. I waited to see if Grandpa would tell him. They seemed to have this strange bond that had grown from the moment they met each other. Every time Travis had come to visit, he and Grandpa would take these long walks, just the two of them, and Travis would always come back smiling and looking like he was ready to take on the world. I had an idea of what those talks were like because I had gone on a few of them with Grandpa, and so had David. David and I never shared with each other what Grandpa told us. We kept it to ourselves, like it was a treasure map to life. Now Travis was a part of that treasure.

Moving In

TRAVIS MOVED INTO GRANDPA'S HOUSE THE SAME DAY HE WAS released from the hospital. Peter knew that he was in good hands and helped move Travis in even though Travis only had a backpack full of clothes, three boxes of books, and a box of CDs to carry inside. He took the spare room above the garage, where Grandpa kept a single bed, an old couch, and a desk. I always wanted that room, but Grandpa cut me off before I could say anything. "Travis is almost eighteen, Neil. He's a man now. It's time for him to have his own space."

I guess I couldn't argue with that. I was just happy to see Travis more often, and with him came Lux, which was even better. Travis's dad got seven years in jail after Travis testified that the severe beatings had been going on since he was six. The bastard couldn't buy his way out of this one.

Travis's mom called him from Europe and said that she would be staying there with a man she'd met. Their house went up for sale, and his mom took the money and put $50,000 of it into an account for Travis for college. After the transfer was completed, he and Grandpa took a long walk.

I knew Travis hated his dad and wasn't fond of his mom, but it had to hurt him. He lost two parents within a matter of days.

However, as I watched through the living room window at Travis and Grandpa talking on the front porch and Mom laughing at their conversation, I knew Travis had gained a family that would love him no matter what. Maybe that would be all he needed to keep going.

Chicago

WE TOOK THE SCHOOL VAN TO CHICAGO. IT WAS OUR ANNUAL trip as a club. Travis, Lux, H, and Melanie would graduate in two weeks. Mr. C, we found out in yesterday's meeting, had taken another job in Missoula, Montana. When he told us, he had said, "I just need my mountains again." I understood. He needed his mountains like I needed my woods. I would miss him. I would miss them all. Suddenly, in the back seat of the van traveling on the interstate to Chicago, I felt lonely. It was the loneliest I'd felt since late fall, just before I became a part of the Polar Bear Club.

We arrived in Chicago around nine thirty that morning. We were staying overnight in a hotel close to the lake. I had never been to Chicago, and I kept looking out the window for Lake Michigan, but instead I just saw a bunch of old buildings and people walking everywhere. There were not very many trees in sight.

We pulled up to a brick, two-story building that had a sign on the outside saying "Community Center." A man walked out, and his muscled arms waved rapidly to us from above his head. His dark brown eyes matched his skin, and his head was shaved. Mr. C jumped out of the van and hugged him like he hadn't seen him for years. We all shuffled out and stayed silent while they hugged each other and looked at one another without saying anything. Both men had tears in their eyes.

Mr. C finally said, "You haven't changed a bit."

"Just a little more around the midsection," the man replied.

Mr. C laughed, then turned to us. "This is Fred Johnson. He's an old Army buddy."

We all looked at each other. We had no idea that Mr. C had been in the Army. H seemed especially interested because he and Mr. C were supposed to meet with an Army recruiter next week.

"Two hours away, and we haven't seen each other in ten years," said Fred. "Can you believe that shit?"

Fred put his muscled arm around Mr. C's shoulders and led us into the building. When we walked in, kids probably around thirteen years old all the way up to eighteen were doing schoolwork. The room was large, set up like a classroom, with eight round tables that had four chairs around each of them. On the far side of the room was an open kitchen, with a stove, refrigerator, and faded wooden cabinets. There were twelve students that stopped what they were doing and looked us over as we entered, but no one said anything. Adults sat at many of the tables with the kids, with some of them teaching up to three students at their station.

"They're all volunteers," Fred said as he saw us observing. "They give up their time to help us teach. It's all people who have once worked as teachers, engineers, police officers, nurses, park rangers, you name it."

"How does that work for the kids?" asked Mr. C.

"They get all of their subjects taught to them by people that have been in the working world. It's real life, so the kids respect them more than teachers that haven't had a lot of real-world experience with certain topics."

We all nodded our heads in agreement. "I wish our school was more like this," said Travis.

Fred turned to him. "I think most of us need to be taught by people that have experiences, but also by people we respect."

H left us and sat down at a table with a group of students. They kept reading aloud with the adult they were with and ignored him. As a big kid with black eyeliner and dressed in all black, he probably freaked them out. We left him there, just watching the lesson, and took a tour of the building, which we found out used to be the old fire station. The gold pole remained in the center of the room.

"Why are the kids here instead of at school?" asked Lux. "Do they get credit?"

"This is the last resort. These are kids that haven't been making it in our public schools. They are either credit deficient, truant, or have been expelled and are trying to turn their lives around," said Fred. "I started this program after I got out of the Army and graduated college. I was a kid just like them, misguided without a lot of direction, and I want them to have a chance."

We visited with Fred for another hour, then found out that he and Mr. C would be meeting later for dinner. "You guys will be okay for a few hours on your own tonight, right?" Mr. C asked. We all agreed a little too quickly, eliciting a suspicious eyebrow raise.

On our way out the door, we found H with another group at a different table. He came up to Mr. C with a contemplative look on his face. "What is it, H?" asked Mr. C.

"It's weird," H said. "I never really had a clue what to do after high school. I figured I would end up drifting around or joining the military, but I think I might want to teach."

"You'd scare the shit out of the kids," said Melanie. Mr. C cut her comment off with a stern stare. One of his pet peeves was diminishing someone else's dream.

"Fuck off, Mel." H flipped her off, then hung his head like he felt bad for his reaction.

"Stay with me, H. Don't let this feeling go." Mr. C put his arm around H's shoulder. "You would make a great teacher. You would connect with a lot of kids and help them through some rough times. Don't ever let anyone tell you different."

H smiled, leaned into Mr. C a little, and then we all got back into the van. H looked back at the school as we drove away.

We checked into our hotel, which overlooked the lake as well as a park with some piece of art that looked like a silver sperm. Travis and I shared a room since Mr. C told Lux and Travis that there was no way they were sharing a room after they requested it. Our room was right next to H, Devo, and Eric. We all opened our doors at the same time, and as they walked into their room, H said to Devo and Eric, "You both might end up dead in your sleep." Travis and I looked in their room to see their reaction. Devo looked at Eric and gestured toward H, then they both jumped him from behind and tried to wrestle him to the floor. H flipped Eric onto the bed and pinned Devo to the floor with his knee on his chest. He held him there until Devo stopped squirming. H let Devo go and then looked up at me and winked.

Lux and Mel were staying together, and before they walked into their room, Devo yelled down the hall, "Let us know if you have a pillow fight!" All of us boys were thinking the same thing: two girls in a hotel room walking around in their underwear. It wasn't perverse, it was just our imaginations running away with us. It was high school.

I tried really hard not to think about Lux that way. I still felt guilty about our kiss. We never told anyone, and we never talked about it. It was just something that happened, and I wanted to kiss someone again now that I knew I wasn't bad at it.

We were on the tenth floor, so after I was settled in, I stuck my forehead up against the cold window and looked down at the ant-like people scattering around the park and the city streets. I wondered who they were and where they were going. I wondered what their dreams might be and if they still had hope. Travis came up next to me and stuck his head to the window too.

"It's peaceful from here," he said. "I'm not sure if I could live in a city like this. Too big and too much bullshit."

I glanced over at Travis and hesitantly asked, "Are you still going west?" Our breath fogged the window as we spoke. The May air was cool, especially this high up.

"Yeah, your grandpa has been helping me with where to go. I guess he has a friend who owns a working ranch, so I might stay there and work. I just want to get away." Our heads stayed against the window. "Look at them. Do they really know what they want? Do you think any of them are living the life they wanted or thought they wanted when they were our age?"

"I'm not sure," I said. "I don't know how many people actually do what they want to do."

"It would be interesting to take a survey of a hundred people on the street and ask them three questions: Are you doing what you thought you would be doing when you were eighteen? If you are, how did you maintain your motivation to stick to your true self? If not, what happened and why did you give up on your dream?"

Travis paused, a gleam of inspiration in his eyes. "Let's do it," he added. "Let's go down there and find out about lost dreams and lost hope and try to avoid everyone else's mistakes. That should be a class." He pulled his head away from the window, went to the dresser, and started digging around for a notebook and pen. "Let's go," he said, holding up hotel stationery and a pen. "We'll ask the questions and, based on their answers, tally them under the headings 'Lost' or 'Found.'"

H was standing in the hallway when we walked out. We told him where we were going and asked if he could tell the rest of the group that we would meet them at the art museum in an hour.

"Yeah, I'll tell them, but those two bastards might not be around if they keep jumping on me."

"Why are you out here?" asked Travis.

"I was going to take a nap, but they tried to throw a blanket over me and hold me down, and then Devo started dropping ass. I really might kill them."

We left the hotel and immediately were surrounded by busy people: tourists trying to rush to their next destination, shoppers overindulging on designer clothes, business people talking or typing on their cell phones, and a few people begging for change. I had the feeling that if people were honest with us, we would be tallying a lot on the 'Lost' side of our survey.

"Let's start," said Travis.

I was worried that we might be looked at like we were crazy, but Travis had a way of approaching people that transfixed them and made them comfortable. He picked a man in a suit and tie walking briskly in our direction.

"Sir, would you mind answering a quick survey about dreams and lost hope? It will take two minutes of your honesty." Travis smiled at the man, who stopped walking.

"Okay," he said, looking at his watch. "Two minutes."

"Are you doing what you thought you would be doing when you were eighteen?"

The man laughed. "Not even close. I thought I would be playing baseball for the Cubs."

"When did you lose your dream?" asked Travis.

"When they didn't call me up from the minors," the man replied. "I couldn't hit the curveball."

"You tried to live your dream. You tried to do something that less than one percent of the population would even attempt." The man nodded. "I would say that just by your attempt, you succeeded," said Travis.

"Perhaps," the man mused. "I didn't quite make it, and now instead of wearing a uniform, I wear a suit. Feels like a sellout sometimes." The man walked away, a distant look in his eyes.

"Lost," said Travis. I put a tally on the 'Lost' side of the paper.

The next person Travis went up to was an older woman with gray hair and green walking shoes, and when he started talking, she paused her slow pace. Her wrinkles formed deep lines next to her pale blue eyes.

"Ma'am," said Travis. "Could you answer my survey? It will only take two minutes, and it will help two young men figure out about lost hope."

The woman's face broke into a smile. "Go ahead. I'm not in a hurry."

Travis altered his question. "Have you lived the life that you thought you would live when you were eighteen?"

"Well, that's not a question that can be answered in two minutes," she said. "I would say yes and no." Travis looked at her quizzically. "What I mean is that I have loved a man and he loved me, I had a beautiful child who passed away three years ago, and I have traveled all over the world."

"I'm sorry to hear about your child," Travis replied. "It seems like you've had a pretty good life otherwise. Would you do anything different?"

"Worry less," she said. "Everything works itself out. However, I guess . . ." The woman paused. She glanced at Travis, who grinned, coaxing her into telling more. "I would have taken a chance and tried to be an actress. I loved drama while I was in high school."

"Why didn't you go for it?" asked Travis.

"It seemed silly. At least that's what my parents told me."

"So you listened to them and not yourself?"

"I suppose," the woman responded. "Still, I have no regrets."

Travis nodded. "Where is your husband now?"

"Oh, he was killed in the war," she said. We had no idea which war, but we didn't push the subject. "Like I said, boys, I have experienced love and experienced being a mom. Loss is a part of life."

Travis quietly said to the woman, "Thanks for answering our questions."

"You're quite welcome, young man. Remember, having experiences, good and bad, in life is everything."

She walked away, and Travis seemed sad all of a sudden, staring blankly at her with slumped shoulders. "I guess 'Found,'" he said.

He thought about talking to a homeless man, but figured that would be stacking the survey toward the 'Lost' side. We talked to twenty other people as we worked our way toward the museum, and then we noticed a familiar face sitting on a bench by the museum steps. It was Mr. C.

Mr. C glanced up as we walked toward him. "How's it going?" he asked.

"It's okay." Travis shrugged. "We're conducting a survey."

"Well, the others are on their way. What kind of survey?"

"About hope and lost dreams," said Travis. "Will you take it? You would be our twenty-first person, and then we can add the tallies."

"I suppose," said Mr. C. "I try not to think too much about lost hope."

Travis started with the same question, but versed it differently again. "Did you know when you were eighteen that you wanted to be a counselor?"

Mr. C smiled. "When you are eighteen, you still feel capable of changing the world. Optimism and feeling invincible are your fuel."

"What did you want to do?" I asked him. It was the first time I had asked a question regarding our survey.

"I was in love when I was eighteen," he replied. "At the time, that was all I wanted."

"That's not really a job," I said.

"No. Love shouldn't be a job. You mentioned hope and lost dreams." Mr. C shifted on the bench. "My only hope when I was eighteen was to marry the girl I loved. That was it."

"What happened?" asked Travis.

"She went to college in Dublin. I tried to go with her, but I didn't have the grades or interest, and I couldn't find any work there. We were very much in love, but she had her dreams, and I didn't want to stop her. I joined the military because I was lost and needed to leave and it was the quickest way I could think of at the time." Mr. C stared out toward the passing cars before him, like he was trying to see through the building across the street.

Travis must have seen the look on his face. "I'm sorry that I asked. Where is she now?"

"She became a writer and lives in London. She's somewhat famous." He leaned toward us. "I may end up a 'Lost' on your survey, but she would be a 'Found,' and that's enough for me, even if it was just for a short time. That's what love can do for your life."

I knew right then that our questions were bullshit. Life is not as simplistic as either being lost or found, or living your dream, or living a life that you didn't think you would. Perhaps life is all experiences, good and bad, like the older woman said, and the way to live a good life is to experience as much as possible. Travis walked over to a garbage can, ready to throw the survey away, but then he folded the paper and put it in his pocket. Maybe he was thinking the same thing that I was. Maybe life should just be lived and everyone should be considered Found.

Lux, Mel, H, Devo, and Eric all walked towards the museum. We climbed to the top of the steep steps together. Before we entered, Lux gently held Travis's hand and said, "You okay?"

Travis looked deeply into Lux's eyes, and I heard him say, "Found." Then he smiled.

We went into the museum and walked around wearing headphones that led a tour through each piece of artwork. It was nice to escape inside the headphones for a while. It reminded me of my time not talking, and in a way, I missed it. The headphones gave me the same excuse to escape. As I studied all of the paintings, I actually enjoyed most of them, especially the impressionists. Those paintings seemed to catch a glimpse of life in simple times with mostly outdoor scenes full of bright colors. Looking at them brought me back to walking in the woods when fall turned the leaves fiery red and orange. Vincent van Gogh's *The Potato Eaters* haunted me with its image of poverty and depression, but most of all, it hit me with the closeness of the family that was eating together, seemingly unbroken. I wondered how the people in the painting would answer our survey.

Lux and Travis held hands while they looked at the paintings. Travis put his arm around her when they saw a painting called *The Kiss*. In the painting, two people were holding each other, covered by a gold blanket, and the man kissed the woman softly. I felt guilty looking at it. It brought me back to my time with Lux getting chased at the zoo, with us lying together under the leaves and me holding her.

Suddenly, an arm wrapped around my waist. I half expected to look over and see Lux, but she was with Travis. It was Melanie.

"Hi, Mel," I mouthed. She smiled and took off her headphones. I knew she would struggle with not talking during the tour.

"You like this one?" she asked. I nodded, and she put her arm around my waist and pulled me closer to her. "I do too." Her smell was similar to Lux's, but I was not an expert on how girls smelled, so maybe they all smelled sweet like strawberries. "Come with me." Mel pulled me along until we found an empty gallery where no one else was.

I took my headphones off so I could hear her. "Maybe we should stay with the group," I said. "It's a pretty big museum." As soon as I said it, I wanted to take the words back. I sounded so uncool.

Mel put my headphones back on me, then put hers on, and I stared into her eyes. She was very pretty. Her eyes were a deep brown that I felt like I was sinking into. As we stood there in the vacant room, Mel pulled my shirt toward her and kissed me hard. Her tongue moved deep into my mouth, and it felt like she was trying to choke me with it. The gum that she was chewing almost passed over to me, and I just about gagged, but this was my second kiss and Mr. C said to get all the experiences I could in life. I'm not sure an open-mouthed tongue-lashing was what he meant though.

The kiss went on for a couple of minutes, and as she moved her mouth fast against mine. This was so different than the kiss I had with Lux. That first kiss was soft and sensual, and I wanted more because it made me feel wanted. This kiss beat the shit out of my teeth and lips and tongue, and it seemed slobbery and forceful. Mel's tongue piercing hit my teeth several times, and as the sound reverberated in my head, I wondered if I would need dental work after this. Then, she stopped and just walked away, leaving me standing in a room full of paintings of naked women and sad old men. I got the hell out of there and realized that I had the same noticeable problem that I had when Lux kissed me. I looked around and found a painting of a wrinkled old man bathing, and that fixed my problem.

I never saw Devo, Eric, or H the entire time we were there. I guess appreciating art wasn't their thing. After moving through the next few rooms of paintings, I finally caught up to Travis and Lux, and they smiled as they crowded me, hugging me on either side. I wondered if they could smell Mel on my shirt or if my mouth was red from being kissed so aggressively. Lux held my hand and guided me to the next exhibit while Travis held her free hand. She snaked us in and out of benches and people, and it felt like we were floating. The colors of the paintings flashed before us, making us dizzy as we sailed from one to another.

I loved them both so much that every time I saw them, I realized how awful the summer was going to be without them. Lux had told Travis that she was going west with him. Apparently, he didn't respond right away, and he told me that was a mistake. I didn't know if he meant Lux going west was a mistake or him not responding to her, but when she didn't come to our house for the next two days, I figured it was the latter.

Mr. C was waiting for us at the museum exit. He pulled Travis aside and spoke to him in private for a moment, then came back to us and said, "H and I are going back to meet Fred. Travis knows the way back to the hotel." Mr. C handed us tickets to the Field Museum, then leaned towards us as H waited by the door. H, Devo, and Eric had been hanging outside the museum. "I need to keep this going. I've never seen H take an interest in very much." He winked at us and grinned.

H and Mr. C jumped on a city bus and left. They would be gone until after dinner, so we were on our own for a few hours. We all agreed to meet back at the hotel before dinner.

Standing on the sidewalk, Travis faced us. "Let's skip the Field Museum and head back."

"What for?" I asked.

"I brought some beer in my backpack. Let's go have a few."

I was anxious and started fidgeting with the strings on my hoodie. The only time I had ever had a beer was with Grandpa, and that was just half of one. It couldn't be much different than wine, right? Lux and Mel must have liked the idea because they walked ahead of us, holding each other's arms and laughing a lot. Lux would occasionally whisper something to Mel, and then they would both stare back at me. Mel's stare worried me. If we were going to kiss anymore, I might have to request that she remove her tongue piercing. I wasn't sure my teeth would last another make-out session.

Travis placed his arm around me. "So, here's the deal." I looked up at his slanted grin. "We'll have a couple of beers in our room, and then Lux and I are going to go to their room. We want to have some alone time together."

I nodded. My throat was dry. "What about Mel?"

"Well, she will most likely stay with you." Travis reached into his pocket and pulled out a condom, then handed it to me.

"What the hell?" I shoved it back. The condom scared the shit out of me. Travis may as well have handed me a loaded gun.

"Oh no. Your mom and grandpa said to take care of you, and this is part of that agreement."

"But . . ." I was about to say that I didn't want to, but the truth was, I did. I really wanted to. I was scared out of my mind. I'd only ever kissed two girls, one I loved and the other I was scared of, and she was the one the condom was supposedly for. "What if she doesn't want to?"

"Oh, she wants to." Travis gave the condom back to me and said, "Just in case. It's like one of those fire extinguishers that says, 'Break seal in case of emergency.'"

We walked up into our room, and I started thinking about David. I wanted him to be the one to hand me a condom and tell me about girls. It was times like this that I needed a big brother to ask questions. I felt completely comfortable with Travis, and I loved him, but he wasn't my real brother.

I took a sip of beer and was taken back by how strong it was. It was different from the ones that I've shared with Grandpa. It was darker and almost smelled of chocolate. The first beer went down well, too well. I grabbed another one from the twelve-pack, and Travis said, "Take it easy. We'll see Mr. C in a few hours."

I sipped slowly on my second one. Lux and Travis sat on Travis's bed, and Mel sat on mine with me, and then she moved her hip next to my front pocket with the condom in it. I started to move my leg away from her, but she placed her hand on my knee and held me there. We played music on the iPod dock that Travis brought with him. Beck sang about a lost cause. That was all of us, lost, looking to be found. I wondered if Travis played it on purpose or subconsciously.

Lux grinned, her face slightly red. "Let's play a game."

The effects of the beer were clearly hitting her. She was laughing much more than usual. The beer was making me less tense, and it scared me how good I felt when I drank it. I had seen the effects of alcohol on my dad, and there was no way I would become him.

"Truth or dare," said Lux.

"Dare," said Travis. "What else?'

"Do your sexiest dance move next to the window."

Travis stood up and improvised a dance that looked like he was shaking biting ants off of his legs and arms. Lux and Mel cheered him on.

Travis looked at Mel. "Truth or dare?"

"Of course, dare!" said Mel.

"Okay. Give Neil a long, slow kiss." Travis emphasized the 'slow.' I had told him on the way back to the hotel about the kiss massacre in the museum.

Mel smiled at me, and I just waited for her to make the first move. My teeth still hurt from our first kiss, and I was nervous about the tongue ring. I glanced over at Lux, but she just winked at me. She was the master of the slow kiss. At least, as far as my limited experience told me, she was.

"Shit! I think we'll do a double dare." Travis leaned in and kissed Lux.

Mel took my face and turned it toward her. I watched as she closed her eyes and moved her mouth toward me, the tongue ring protruding from her mouth just before it entered mine. This time, her lips felt soft and her mouth moved slowly. I could tell she was trying to be gentle like Travis said, but her tongue started moving faster, and I had to pull back because my front teeth were getting hacked up.

"What?" she said. I gently felt the inside of my mouth with my tongue. "Listen, you little shit. You're making out with a senior here, so you better enjoy it."

"Sorry! I didn't know it was such a privilege."

I regretted my outburst right after I said it.

Travis and Lux looked up. "Everything okay?" asked Travis.

"This little freshman pulled back from my kiss like he was judging me with all of his fucking experience." Mel flipped me off. I guess she wasn't used to boys stopping her advances. I did have one experience, and it was great, so I guess I did judge her a little. It wasn't bad. It was just different.

"Well, by the looks of him, you did something right," Travis chuckled. Let's just say that my pants were bulging out a little more than usual. "Well, this party just got interesting."

Lux playfully hit Travis. "I think we might head down the hall." She took Travis's hand and pulled him out the door.

After the door closed shut, Mel turned to me and smiled. I guess she liked that she made me excited. She climbed onto my lap and started to kiss me again, but this time harder, like in the museum. I didn't want to hurt her feelings again, so I just let her beat the shit out of my mouth. She unbuttoned her shirt and guided my hands to her flesh. It was my first time having my hand in anyone's shirt, and it was softer than I thought it would be. I was having many firsts lately.

Mel pulled her face back. "I have a condom," she said. I guess Travis didn't have to give me one. She started to unbutton my pants, but I stopped her.

"I'm sorry," I said.

She paused, her face inches from mine. "What the fuck?"

"I just can't," I replied.

"What the hell do you mean? You just can't stop like that." Mel reached down and grabbed my zipper.

"No!" I pulled her hand off me and held it. "I don't want to do this. I like you, but I don't love you."

Mel fell back on the bed, and her body bounced with laughter. At first I thought maybe I'd made a mistake, but I knew I was doing the right thing. "I just don't want to be disrespectful."

"Listen." She rolled over and stared at me. Her hair fell in front of her right eye, which turned me on for some weird reason. "I don't love you either, but it's just sex, and it's sweet that you want to respect me. Honestly, you're the first." A strange look crossed her face, like she was trying to remember something. Then, a single tear ran down her cheek.

"Are you okay?" I asked, grabbing a tissue from the top of the dresser. "Mel, I didn't mean to hurt your feelings. I just . . ."

"You didn't hurt my feelings. Not at all. You just made me realize that there are still good guys out there."

Her response surprised me. Was I considered a good guy? "I don't want you thinking that I'm not attracted to you. I am, but I don't feel right having sex with you when we just had our first kiss today and we both have been drinking." I felt lame because most of the other guys at school would think I was a wimp, but I didn't give a shit. Grandpa taught me how to treat women, and I was following his advice.

Mel sat up next to me and hugged me, but it wasn't sexual. I held her as she cried. Her red hair tickled my chin, and my t-shirt was getting wet, but I realized that Mel hurt for more reasons than the Polar Bear Club or I knew. I had heard about her reputation, but I didn't want to believe it. Mel always put up a front, like she didn't care about school or people or herself, but this was a different side of her. Maybe it was her true self coming out. We talked for a while longer, her head on my chest, and I just held her. We drifted off to sleep.

I felt someone pinching my earlobe and trying to tickle me behind my neck. "Wake up, Romeo." Travis started laughing. "I guess that condom came into good use?"

Not answering, I rose up, looking for Mel. She was gone. Travis didn't ask me any more questions. He wasn't that type of guy. He just acted like he was proud of me.

"Get ready, buddy. Mr. C and H are back. We're heading to dinner and then to the play. Make sure you brush your teeth. Mr. C would be pissed and drive us all back if he knew we were drinking, and H would kill us because he wanted some of that beer."

Travis got into the shower, and I just lay there and tasted beer and Mel and stared out the window. The city lights were glowing, and the buildings across from us were lit up like huge metal trees. If I was near my woods right now, I would take a long walk and cover myself in branches and leaves. Cities made me uncomfortable. Claustrophobic. They were too busy with too many moving parts.

Mr. C gave us a choice. We could either go to the play at the Chicago Theater, where the tickets had been donated to him, or we could go back to see Fred and watch a play performed by the students that he worked with. We all picked watching the students.

We drove back to the youth center and met Fred outside the building. The sidewalks were filled with adult men just hanging out. They stared at us and made a few comments as we walked past, mostly at Lux and Mel, but Fred just shook his head at them, and they all stopped and shuffled away. Fred wielded a certain confidence that I admired and wished I had. Travis had it, and Mr. C had it, and Grandpa certainly had it. I just wondered how they got it.

Fred told us that the play had been written by two of the students. We sat in the gym in the audience and watched a one-act play about a Christmas dinner where the oldest son comes home from a war and surprises everyone, and at the end, he announces he's going back for another tour of duty and the lights suddenly go out in the entire gym. The ending startled me. It was so sudden, and as the lights went out, it seemed like the son's return to war signified his death.

The stage was basically the gym floor of the youth center with a few props. The drama brats in my school would never perform in such conditions. Their parents wouldn't let that happen. We had performing arts centers, trained drama teachers, and money for authentic outfits while these kids pieced together costumes from Goodwill and the Salvation Army and anything else that was donated to them. Besides us, the audience was filled with mostly moms. I wasn't sure where the dads were.

After the play, H, Fred, and Mr. C went to the far side of the gym and talked while the rest of us waited by the door.

"What did you guys do after we left?" asked Devo.

"Not much. Just took a nap," said Travis. He winked at me.

Lux came next to me and whispered, "I heard what you did, or should I say didn't do. Cool move!"

"It wasn't a move. It was nothing," I replied.

"It was good you were honest with her and respected her. Mel has been through a lot."

"We all have. That's why we're in this fucking club." I found myself getting defensive with Lux. Maybe it was because I realized that I wanted to lose my virginity, but I wanted to lose it to someone that I really liked, like her. "Sorry, Lux."

"It's okay. I wasn't trying to pry or insinuate anything," she said. "I just think it's cool. Most guys would jump all over Mel, and they have. She's hot!"

"How about you? How was your evening?"

After I asked, I wanted to take it back. I didn't actually want to know.

Lux just ignored the question and stared at me like I had something on my forehead that shouldn't be there, then grabbed my hand and led me away from the group. I looked back, and Travis nodded at me.

When we got outside the community center, Lux turned to me, getting right in my face. "What's the problem?" It was the closest I had been to her since we kissed. I loved her light blue eyes, and her skin was smooth except for a tiny scar above her right eye. The imperfection made her even more attractive. Most of us called them flaws, but I called them truths. It was like seeing a dead tree in the woods. The tree was once beautiful, but now it waited to fall, where it would vanish into the soil and make it richer with life.

"Nothing. I'm just . . ."

"Spit it out because you're not going to keep doing this shit."

"What shit?" I looked directly at her and felt my shoulders tense and breathing increase. I didn't like getting angry at Lux.

"Where every time Travis and I kiss, you start acting like a jealous ass."

So, she knew. I didn't know how to respond. I loved her, and I loved Travis. I couldn't help what I felt. "Does Travis know?"

"Know what?"

"That I'm jealous of you two. That I love you! That we kissed. Does he know?"

"You love me?" Lux slightly grinned, and when I looked down, she moved on. "Yeah, I told him all about the night at the zoo. He's okay with it. He says you're like a little brother to him, and it was just a kiss."

"It was more than a kiss to me. It was my first, and I . . ." I felt myself going to that place where I hated to go. That place where I killed fish. "And he's not my brother. My brother is fucking dead. My brother left me. Everyone leaves." I started pacing back and forth.

Lux just stood there and watched me unravel. My head filled with heat from the adrenaline, and I started to hyperventilate. I turned to leave. I needed to get away. It was my fight-or-flight response, and I wanted to fly.

Then, strong arms held me from behind. Travis. He gave me a bear hug, and I tried to free myself, but he just held on tight. Turning, I put my face in his chest and cried. I was sick of feeling this way. I was sick of feeling hopeless even when I had friends and a mom and a grandpa who loved me. I knew I had a lot to be happy about, but I couldn't find happiness, not enough to lift the darkness that had taken over my brain.

"I just want to feel normal!" I screamed out. Travis held my shoulders and moved me out in front of him so he could look me in the eye.

"This is your normal, buddy." He smiled, and I couldn't help but smile back. "This is my normal, our normal, and it's okay." He looked over at Lux. "Maybe everyone else is fucked up. They hide in their bright, little lives while we live in ours and experience the pain."

"I can't handle you leaving me."

"Oh, I'll never leave you, Neil."

I pushed him, then grabbed the collar of his favorite Nirvana shirt. Travis put his hands up in surrender. "Dude, love you, but watch the shirt."

I grasped tight. "Never try to kill yourself again!" Travis nodded his head and grinned. Then he hugged me and didn't say anything. It wasn't good enough for me. "Just don't . . . I can't take losing another brother," I said.

Travis took a deep breath and said, "No. I think that's over with now."

We got into the van and headed back to the hotel. Everyone was tired, and no one spoke. Mel sat next to me, and it was one of the only times I had seen her quiet.

"Where's H?" asked Devo.

"Staying here," said Mr. C. "Fred offered him a job and a room to stay in. He'll be tutoring kids six hours per day."

Devo's eyes widened. "Wait, he's just a kid himself! Doesn't he need to return to school?"

"H is nineteen," said Mr. C. We all looked at each other. "He was held back when he was little, but he could have had the credits to graduate last fall if he wanted to. He was just taking classes to stay in the club. He's a 4.0 student."

The group sat in silence. How could this big kid who looked like a goth superhero be a 4.0 student?

"Don't we get to say goodbye to him?" asked Devo.

"H said that he didn't want to go through all the emotions of goodbyes, so he told me to let you all know that he would take a bus up next week to see you," Mr. C assured us. "This is going to be an amazing experience for him."

I stared at the city lights through the tinted window of the van. People come and go so quickly in our lives, and it scared me to think that the majority of people we meet won't be around someday. Most will just vanish for no rhyme or reason. That was probably why Mom had so few friends and why Grandpa kept to himself. Losing people hurts, no matter if they're living or dead. However, the ones that stay through all the muck that life can bring will be there through everything, waiting to help pick you up when you fall. That is what makes everything worthwhile.

After we arrived back at the hotel, we all went to our rooms and vanished one by one from the hallway.

I saw Travis sneak out of the room around midnight. Next thing I knew, Mel was lying next to me. She placed her head on my chest, and we lay there with the lights from other buildings trickling through the window into the room. This was new territory for me. I put my arm around her because it seemed like she wanted to be held, and we stayed like that all night, never saying a word.

When the morning light broke, Travis came in and tapped Mel on the shoulder. She got up and kissed my cheek, then said, "Thank you!" I stared at her, confused, as she snuck out of the room.

"Lux told me what happened with Mel," said Travis. "She needed to meet a guy like you just to show her that not all guys are horny assholes."

"Are you a horny asshole?" I asked him.

Travis smiled and said, "Just for one person."

Travis took his meds and fell back to sleep. Later that morning, we left Chicago and H behind. Chicago provided me with my second kiss, my almost lost virginity, my first full beer, great art, and the realization that it was okay to love Lux and just be her friend. What Chicago didn't offer was a chance run-in with my dad. I never mentioned to anyone that Dad had moved there, and I was thankful that Chicago was big enough that the chances of seeing him were very little. As I walked the streets yesterday, he was always on my mind, and I imagined what our interaction would be like if I did see him.

The skyline faded away through the window of the van, and I knew he was somewhere among the people running around trying to live their lives. I wondered how he would have answered our survey.

The Great Plan

TRAVIS INTERVIEWED WITH THE RANCHER THAT GRANDPA knew over the phone, but decided after a couple of days that he would just travel. I heard him and Grandpa talking in the kitchen.

"I have the money my mom gave me. I think I'll just take an extended road trip and see what happens," said Travis.

"You should think about using that money for college," Grandpa replied.

"Yeah, I guess that would be practical, but then what about the experiences I would get from traveling? That's an education too. Besides, I can take out loans for college, and I can't do that for a road trip."

Grandpa sighed. "You got me there." Travis knew how to talk to him. He used the word 'practical,' which was a word that Grandpa hated. "There isn't any learning from anything that's practical. Never will be." Grandpa laughed. "If I didn't have responsibilities around here, I would set out on the road too." By responsibilities, he meant Mom and me. I hated being a burden.

Travis pulled out a map and laid it across the table. He wanted Grandpa's advice because there was not a state that Grandpa hadn't been to. I watched from beyond the door in the hallway.

"Two to three weeks after graduation I was thinking," said Travis.

"For sure west." His finger pointed toward Montana, then moved to Wyoming and Colorado.

I wanted to run into the kitchen and yell, "Fuck you! Go ahead and leave me too!" But Travis wasn't my dad, and he wasn't my brother. I also didn't want to do anything that would spoil my plan of going with him. I figured I could travel with him in June, July, and part of August, then fly home from wherever we were in time for school to start again. Maybe Grandpa would come and get me, and then he could get on the road too.

"Definitely go west, Travis," said Grandpa. "Too many people east. West is where you might find what you're looking for. There's a lot of open space out there and mountains that will overwhelm you just by looking at them." He paused as he looked at the map. I could tell by the gleam in his eyes and slanted grin on his face that he wanted to get in his truck and go. "There is a freedom out there that's addicting. You might not ever come back."

I bolted to my room and started to devise a plan so I could go with Travis. It was a struggle to come up with anything good. I could hide in his trunk until he got to Nebraska, and then when I came out, he would be stuck with me. I could freak out and land in the hospital and blame it on Travis taking a trip without me and leaving me, but that seemed childish, and I didn't want to cause any problems.

Then, it came to me. I would get a job, save some money, finish driver's education so I could help with the driving, and convince Mom and Grandpa that going on a road trip was my way of letting David and Dad go. I had read stories about people being able to leave their past behind and heal by traveling on the road. None of it would be a lie. The only difficult part was trying to convince Travis because he was probably doing his own healing and I wasn't sure he wanted a partner to do it with.

Shit! What about Lux? Would she still go to college, or would she leave with Travis like she mentioned before? I loved Lux, but if she went, I don't think Travis would want me tagging along. So, my plan was simple: find a job, get my driver's license, talk Mom and Grandpa into letting me go, convince Travis that he should take me, and get Lux to go to college. I had one month. Lives could be made or ruined in a month.

Working Man

A WEEK AFTER I CAME UP WITH MY PLAN, I STARTED WORKING at Simon Says after school. Devo's sister gave me the task of cleaning and bussing tables, which paid a quarter above minimum wage. I hated the feel of my skin and face after working in a grease pit all day, and I always smelled like French fries. Each time I walked through the door, Grandpa would say, "You always make me hungry. Just the smell of you clogs my arteries."

I found out how gross people are while working there. They use too much mustard and drink too much soda. The worst part of the job was closing, where I had to take the mats by the dishwasher and stove out back and spray them off with a hose. My hands never seemed to get clean after that, and the hose just sprayed off the food, not the grease. I started getting acne, but if I could earn some money for the trip, a pimple or two was worth it.

I also picked up a job on the weekends with a friend of Grandpa's who delivered hay to horse farms. All I had to do was move the hay bales from the barn to the truck, stacking them in the back, then the easy part was throwing them in the horse stalls when we delivered. I earned about eighty dollars each Saturday for four hours of work, and my arms and shoulders were getting strong and toned from tossing the hay bales. It made me look more like David.

My grades slipped a little from A's to B's in three of my classes, and I didn't think it was that big of a deal, but the teachers in each of those classes kept me in after school to see if I was okay. Each of them said the same thing. "When we see grades falling from a good student like you, we get worried. Is there something going on that we should know about?" They were truly trying to be helpful, but I couldn't tell them that I was just tired from working all night and did most of my homework on the bus ride to the diner or on Sunday nights. I was saving about two hundred dollars per week, so a B grade was worth it to me. By the time Travis wanted to leave, I figured I would have about six hundred dollars total.

My plan had to work. I needed to leave myself behind and come back a new person with a new life. Could a road trip erase memories?

The Boyfriend

SOMETIMES LIFE SEEMS TO SPEED UP TO A VELOCITY THAT becomes out of control. I was planning and working and planning some more. Grandpa had a quote by John Lennon in his garage that said, "Life is what happens when you are busy making plans." I think that is true for everyone. I was rushing through school, trying to go with Travis out west, working, and blocking out David, and Travis, Lux, and Mel kept saying how they wanted to graduate and get out of school. Their lives must have been moving rapidly too. Grandpa was a master at enjoying the life that was right in front of him, and he always reminded me and Mom to slow down and be grateful. Mom was looking more relaxed too, so maybe she had finally started to listen. I still needed to open my ears.

When I came home from throwing hay one Saturday afternoon, Mom was sitting on the porch with a man I'd never seen before, and they were laughing and sipping on iced tea. Grandpa was working in the garage on his old Jeep. He'd been working on that ugly car relentlessly the past couple of weeks, but he said that when he was through with it, anyone who owned or ever wanted a Jeep would be envious. I didn't doubt him. As I watched Grandpa tinker, I figured that since he wasn't worried about my mom having tea with a man on our porch, then neither would I.

"Oh, honey, come on over. I want you to meet someone." Mom looked happier than I had seen her in a long time. "This is Evan."

As I shook Evan's hand, I noticed that his eyebrow hair flared out like sharp, little wings, and his nose hair was in need of a trim. His hand was long and bony, and his skinny neck had blue veins sticking out on either side. The bushy salt-and-pepper beard that invaded his face led directly to the largest set of ears I'd ever seen. My first thought was that my mom could do better, but I was judging on looks alone. He seemed friendly, and that was good enough.

"Neil, what do you like to do?"

I was relieved that he didn't ask me if I played sports or had a girlfriend. "I like to draw." I shrugged, not wanting to let this man know too much about me.

"That's fantastic! I would love to see your drawings sometime," he said. This had to be a show for my mom. You know, show interest in the kid. "I'm a graphic designer, but I was trained as an artist. That was a long time ago." Shit, maybe he was actually interested.

"Yeah, I could do that sometime," I replied. After he mentioned that it was a long time ago, I realized that he was quite older than my mom, probably closer to Grandpa's age than Mom's. His wrinkles were not as pronounced as Grandpa's, but he had gray hair. At least the hair he had left was gray. "It was nice to meet you," I said, then went inside.

Up in my room, I watched them from the window. This guy, Evan, made my mom laugh a lot, and I liked him for doing that. She deserved to laugh.

Suddenly, from behind me, I was blindfolded and dragged to my bed.

"What the hell?" I screamed through the fabric. Then a girl

started laughing, a familiar sound that I loved. I pulled what turned out to be a pair of boxers from my face and spun toward her, her eyes about two inches away from mine. "Lux, I hope those are clean."

"Your ass would have been mine," she said, still laughing. When Lux laughed, she opened her mouth wide, and you could see all of her teeth and the back of her tongue. I loved that she laughed with so much enthusiasm.

"I didn't expect an assassin in my bedroom."

"You always need to be on alert." This was another reason why I loved her. I never knew what to expect. "How do you like the guy your mom's with?"

"Did she know you were up here?" I asked.

"No. Your grandpa did. I was already waiting here when your mom got home."

I yelled out the window, "Thanks, Grandpa!"

He said loudly in his slow, usual way, "Hey, Neil. Hope your day was good." And then he went on working.

"Yeah, Grandpa and I have a pact." Lux moved to the window and stared down at the porch. "Your grandpa is a great man. He's just himself. True, you know?" Before I could answer, she continued, "Your mom looks really happy. I'm not sure I've ever seen her smile so much, unless Travis gets her going with his bullshit."

"Yeah. I'm glad. It's just . . ."

Lux finished my sentence. "Weird to see your mom with another man?"

"Yeah. I mean, my dad was no treat. Complete asshole actually. But it's still weird." I moved next to Lux, and we both looked down at Mom.

"I felt the same way when I saw my dad with a new girlfriend," Lux said. "It scared me. I didn't know if she would be this horrible bitch like my mom or if she would take my place and my dad would just forget about me."

"It's hard being forgotten." I looked back at Lux. "But maybe there's some good in it."

Lux nodded, her face turning dark, and her eyes focused on the sky out of my window. "I've been forgotten," she said. "I'm not sure I can find any good in it."

"Yeah," I said. "You're probably right. Who forgot you?"

"My mom was a beauty queen, a for real beauty queen, Ms. Wisconsin when she was twenty, and then after I was born, she turned into an alcoholic."

"Damn." That was all I could come up with.

"By the time I was six, I don't think I ever saw her sober again. That much drinking takes your beauty away, so her attention turned more to my looks, or according to her, lack thereof." Lux felt the ends of her hair. "She hated it that I liked my hair short and dressed in boys clothes. She used to berate me for how I looked." A tear fell down her cheek. I put my arm around her shoulder and held her next to me. "My dad, in between his business travels, finally started to notice how it was taking its toll on me. He was getting calls from my teachers and school counselor saying I was withdrawn and always seemed depressed. It didn't take him long after that, and he left her when I was eight, and I haven't seen her since."

"Are you and your dad cool?" I asked

"I guess. He minds his business, and I mind mine." She wiped her tears. "I mean, he loves me. I know that, and I have always felt safe around him. Still, he was always busy with work, and I was alone. It was so hard to care about myself until I met Travis."

"What do you mean?" I asked.

"Travis made me see myself for who I am. He was gentle, and his love helped mend old wounds." She smiled and placed her head against my shoulder.

I knew what Lux meant. Travis made me care about myself again too. He helped mend my wounds. The world was a better place with him in it.

Planning

MAPS COVERED TRAVIS'S BEDROOM FLOOR. HE HAD MADE highlighter marks all over the pages, circling names of places and roads. A list of names and phone numbers in Grandpa's handwriting sat next to the maps. I had seen them together a lot lately, and it made me jealous. Grandpa was spending so much time with Travis that we didn't hang out as often. I also wanted to spend my own time with Travis so I could talk him into letting me tag along with him for the summer. He was going to have the freedom soon to do what he wanted with his life. I didn't want to rush mine, but at the same time, I wished I were graduating too.

I needed this. I needed a road trip to say goodbye to David because with all of Mom and Dad's bullshit, I never truly had the time to grieve. The road, and Travis, may help me leave my past in the plains and the mountains. The thin mountain air could suffocate my demons and block the noise in my head.

Travis had Fort Collins, Colorado, circled twice and Missoula, Montana, circled once on the maps. He also circled a place in Colorado called Crested Butte. He was definitely headed west.

As I looked closer at the map, I noticed that Travis also had a place in southern Wyoming circled, someplace covered with forests and mountains, but it didn't have a name. It was circled three times. I ran back to my computer to look it up on the internet and discovered that it was a forest called Medicine Bow. The perfect place to get lost.

I had saved $683.58 by the first week of June. I had not spent a penny of my money, which made me feel bad because whenever Travis and I did something, he paid, but he had always paid before. With my new earnings, I would convince him to take me on his trip and that it would be easier with me along. I had two weeks. Two weeks until I could leave my demons behind.

The Return

EXAM WEEK WAS A BLUR. IT WAS TWO DAYS BEFORE graduation. I had studied hard for my exams and was pretty sure I had gotten A's on all of them. With all A's, Mom would be more likely to let me leave. Travis and Lux had crammed for their tests all week in the corner of the library. Lux had said, "We need to finish strong so we can leave this place behind." I wasn't sure if she meant the school, the town, or both.

Devo walked around school with his headphones on, orange, baggy pants from the eighties, a white t-shirt, suspenders, and purple Chuck Taylors. He wore that same outfit every day that week, and when people gave him crap, he would say, "It's my exam outfit. I've gotten all A's wearing it." Then Devo would just move on, confident with who he was. Eric, on the other hand, was a nervous wreck all week. Lux said that his parents put a lot of pressure on him during exams, to the point where he threw up about four times every day and didn't sleep all week. He had to visit Mr. C twice with panic attacks, and they would practice breathing to calm him down.

Ever since Chicago, Mel grabbed me when I walked by. She liked to pull me into a dark corner and make out with me, and I never knew when to expect it. It was like a Mafia hit, except with her mouth instead of a gun. This last time, she scared the crap out of me. I'd forgotten a book in Travis's car and went out during third period to get it. When I opened the rear door and bent over the floorboard, I was pushed into the back seat. At first, I thought someone was about to beat the shit out of me, but instead, Mel jumped on me and started kissing me. When she knocked me down, I figured I was about to get a tongue-lashing, but then she kissed me softly. After a couple of minutes, she stopped, hugged her head into my chest, and then got up and left. Mel was the master of the "hit-and-run make-out session," as Travis started to call them.

The cool thing about exam week was that the Polar Bear Club could spend more time with each other. Exams ended at one thirty every day, and then we all met in Mr. C's office and hung out for two hours, trying to act normal, as if the school year weren't ending. We all knew our club was about to get much smaller.

The Friday before graduation, at two in the afternoon, a tall figure walked through the office door. His hair was shaved to a short stubble, and he wore a black shirt that had an Army logo on it. His big grin was hard to recognize on his familiar face because it had hardly ever been seen before.

"H, my God. Look at you," said Mr. C as he stood and shook his hand. We were all silent for a moment with our mouths wide open, and then the room erupted in clapping and celebratory cheering and whistles.

Travis hugged him. "You look great, man." He stepped back and just stared at H. "You look better than great."

"Okay, you can stop checking me out now." H gave Travis a friendly shove on his shoulder. "I figured I should be here for the last Polar Bear meeting."

"Well, Fred told me you were doing great and the kids love you. He said they connected with you pretty quick and respected what you had to offer them." Mr. C doted on H like a proud father. We all knew it would be a tough week for Mr. C. He didn't want to see any of us go. "Tell us about your experience with the kids and Chicago."

"Wait!" Mel interrupted. "When did you get hot?"

"Always have been, Mel. Just didn't want you attacking me all through school, so I thought I would hold off on showing my hotness until now." H was being a smart-ass, but he did look good. He had always been strong, lean, and toned. His now cropped hair showed off his dark eyebrows, narrow nose, and high cheekbones. H still had a roughness to him, but as Mel pointed out, it was now a handsome roughness.

"Well, where do I start?" H mumbled. He was very intelligent, and I had heard him speak clearly before, but it was only when he was really pissed. He usually mumbled, in a reserved way, when he was asked to say something personal. "The kids down there opened my eyes. So did Fred." He looked over at Mr. C. "Your friend is amazing! The experiences that guy has had. Holy shit!" Mr. C nodded in agreement. "Fred told me about Iraq and then how he came back and spoke at rallies against the war and the book he wrote about growing up as an inner-city kid. He's just cool!" We all sat amazed at what we were hearing. H never spoke about anyone with affection. He tilted his head toward Mr. C and gave him a slanted grin before saying, "Fred also told me about the time the two of you went on a road trip through Europe and ended up staying a week in Amsterdam." Mr. C gaped at H, shook his head, and gestured for him to move on.

H continued, "The kids didn't take to me at first, until one day I just said, 'Listen, I'm not some white guy coming down here trying to save you. I just want to get to know you.' It seemed like they started to open up after that."

He told us about one student that he had gotten to know well. "This kid, they called him Little Frank. He had Down syndrome, and he was so cool."

"Was?" asked Mr. C.

H looked over at Travis, and tears filled his eyes. He struggled to catch his breath. It was startling. I had never seen him cry before, or even show much emotion at all. Travis put his arm around H and squeezed H so tight that his knuckles turned white.

"Little Frank and I went for a walk one day," H spoke softly. "He showed me where he lived. I got to meet his mom and his grandma, and they invited me over for dinner one night, so I went." He could hardly catch his breath between sobs. "When I arrived at the house, his grandma answered the door and said that Little Frank had been hit by a stray bullet when he was playing in the yard. He was taken to the hospital and died." H pounded his fist on the table in front of him. "I should have been there to protect him. I should have . . ." He couldn't talk anymore.

"It's not your fault," said Travis.

Mr. C moved towards H and hugged him, and then we all circled around him. "You couldn't have protected him," Mr. C said.

H told us about Little Frank's funeral and how Fred and the rest of the kids at the school all sang a slow version of "I Want It That Way" by the Backstreet Boys because Little Frank always sang that song at least twenty times a day.

"I really loved that kid," said H as he sat back in his chair and just shook his head, a grin on his face. "Everyone loved him. The kids at school and his family all wore shirts to the funeral with Little Frank's picture on it. They gave me a shirt too. Man, he sure made me laugh."

In such a short time, H had experienced a lot. They weren't all great experiences, but nevertheless, he was experiencing life. I wanted that. "What's with the Army shirt?" I asked. I didn't want to sound insensitive by taking the subject away from Little Frank, but I could tell that H wanted to change the topic by the way he stopped looking at all of us.

"Well, I joined after about a week in Chicago." He was mumbling again. "I listened to Fred and what he told me about his life, and I just wanted to experience something special, something that a lot of people don't. I guess I wanted to sacrifice my time and serve something greater than myself and see what it was all about. Plus, I decided that school wasn't for me, and hell, I don't have the money to pay tuition anyway."

"Well, the Army will provide for you, and you can earn some money if you decide to go to college," said Mr. C.

"Yeah, Fred said that he would always have a place for me when I'm done. I leave for basic next week," H replied.

"Shit, so soon?" asked Travis. "We need to hang out."

"I'm going back to Chicago tomorrow. I want to be with the kids a few more days and say goodbye. They're awesome kids. Showed me a different way. They made me earn their respect by showing up and being there for them every day and by being real. They didn't want anything from me except to show respect back."

We were all happy for H, but with his visit and early departure, it brought reality to what was happening. The Polar Bear Club would never be the same. This time together, right now in Mr. C's office, would disappear like smoke in the wind. Graduation was in two days, and then my friends would be leaving for something that they hoped would be better. I felt like time was running out for me to convince Travis to take me west with him. Did that mean our friendship was running out of time too?

Mom

TRAVIS TOOK US HOME AFTER SCHOOL, RAN UP AND GRABBED a clean shirt, then left for Lux's house to take her out to eat. He had put on a blue, button-down shirt that matched his eyes, a big change from the band t-shirt and jeans that he normally wore.

Mom was sitting on the porch with Evan. Maybe this was going to become routine: me coming home to find Mom laughing with Evan and drinking iced tea on the porch and Grandpa in the garage working on his Jeep. I still enjoyed hearing Mom laugh. She had dreams once too, and I hoped she was dreaming again.

Mom used to sing and dance, which was not unusual for teenage girls in the eighties, but she was actually good at it. She had what Grandpa called "a gift of extreme capabilities." She went to dance school every night, sang at school events, and recorded at a local studio. Grandpa and Grandma had to pay for the recordings, but they believed in her talent and wanted to give her every chance to succeed. Grandpa kept pictures in a trunk in the attic where Mom was dressed like Madonna and one where she was in the midst of a song and dance at a Madonna concert. When I asked her once who had taken the picture, she gently smiled and said, "Your dad. He hated going to that concert, but he loved watching me dance. We were only seventeen. Our entire lives were ahead of us."

Mom was also a good student in school. She had A's in most of her classes and was on the student council and in the drama club. Her senior year, she received a scholarship to a performing arts college in New York City. She was prepared to have a long-distance relationship with my dad because, at the time, nothing was as important as dancing and singing.

So what happens to a girl who has her life before her and her dreams within grasp? What becomes more important than dance or song? A child, one that comes into this world perfect and innocent that you can sing to every day and dance to sleep.

One dream turned into another. They named him David, but Mom called him Kelly, after Gene Kelly, her favorite dancer. Then, somewhere along the line, she and Dad stopped having fun and stopped loving each other. They stayed with each other for their kid's sake, and Mom stopped singing, she stopped dancing, and her dreams vanished.

As I watched Mom and Evan, I had hope that she would find happiness and go after some sort of dream again. I had hope that she would find love again and move on with her life. If she could find that peace with Evan, then maybe it would be easier for me to leave with Travis. Mom needed to heal as much as I did. She lost the same people I did. I had hope as she gently sang along with the music that filtered in from Grandpa's stereo in the garage. While she sang, Evan tapped his foot and held her hand.

Graduation Gift

I WOKE UP THAT MORNING TO GRANDPA SHAKING MY BED. "Come on. It's time to give Travis his gift."

"What are you talking about?" I looked at the clock, which read six. "Grandpa, I only got him a book."

"No, my gift to him." Grandpa took off out the bedroom door and down the stairs.

I put on a shirt and went downstairs. Grandpa was like a kid on Christmas morning. Mom was making pancakes and had stacks of them staying warm on the stove top. When I followed Grandpa outside, the Jeep he had been working so frantically on sat in the middle of the driveway. It had been repainted olive green, the row bars had new padding, and the larger-than-normal tires were almost new. Seat covers protected the torn seats. He started it up, and the engine roared awake followed by a steady rhythm of gentle rumbling.

"Wait until he hears this stereo," said Grandpa.

Travis was still asleep in the loft when Grandpa turned the stereo up as loud as it could go. Jimi Hendrix's "All Along the Watchtower" rang out. Within moments, Travis emerged with Lux right behind him. Both of them were wearing pajama bottoms and t-shirts, still groggy. Lux's hair stood in every direction, looking like it was trying to escape her head. Grandpa wore a big, crooked grin and leaned up against the Jeep.

"What is this?" Travis asked Grandpa. "Looks great. You're going to love it."

"No, *you're* going to love it!" Grandpa stood aside for Travis to inspect his new Jeep. Travis slowly walked over to it. He just stared at his gift, dead silent, then turned to Grandpa with tears in his eyes.

"I can't . . ."

Grandpa cut him off. "You can," he said. "It's a gift from all of us."

"It's too much," said Travis.

"No. It was mostly just time. People owed me the parts, so the rest was virtually free. Now, enough of this, you enjoy it, son."

Travis was overwhelmed by the gift, but I think he was even more overwhelmed when Grandpa called him "son." He hugged Grandpa, then looked over at me and waved me into their hug. I went without hesitating. When I looked up, my mom and Lux were crying too. Travis went over and hugged my mom, lifting her into the air.

"I love you guys. I love my adopted family!" yelled Travis at the top of his lungs. We all laughed because that's exactly what we were. Lux joined in on the hug fest. She was a part of our adopted family too, a bunch of misfits that never cared to fit in anyhow.

Grandpa gave Travis a quick tour of the Jeep. He showed him how to use the four-wheel drive and the iPod dock that he had installed and how to put the black cover on and off. Grandpa had also attached an old Army first aid kit to the back of the spare tire. "You are ready for some mountains," he said.

After Grandpa mentioned the mountains, Lux walked quickly back towards the loft with her hands cupped over her mouth. "She's not happy I want to leave," Travis spoke softly.

"I thought she might go with you," my mom replied.

"No. She has to leave for college early. I guess she's taking a summer class."

This was my chance. I needed to tell Travis that I wanted to go with him and show him my money and ask in front of Mom and Grandpa. But then I thought about it. Would I be selfish to ask right after we found out that Lux wasn't happy? I stood quietly, acting like I was checking out the Jeep.

"Neil, can you go see how she is?" Travis asked. "I think she might talk to you right now more than me."

I felt bad because I thought Travis should go talk to her, but I wanted to help. "Yeah, I'll go."

Grandpa continued to show Travis around the engine, and Mom went inside to finish cooking breakfast. Walking up the steps into the loft, I heard Lux crying. I knocked on the door.

Lux was on a bench glaring out the window. When she saw it was me, she wiped her tears and frowned. "He sent you to calm me down? How fucking lame!"

"I guess," I said. "I just want to make sure you're okay." I sat next to her on the bench. We both looked out the window as Travis and Grandpa checked the oil. "He's pretty excited."

"It just seems like he wants to leave and forget about all of us," said Lux.

I peered at her. "I meant my grandpa is excited, but yeah, I think Travis wants this road trip. It seems like there are some things he wants to leave behind, but I don't think it's you at all." I wasn't sure if I was being comforting or not. "Do you want to go with him?"

Lux looked at me and grinned. "I have my own demons to leave behind, and there are a few things I need to prove to myself." She wiped her eyes and smiled down at Travis. "I just love him so much. Look at him. He's full of life. It's like he's a little kid that just opened his favorite toy. I'm just worried that if he goes west, I'll never see him again."

Lux was right to worry. The fear of never seeing Travis again was the reason I wanted to go with him in the first place.

Commencement

MOM, GRANDPA, AND I SAT DOWN IN THE GYM FOR THE graduation ceremony. Travis reserved seats for us in the family section, which were in the bleachers on the right side of the gym. We were up high enough that we could see everyone.

For some reason, I thought H would be around, but I should have known better. He had said his goodbyes at the last Polar Bear Club meeting, so he was out of our lives forever. Devo wore a black, three-piece suit under his gown, and its pinstripes made him look like a 1920s gangster. He even wore a white tie with a white carnation pinned to the side. Mel looked beautiful in a yellow sundress with white flowers. She had slipped me a note while we all were hanging out in the parking lot just before we had to go inside, and she whispered that she had a gift for me later. For one thing, it was her graduation, so I should have been giving her a gift, and two, my palms started sweating. Lux wore a black suit with a red silk shirt. "I'm going for Annie Lennox," she had said. I had no idea what that meant, but she looked good.

There was something edgy about Lux today. I figured it was Travis getting the Jeep because it made his trip west more real than ever. She was rather stoic during the commencement speeches and stared at the floor the entire time. When she finally walked up to accept her diploma, she just kept walking after she took it from the principal. She walked down the aisle on the opposite side of the gym from us, strode out the door, and then she was gone. We all noticed it, but I guess everyone figured she was going to the bathroom or needed some air for a moment.

Ten minutes later, after two more boring speeches about moving forward in life, she still wasn't in her seat. I caught Travis looking at me, and he shrugged, gesturing toward where Lux had been. I just shook my head and shrugged back. I was hesitant to go and look for her because she probably wanted Travis to do it, but he was stuck in the sea of graduates. Panic suddenly came to me, and I started to breathe faster. The fear of loss was embedded in me, and after seeing Travis shrug and the look of worry on his face, I had to go find her.

I glanced over at Grandpa, and he nodded, gesturing in the direction Lux went. I stood and went to the door that she walked out of, which led to the commons. Lux wasn't there, and she wasn't in the bathroom when I had an older lady check. My breathing grew heavier, and my palms started to sweat for the second time today. I ran outside and frantically looked around, but I didn't see her anywhere in sight. I sprinted to Travis's Jeep and fell into the passenger's seat, exasperated. Nothing!

I slowly wandered back toward the gym, not really knowing what to do. People were filtering out from all of the doors, and I desperately tried to get through the onslaught of bodies. Finally, I saw Travis hugging Mom and Grandpa as they stood in the gym. His attention immediately turned to me. "Did you find her?"

"No," I said. "I checked everywhere."

"She's probably just upset," Mom assured us. "A girl needs some time to relax and breathe."

Travis and I looked at each other, and we both frowned. Devo, Eric, and Mel had now moved next to us. None of them had seen her either. The next to join our circle were Mr. C and Peter.

"Congratulations!" Mr. C hugged us all even though some of us didn't graduate. "So, our little club is officially over."

"Oh, there is email," said Eric. "Besides, you still have Neil and me, and we'll have enough issues." Apparently, Eric forgot that Mr. C was leaving. We all laughed uncomfortably, then went silent.

It was really bothering Travis that Lux had left. I hadn't seen his face look so distraught since he was in the hospital, and he started fidgeting and paced the gym floor until Mr. C placed his arm around him.

Devo was tuned out, listening to his music. His mom hadn't shown, and music was his way to cope. With a sad expression on his face, he waved at us all and said softly, "I'll see you at the diner later." His sister was working there today, and apparently she had a cake for us.

Devo walked out the school door and across the parking lot. Mom wanted to go after him, but I put my hand on her arm. "Just let him walk it off," I said. "He's okay."

She sighed. "Honey, I just can't believe his mom didn't show up. This is one of the most important days of his life."

Mom was clearly upset. She had, to my surprise, become the Polar Bear Club's mom. Lux had practically been living with us in Travis's room. Devo would show up on the couch every so often. Grandpa made him a key after he found him sleeping on the porch one night. I have woken up to Mel and Mom having breakfast and talking about female stuff. Even Eric spent the night sometimes. He would just show up. My mom always called Eric's parents when he came because they actually cared about where he was, but everyone else's parents could care less. They never returned Mom's calls.

We all left the school and agreed to meet at the diner in an hour. The diner was our hangout, and now that everyone was moving on, it was going to end. Maybe another group of kids would make it their hangout in the years to come. What would I do? I could join them, but maybe the diner would just become a memory to me as well.

Travis didn't talk as he drove us home. Grandpa wasn't the type to try to fill the silence, so he let it sit in the air. Mom just kept looking at Travis, clearly worried. Once we reached the driveway, Travis parked the Jeep and leapt out, running to his room. I waited at the bottom of the loft stairs, waiting for some confirmation that she was there. All I heard was, "Shit!"

I went inside to change, then hurried out to the Jeep, but it was gone. Travis had left without me. Did he find something? Did he not want me there? I became selfishly paranoid, but then realized that he probably was freaking out wondering where Lux had gone and just forgot to wait.

I turned around and saw Grandpa open the door to his truck, keys in hand. "Let's go," he said. "I'll drive you."

I ran over and got into the passenger seat. "Grandpa, do girls always do this?" I looked out the window as we passed the houses. "Do they drive you crazy with worry?"

When I looked over at him, he had a grin on his face. "Not always, but it's worth it," he said. We were quiet the rest of the way.

Grandpa tried to not go more than five over the speed limit for the three miles it took to get to the diner. He dropped me off next to the curb out front. "Let me know when you find her," he said, then drove away.

Travis's Jeep was parked in front of the diner with one wheel up on the curb. I didn't know what to expect when I walked in. Would he be manic? Was he about to melt down and end up in the hospital? This time it would be the adult hospital.

I cautiously walked in. Travis was pacing around the diner with a note in his hands. Devo had his earbuds in and just watched. Mel was crying. Eric hadn't arrived yet.

Devo's sister tried to calm Travis down. "She will show, Travis. It's going to be okay."

"Where is she?" I asked. "What happened?"

No one answered me. I felt like they were ignoring me. I was sick of seeing Travis freak out, and this was not a time for him to end up in the hospital. "Where the hell is she?" I yelled so loud that I startled even myself. Everyone stopped and turned their attention to me, except Travis. He just kept walking around the diner. I stepped in front of him and grabbed him by the shirt.

"Stop acting so fucking crazy. Stop pacing around. Get your shit together, and let's find Lux."

He handed me the note.

Come to your beloved west and find me and tell me you want to be with me. If you don't, then I'll just figure my life out without you. Follow the clues that I left you and then see if you can follow your heart. The first clue is at the zoo next to where the sea otters swim. Neil knows. Come find me.

Love,

Lux

"Okay." Travis walked toward the door. "Who's with me?"

Devo stood up. "Wait! We need to make a plan."

"Count me in," said Mel. "I've known that crazy girl since I was six."

"I'm with you," I said.

We sat down at the booth and mapped out our plan. "We have to be efficient," said Travis. "We need to get to wherever her clues take us as fast as possible. That means you guys will need to help with the driving."

I was afraid that Lux was in one of her bouts of depression, but then she wouldn't have the energy to drive out west and play this game with Travis. She loved Travis, that was clear, and it seemed she was doing this to see if he loved her too. What better way to make him prove it than by chasing her across the country? The next obstacle for me was to convince Mom that I should go.

Travis and I pulled into the driveway of Grandpa's house, and he hopped out of the Jeep and ran upstairs, yelling, "We're leaving in one hour!"

I sat in the Jeep, figuring out what to say to Mom. Grandpa was working in the garage on a Volkswagen Beetle that he had bought for a couple hundred dollars from a friend of his. I had a suspicion that the Beetle might be for me when I got my license in the fall. Watching Grandpa work, I decided to tell him about Lux first because he could help convince Mom to let me go. As I walked up to him, Grandpa glanced at me with concern in his eyes.

"Can I talk to you?" I asked.

Grandpa immediately put his tools down. "By the look on your face, we should take a quick walk."

Grandpa and I had only been on two walks like this before. Once was after David died, where he talked to me about loss and grieving. The other time was when Dad walked out on us. He explained what real men are like and how they should respect women and take care of their families. I had no idea what he would say this time, but I had less than an hour.

"So, what's going on? I saw Travis running upstairs." Grandpa sipped on a bottle of beer as we walked.

"Lux is gone," I said. "She left graduation."

"Yeah, I saw that. Complicated girl, that one."

I put my hands in my pockets and kicked a small pebble with the side of my shoe. "She left a note at the diner that said she was going west and that Travis needed to find her. She's leaving clues along the way. The first one is at the zoo." Hesitating, I looked at Grandpa. "Travis wants me to help him, and he's leaving in one hour."

"Boy, that's a tough one. Your mom is doing better, but I'm not sure she'll let another boy out of her reach."

"Yeah. She's been protective." I almost started to cry. "I need to get out of here for a while, and these guys are my friends. My only friends." My breathing became heavy. Grandpa handed me his beer.

"Take a sip," he said. "I think a trip west might do you some good. Besides, Travis is a grown man now. It's not like anyone will bother you."

"Devo and Mel are coming too."

Grandpa laughed. "Well, now I know no one will bother you. No one in their right mind would mess around with Mel. She would talk them to death." He took the beer back. "Mel's a good girl. I'll talk to your mom."

We turned around to head back to the house. Grandpa said, "Double time. You're leaving soon," and we started jogging. Grandpa seemed sure that Mom would let me go after he talked to her. I wasn't as confident.

Mom was sitting on the porch drinking iced tea. She smiled as we walked up, but she had a strange look in her eyes. "Where have you two been?" Slightly out of breath from keeping up with Grandpa, I reached down and hugged her. "Well," she said. "I can tell two things from that hug: you want something, and Grandpa let you drink some of his beer again."

"Truth is, I need a favor," I replied.

Grandpa placed a hand on my shoulder. "Let me," he said. He looked Mom square in the eyes. "The boy needs to get out of here for a while, and I think we should let him."

"What?" Mom shot out of her chair.

"Lux left, and they need to go find her. I just think it would be good for Neil to get away for a while."

Mom's eyes were big, and her hands were on her hips, which was something she did when she wasn't happy. "Neil, you're too young, and we don't have the money." She shook her head.

I pulled just over six hundred dollars out of my pocket. "I've been saving everything I've made."

"You already knew this would happen?" asked Mom.

"No. I just wanted to go west with Travis for a while. I had no idea Lux would do this."

"What kind of girl plays these games?" Mom liked Lux, but I could tell she was disappointed. It grew quiet, then suddenly Travis was standing next to me. He placed his arm around my shoulders.

"He will be okay," said Travis. "I agree. It might be good for him to get away." Two men that I respected were standing on either side of me. I felt secure and supported and loved. "Besides, she left us clues. I bet we find her within a couple of days. This is just Lux playing her games. She's always been a little out there. That's why I love her."

Mom smiled. "I'm glad that's why you love her. She has spirit." She looked at me and reached for my hand. "You really need this, don't you?" I nodded. Tears welled up in her eyes. "I sometimes forget how hard all of this has been on you. You're lucky to have friends like these."

"I'm lucky to have you, Mom," I said, hugging her again.

"You are becoming such a fine young man. Okay, you can go, but you have to call me every night." Mom stood and put her hands on Travis's broad shoulders. "He's the only baby I have left. Take care of him."

"Like a brother," Travis replied.

•

Clue One

I PACKED THREE SHIRTS, TWO PAIRS OF SHORTS, TWO PAIRS OF socks, three pairs of underwear, and one pair of pants in my small backpack. Grandpa entered my room as I zipped up the bag and handed me a knife in a green sheath.

"Careful with that. It will slice your hand clear off," said Grandpa.

I grabbed the handle and pulled out Grandpa's knife that he had since the war. The handle was brown and had grooves that molded onto my fingers to make it easier to hold. The blade still had a shine after all these years and looked about five inches long. Usually when we went camping, he would bring it along, so I had held it before. It was a special knife, and I knew it meant a lot to him to give it to me. He grinned at me, and I felt like when he passed me the knife, it was like my initiation into manhood.

"Thanks, Grandpa," I said. "I'll take care of it."

"Keep it in your bag until you need it, because that thing is not exactly legal," he replied, winking at me. "I packed a small tent and two sleeping bags in the back of the Jeep and attached a first aid kit to the spare. You guys are all set."

I hugged him hard, almost lifting him off the ground.

"Boy, you're getting strong," he said. "Listen, you can experience a lot on the road, good and bad. Just enjoy it. Enjoy the freedom and take in the sights, even the flatlands. When you get to the mountains, if you don't find her by then, breathe deep and remember how small we truly are. Remember David and how much he loved you, and he will be there with you."

"I will," I said.

"The mountains can help you find your way."

The two of us walked down the stairs and outside to the Jeep, where Travis and Mom were waiting. Grandpa gave me another two hundred dollars and hugged Travis. Mom squeezed me tight. I thought she would never let me go.

Mom hugged Travis, and I heard her say again, "Take care of my baby. He's the only one I have left." Travis nodded to reassure her.

We got in the car and drove toward the zoo to find the first clue. Devo and Mel were meeting us there. The Jeep would be full with all of us; luckily, Grandpa had welded a rack that hung off the back that we could strap our bags to. We placed trash bags around everything as well as a small tarp that would lie under the tent when we set up camp. Grandpa had shown us how to secure everything and tie knots that would not come loose with the wind. I think Grandpa would have come if we had asked him, but he was a believer in people finding their own adventures. This was ours.

Devo and Mel were in the parking lot of the zoo waiting for us.

"To the sea otters," Devo said. He turned his music off and tucked his iPod in his backpack.

When we got to the exhibit, everyone stopped. The only sound was the little kids laughing at the antics of the sea otters. I remembered laughter like that. Would I ever forget how David and I once were? Would our laughter drift? Would the memory of him fade away where I would only remember pieces of who we once were? These thoughts terrified me.

We looked around the area, expecting a clue to be visible, which was silly and not Lux's style. Travis ran his hand under and behind the sea otter sign, but there was nothing. Mel went to a bench that was painted with tiger stripes and felt around it. She found nothing. Devo looked through a flower bed, walking softly not to trample any. Nothing.

I walked over to the machine that made the plastic zoo animals and felt underneath and in the back. My heart was racing in anticipation. Then I felt an envelope that was heavily taped to the machine, out of sight for anyone to see.

"I found something!" I yelled. The parents of the kids stopped watching the sea otters and grabbed their kids' hands. I guess I yelled too loud, and they probably figured a crazy high school kid was about to go off or something. "It's a note!"

Travis came running over, and I handed the envelope to him. As he looked at the front of the envelope, his face dropped. In black marker, it said, "Neil." How did Lux know that I would be here with Travis? I felt excited that one of the clues was addressed to me but embarrassed because I figured they would all be for Travis. Travis looked at the ground as I opened the letter and read it aloud:

Neil,

I am giving you this first clue because you will understand, and I want to give Travis an opportunity to actually find me. You probably think this is some foolish tease or that I went nuts. Neither is true. I just want to see if Travis actually loves me, actually wants to spend the rest of his life with me like he always says. I want him to come after me. I hope I didn't disappoint anyone, including your mom and grandpa. You can find the next clue at America's Stonehenge. Travis will be motivated because he can see some vintage cars there. Hopefully they won't keep the Brown Bomber. Go west! If no one comes, then I understand that my life will be mine to live, and if that's the case, I bid farewell.

Lux

Travis stood in front of me, tears forming in his eyes. "Why these fucking games? Why now?"

I grabbed his shoulders and squeezed them. "You don't have time for that." I shook him. "We need to go find her."

Mel took my arm as I walked back to the Jeep with the clue in my hand. She had a mischievous grin across her face. "I never knew you could be such a hard-ass." She walked against my hip until we reached the Jeep.

I pulled out the map of the United States, then grabbed Travis's phone to use the internet. When I looked up "America's Stonehenge," I got information on some place out east, but that couldn't be it. Lux said, "Go west!" She also said something about vintage cars, so I searched for America's Stonehenge and cars. "Holy shit!" I said excitedly. "Alliance, Nebraska, at a place called Carhenge."

I showed Travis the pictures. He smiled. "You think we can beat her there?"

"She just left this morning, and she's only one driver," I answered. "Maybe."

Travis literally jumped into the Jeep and started it so fast that we all thought he might leave us standing in the zoo parking lot. We dove in after him. Devo seemed more motivated to go on this road trip and find Lux than I've ever seen him about anything. He hated school, but it came easily to him, so his grades were mostly A's. He never worked anywhere all through high school, but he always seemed to have money. He didn't have a girlfriend and wasn't interested in one. Devo just liked his '80s music and hanging out with us. Travis once said, "Devo doesn't need much, and because he's so quiet, no one expects much from him. He just drifts through life." I liked Devo, and if he was happy with drifting through life, I was happy for him. But I wanted more for myself.

We got on the interstate and drove without saying much of anything until we crossed the Mississippi River, when Devo took out his earbuds and said, "Mark Twain suffered from color blindness. You wonder how he could write about a place that might not have been true to his eyes." We all looked at each other. "Maybe he had someone describe the colors to him," Devo continued as he put his earbuds back in. We all looked over the bridge at the large, muddy river, and I think we all wondered the same thing. Was Lux safe?

Iowa City was a cool town. We pulled into a gas station that had a choice of two fast food restaurants, so Mel and I went in to get some burgers while Travis filled up the Jeep with gas. Devo had his head back on the headrest and slept, not waking even when Travis had slammed on the brakes in the parking lot on purpose and Devo's head had come forward and slammed back into the seat.

After filling up, Travis went in to see the cashier. Within two minutes, he came running out, his eyes wide, and yelled, "Let's go!"

"What the hell," said Mel. "Did you rob the place? We've got burgers."

"She was just here," Travis frantically replied.

"How do you know?" I asked.

"The cashier asked where we were from. When I told him, he said we were the second in the last hour. I asked him what the person looked like, and he described Lux. I think the perv got a boner from watching her fill up gas."

We hustled back into the car and started rushing down the interstate again. I wondered what she would do if we caught her or got to Carhenge before her. Lux had a plan, and she would be devastated if she didn't get to carry it out. Would it be enough to have Travis chase her down and find her in Iowa?

I secretly hoped that either Travis would slow down or Lux would speed up. I wanted to find her, and I wanted her to be safe, but I also wanted to be on the road. Lux wished to be found, but I think she needed to be chased even more. Her clue was too easy, and she knew we would find it soon after she left.

"You know," said Mel. "Young women aren't safe on the road alone. There are a lot of creeps out there just waiting to prey on us."

Travis looked deep into the rearview mirror, his face turned to fire. "Shut the hell up. How could you say that?" He pushed the gas pedal all the way to the floor, but the old Jeep had a hard time going any faster than sixty miles per hour.

We came into Omaha, Nebraska around ten o'clock that night. Travis didn't let anyone else drive all day.

"She would stop," Travis said aloud, trying to reassure himself. "I think she would want to sleep so she had the energy to keep this little game of hers going."

Travis thought this was a game. I wanted to tell him that he was wrong. This was a test. It was the kind of test that Grandpa always talked about. He would say, "Life will throw at you more than you think you can take. It's up to you to pass the test and keep moving forward. What's important are the experiences and recognizing that you are being tested."

We stayed in a cheap motel that looked like it had been there since the 1950s. The white shutters had been worn down by the Nebraska winds, and the doors had all been repainted white, but the red paint underneath could still be seen, so they were actually an ugly pink. We got two rooms, one for Mel and the other for Devo, Travis, and me. There were only two other cars in the parking lot. We placed our bags in our rooms, then sat in the plastic lawn chairs in front of our rooms, looking at the Nebraska sky.

Travis was quiet. "There's no telling where she could be right now," he finally said. "Why would she do this?"

I had an answer, but I didn't know if Travis wanted to hear it, so I stayed silent. Devo was listening to his music and looking at pictures on his phone that he had taken throughout graduation. It seemed like the ceremony was a week ago. Suddenly, he sat up. "Lux," he said.

Travis's eyes immediately searched around the parking lot and out to the road. "What the hell, Devo! Not cool!" He looked like he wanted to come out of his chair and kick Devo's ass.

"No. The picture," Devo replied. He held his phone up for us to see. Lux was sitting next to Devo, and he had taken a close-up of her profile. She was crying and looking down at the floor. She looked discouraged but beautiful.

"Go to the next one," said Travis. He knew that when Devo started taking pictures of you, he wouldn't stop at one, even if you were crying. Devo liked to keep clicking the camera until you started yelling at him.

The next photo came up, and she was holding a piece of paper for Devo. It read, "*I am leaving because you said you would stay with me forever.*"

Travis grabbed Devo's phone. "There has to be more." His compulsiveness was showing. The next note read, "*Show me how much you love me. Come for me.*" Travis grabbed Devo's shirt and twisted it in his hands. "You dumbshit! You saw these notes? You saw her crying?"

"No!" said Devo. "I was just taking pictures. I didn't read what she wrote, and I thought she was crying because of the ceremony."

Travis let go of Devo's shirt and swiped to the next five photos.

"*Do you truly love me?*"

"*Do you want to be with me?*"

"*My heart is with you.*"

"*But it's broken knowing that you would consider a life without me.*"

"*Come find me, please. Otherwise, I will take that as a no.*"

Travis stood and started pacing. He was about to lose it. "I do love her, she knows that." He stopped in front of Devo and studied him, breathing deeply. Devo turned his head and squinted like he was ready to take a punch to the face. "I'm sorry I grabbed you," Travis quietly said. "I would never hurt you, Devo." He looked at me. "I would never hurt any of you. It's just, she can drive me to madness."

The light in Mel's room came on and filtered out from the crease in the curtain. Suddenly, Mel opened the door to her room. "Can you guys keep it down? It's bad enough I have to drive across the country with a bunch of stinky boys, but please let me get some sleep." She looked at Travis and simply said, "We'll find her. I know that girl. Now go to bed."

"I guess you do love her then," I said. "I think that's what love does. It drives us to madness, and it can hurt, but it feels great when we have it. It's just losing it that destroys us."

I had often thought over the past two years how easy life would be if I didn't love the people that came into my life. David's death destroyed me. My dad, though I hated him most of the time, left my heart empty. I was worried about my mom and her life because I could not imagine how difficult it was for a parent to outlive their child. Grandpa was getting older, and someday I would have to say goodbye to him. I loved Travis as a brother, so when he decided to leave, I felt like a part of me was dying. Now Lux had left. She may as well have written those notes to me. I loved her so much, and now she was on the road alone.

I had tried to stop loving when I stopped speaking. I never wanted to experience the pain of loss again, but that was impossible. It is impossible not to love because there is so much to love. Still, sometimes it would be easier to just shut the world out and never experience loss, but that wasn't real. Loss is a part of living. I just hated that part.

"Okay, let's try to sleep until five and then go. If I know Lux, she'll sleep until at least nine." Travis went into the room. For some reason, Devo decided to sleep in the back of the Jeep in a sleeping bag. He fell asleep within minutes. I stayed in the plastic chair and looked at the stars and the empty highway. I was exhausted, but my mind was full of a thousand thoughts. No sleep was going to come to me tonight.

With the stars blinking over the Nebraska sky, I thought about David and his suicide. Why didn't anyone want to talk about suicide? I guess no one wants to talk about how desperate someone can become to actually do the unthinkable. Yet it happens all the time. The stars held no answers for me as I drifted off to sleep.

A Very Strange Place

WE ARRIVED AT CARHENGE BY TEN THE NEXT MORNING. NO one was there except for a deer running across the field. When we approached the cars, none of us said a word, but we all had the same look on our face: raised eyebrows and our mouths slightly open. The cars all stood as a replica of Stonehenge in England. They were painted gray to resemble stone, and some had rust on their hoods. It was a bizarre sight in the middle of nowhere, like aliens had landed and decided to make a monument to screw with our heads.

"This is wicked awesome," said Devo. He admired anything vintage, and all of the cars were.

We all walked into the middle of the gray, steel circle and naturally made our own circle with our backs to one another. All we heard was the wind whistling through the cars.

"Alright, spread out and look for it." Travis was determined to find the next clue.

"If we don't find it, I say we hide and wait for her," said Mel. "She usually sleeps until about now." Mel had a point, and we all agreed. It was rare for Lux to get up before nine, even during the school year, and then she usually struggled to actually get up for at least another hour.

The cars were mostly from the '50s and '60s. I started taking pictures for Grandpa because he would love this. He loved old things, and bizarre things. This was definitely bizarre. We each took a car and started checking the obvious places in clear sight for the clue, and then we started looking deeper into the crevices around the car. The cars had a strange smell to them, a mix of earth and metal, with the feeling of isolation.

A couple of tourists showed up within twenty minutes of us looking, and we still hadn't found a clue. It was getting hot, and I could tell that Mel was becoming increasingly annoyed.

"If that little bitch thinks we're just going to chase her little ass all over the country, she can . . ." Mel stopped herself when she caught Travis looking at her.

"Isn't that what we're doing, chasing her all over the country?" I said, trying to disrupt the exchange that Travis and Mel were about to have. Travis just mumbled and kept searching.

"Say, isn't this the darndest thing you've ever seen?" A man with a rich Southern accent said to Devo. His jeans were faded, and he had a scruffy beard that he had probably grown for six or seven days. His t-shirt displayed a red, white, and blue eagle that had its talons out, about to land on a map of Iraq. His wife was in shorts and white sandals with a bright pink t-shirt that depicted a woman riding a horse. The shirt said, "Don't Stand Between a Woman and Her Horse."

"I guess it is," Devo replied to the man.

"You boys must really like it the way you're admiring the cars. Looks like you're searching for treasure." The man caught sight of Mel. "My apologies, and ladies too."

Devo started, "We actually heard a rumor back home that Bonnie and Clyde hid millions in these cars and it was never found."

"Well," the man said calmly. "That certainly would be something."

Devo smiled. He thought he had the man going. "Yeah, if you help us find it, we'll give you a share."

"I would be obliged if you'd share it," the man replied. "Problem is, Bonnie and Clyde were robbin' banks and dead long before these cars were put here." He smirked back at Devo, then reached into his back pocket, pulled out a big buck knife, unfolded the blade, and started cleaning underneath his fingernails.

The blade was shiny and looked to be around four inches long. "Shit!" I said loud enough for Travis to pull his head out from under a truck.

"Now, the way I see it, you might be just messin' with me because of my accent, and then you might be vandalizing this place. Tell you the truth, I don't appreciate either one."

Devo's eyebrows curved up over his white sunglasses. Travis slowly walked over and stood between Devo and the man with his fist clenched, ready to protect us.

"Oh, honey, stop messing with that boy," the man's wife scolded. "They aren't doing anything wrong. Besides, they got this pretty girl with them to keep them in line."

Mel smiled at her, and the man put his knife back in his pocket.

"Sir, the truth is . . ." Travis hesitated, then smiled at the woman. "Truth is, I'm chasing my girlfriend cross-country, and she led us here to find a clue about her next location." He paused. "Problem is, we've been looking and can't find it."

"Well, isn't that the sweetest thing," the woman beamed. "Not sure I've ever heard anything so sweet, you chasing that girl. Hell, last time this slug chased me was when I took the last piece of fried chicken." The man put his arms around her waist. She smiled and grabbed his toned forearms.

"Well, son, I'm sure glad I didn't have to cut you up for vandalizing," said the man. "But, I guess we could help you find that clue. What do y'all think it'll look like?"

Travis pulled the light blue piece of paper from his back pocket. "You don't have to do that, but the first clue was written on paper like this."

"You looked through all these cars?" asked the man. He scratched his head. "Describe your girl. That might help us."

The couple looked determined to help. Perhaps they understood what young love meant. It was obvious that they were very much in love, and they didn't need to ask any questions about why we were chasing this girl. They just realized that Travis was determined to find Lux, and anyone willing to chase after his girlfriend must be in love with her.

We all stood there, waiting for Travis to speak.

"She's . . ." Travis started. "She's a pain in the ass with a smile that would make a convicted murderer repent. Her hair has its own mind, especially in the morning, and when she talks, it makes you wish you had an extra ear just so you could take in what she's saying even more intensely." Travis looked out over the large grassland, and after a long pause, he continued. "She's real. What she says she means, and she doesn't try to fool you. What's standing right in front of you is what you get. She loves to be held on stormy nights, and she giggles in her sleep." He turned and looked directly at me. "I love her eyes. They're soft and light blue and make you want to go blind staring at them as if they'll be your last memory. But what I love most, the thing that makes me want to chase her all over this country, is that she truly cares for others."

There was silence. Mel was crying, Devo just stood there with his mouth open, and I found myself nodding my head, agreeing with everything Travis said.

"Oh, doll," said the woman as she moved toward Travis. She touched his face with both hands. "You need to hang onto her, honey."

"Hell yeah, that sounds like quite a girl," the man agreed. "We better get looking."

We all searched the cars again, this time with more intensity. No one spoke a word. I searched a car that was partially buried, looking around the tires, underneath, on top. After Travis described Lux, I realized how much he truly loved her and how much they were alike. I was glad I was here, but I had to rethink my purpose. I loved Lux, and I wanted to be with Travis, but my purpose should be to want them to find each other and be together and live a happy life.

Suddenly, I found myself searching harder, almost frantically. I climbed one of the cars in order to get to an old Cadillac that sat on top of it. Reaching the Caddy, I held onto the hood like a monkey and then planted my feet so I could get a better look. I felt underneath by the trunk and worked my hand up the length of the car. The fall from that height would have hurt. Travis stared at me with curiosity as I swept my hand underneath the left quarter panel.

"Holy shit!" I screamed, pulling out an envelope from under the car. It was duct-taped where the engine would have been and sealed in a clear plastic bag, most likely so it wouldn't get wet if it rained. "I got it!" I yelled again. I wanted to leap off the car, but getting hurt might mean the end of my trip. Travis was standing underneath me, so I tossed him the envelope and climbed down.

Travis held the note in his hand and stared at it like it was about to catch fire. He felt the edges of the plastic that the envelope was in and the gray tape that held the bag closed, then looked up. "I'm worried about where she may have gone next."

"Hell, son," said the man. "She's not going to go anywhere that you can't find her. That's the point. She wants to be found."

It was clear right then to Travis that Lux did want to be found. He nodded his head at the man. "You're right!" Travis ripped open the clue and read it aloud:

Travis,

If you've come this far, I'm thinking you are willing to go a little further. I'm hoping that this trip will give to you what it's giving to me . . .

"Yeah, a fucking heart attack," said Travis.

See if you can discover it along the way . . .

Travis looked back up. "Discover what?" We all just stood silent.

Remember when we talked about being invincible and how we felt like we could do anything together? Remember when we would camp next to the river, walk out into the moonlight, yell at the stars, and jump from the bridge into the water? Remember last year when all we talked about was running away together after graduation and living how we wanted to live? Do you remember when we looked at the map, and as we kissed and laughed, you said we would go where your finger landed, and with your eyes looking at mine, we smiled and looked at the map at the exact same time? Well, go there now.

I hope you remember,

P.S. Before you go there you must stop at Carry-On Café in Breckenridge. Something awaits you there that will warm you.

Lux

"That's so romantic," said Mel.

"It's nuts!" said Devo.

"She wants you to go after her, honey," said the woman. Her husband reached for her hand. "We all want that from our men."

"Well," I said. "Do you remember?" Everyone was getting off track with their own thoughts about what romance was, and I just wanted to go after Lux. "Travis!" I said louder.

He shook his head. "Yeah, I remember. I promised her that night that we would go there. I promised her we would make a life together and just have fun and not worry about the shit that other people do. No kids, no bills, just fun."

No one said a word. We all waited.

"San Francisco!" said Travis. He slowly brushed his fingers through his hair and shook his head like he couldn't believe it.

"That's a big city," Devo replied. "How are we supposed to find her?"

"Well, after I pointed to San Francisco on the map, we went and bought another map of the city and did the same thing. Kissed, closed our eyes, and pointed."

"Where did you end up?" I asked.

"North Beach. Washington Square."

Travis shook the man and woman's hands and then walked towards the Jeep. None of what was happening seemed strange to any of us. Maybe it was because it was Lux and she was always doing crazy shit, or maybe it was because we were all just kids and doing crazy, impractical things came naturally and didn't bother us like it did with adults. Either way, we were going to San Francisco. The way I saw it, everyone had their time when they needed to go nuts.

The Continental Divide

WE PASSED THROUGH DENVER DURING THE NIGHT. THE AIR was cool, and there wasn't any humidity. We passed one small town after another as we climbed up the interstate closer to the mountains. It was too dark to see anything, but every so often, the clouds would break and the moonlight would reflect off the white-capped mountaintops. It was haunting to see something so big and know you are driving through it. We could have been swallowed at any time.

We drove into the mountains with the radio playing. One station was airing a tribute to the bands of the 1990s, and Travis was singing every lyric. The radio system that Grandpa installed for him shot out of the open-air Jeep so loud that passing cars glanced over. When Pearl Jam started singing "Breathe," Travis stopped his serenading and turned the radio down. He looked over at me and asked, "You've been laid yet?" He glanced in the rearview mirror at Mel, who was asleep on Devo's shoulder. Devo had his earbuds in, listening to his own music.

"No." I was at a loss with what else to say. I almost felt like apologizing because it seemed like every teenager was having sex except me, but I knew that wasn't true. But it still seemed like it. Travis must have recognized how I felt as I looked down at the floor mats.

"Well, you've got plenty of time. Don't rush it."

"I guess I just never had the opportunity. Well, besides . . ." I stopped myself and looked back at Mel. "I just couldn't then."

"Well, I'm sure you could have." Travis laughed.

"Smart-ass." I shoved his shoulder.

Travis peered over at me. "I know it's important for you to find the right person, but it's also important to have experiences in life. It's just sex."

"It's easy to say that when you have it all the time." I said, jealousy in my voice because I often pictured myself with Lux.

"Yeah, well, she's the only one. She will always be the only one."

I was stunned. Most girls thought Travis was hot, and they looked at him all the time. A few of them even talked to me at school to find out more about him.

"Really?" I asked. "Lux is it?"

"You seem surprised." Travis smiled. "Two things: I love Lux, and I knew she was 'The One' the minute I met her, and not many girls want to be with a crazy fuck like me." He laughed, but I didn't. If they didn't want to be with him, they certainly wouldn't want to be with me. Maybe I would never meet the right girl.

Travis turned the radio back up and Soundgarden sang "Fell On Black Days." I turned my head towards the window as tears erupted in my eyes and the cold, thin air perpetuated it. I just had a conversation with Travis that I should have had with David. David was my big brother, and he was supposed to talk to me about girls and sex, but at that moment, I appreciated Travis taking on that role. I missed David, and thoughts of him always crept up on me, like he was there in my head reminding me of our short time together.

We rode into the town of Breckenridge without speaking, and as Mel moaned and stretched, Travis nudged my leg and mischievously grinned. I just kept a straight face, not wanting Mel to know what we were thinking. I was always afraid that girls would realize how much we thought about them. It was better to just sit and look stupid.

It was too late to go to the café and get the next clue. We were not sure what this clue would be since we knew our next destination would be San Francisco. We pulled up to the curb and looked at the hours on the front door. They would open at seven in the morning.

We stopped for food and gas. Travis came out of the market with four gallons of water, trail mix, and hot dogs and buns. "Grandpa said we'd need to stay hydrated when we got to the mountains."

It was still uneasy hearing Travis say "Grandpa," but he was family. Then I thought about what he just said. "What do you mean 'when'?"

"What?"

"You said 'when' we got to the mountains. How did Grandpa know we would come this far?"

Travis and I just stared at each other. Did Grandpa know? He gave Travis the Jeep, which I knew he wanted to give to Travis anyway, but the timing was perfect, and the two hundred dollars. Was Grandpa in on it? Did he help Lux plan? Was this some sort of weird test that he was pulled into? He was always a sucker for romance and love, and Lux could be convincing, even to an old man who had already lived several lives.

"Holy shit!" Travis put the food and water in the back of the Jeep. "You think he knew?"

"Call him," I said. I looked at my watch, which read eleven o'clock. "He might be asleep, but then he never really sleeps."

Travis pulled out his cell phone and called Grandpa. He answered on the first ring.

"Hello."

"Grandpa, it's Travis." Travis put him on speakerphone.

"Where are you, boy?"

"In Breckenridge. We're doing okay. Going to find a place to camp soon."

"Stay in White River National Forest. You can camp cheap. Watch out for mountain lions. Those damn things will grab you up. They would at least grab Devo's skinny ass and run off with him." Grandpa paused. "So what's up? Everyone okay?"

"Yeah," said Travis. "I'll just get right to it."

"That's the way I like it," Grandpa replied.

"Did you know Lux was leaving? Did you know she had this planned and that we would be following her through the mountains?"

Grandpa hesitated. "Travis, you need to listen up. All of you do. I know you have me on the damn speakerphone." He sighed. "Now, a girl like Lux comes along only once in your life. The rest are just substitutes. Some girls find out how much you love them when they ask you to do silly crap like go shopping and help them pick out shoes. Some of them find out by how much you hold their hand and if you look at them when they're talking. Then, there are a few that will test your heart. They will make you go to the ends of the earth and convince you that you are more of a man than you thought you were. They will test your will and see if you have the grit to love them for a lifetime no matter what kind of hardships you may have. Well, son, you found one of those girls."

We were all silent. Mel had tears in her eyes. Devo just listened with his mouth hanging open like he usually did when Grandpa started talking, and Travis stared at the moonlight and the peaks that lay beyond the town. I grinned because it was my grandpa who knew the world so well.

He continued, "So, you see, it doesn't matter what anyone knew or had planned. What matters is that you are on the road on a journey to find out if your love is true and if it will last. That's rare."

"She's been testing my heart for a long time," said Travis. "She's everything to me."

"Then you know what to do." Grandpa cleared his throat and finished the conversation by saying, "Go get her and tell her what she means to you."

"Thanks," said Travis.

"You kids be safe and say hello to the mountains for me." Grandpa hung up the phone, and we started to drive.

We found a site to set up camp right off the road next to a river. The river roared in front of us, then trickled off to a calm pool before moving down the mountain more rapidly. We had two tents: Grandpa's old Army tent that smelled musty and was sewn and patched up several times, and one that Devo took from his house. Devo pulled out his sleeping bag and fell asleep in the back of the Jeep. Before he went to bed, all he said was, "I need to find an outlet in the morning to charge my iPod." It was the most he'd said all day.

Travis crawled into Grandpa's tent. He hadn't said anything since he hung up the phone. He looked a little stunned, which was often how Grandpa left people feeling when he was through talking to them.

I walked down to the river with Mel. We went to the calm area where the water flowed gently and sounded like one of those fountains that you can buy for your garden. It was peaceful. We sat on some rocks next to the edge of the river.

After looking at the water in silence for a couple of minutes, Mel stood up. "I'm not sure if I will ever be one of the rare girls that your grandpa talked about or if I will just be a substitute."

I looked over at her. "Mel, there is nothing ordinary about you." The words just kind of came out, and I felt embarrassed. As I watched her in the half light that reflected off the water and saw the tears in her eyes, I realized that Mel searched for belonging like the rest of us. She wanted to be accepted and feel normal, but the Polar Bear Club was anything but normal. We were all a bunch of misfits in haphazard lives, but we were not boring.

I reached out and lightly stroked her hair. As a teenage boy, I often wondered how I would be at showing affection to a girl. I'd seen plenty of movies. Some guys kissed women hard, and some did it soft. Some took control, and some just let it happen. To me, stroking her hair just seemed right and natural for the situation. Right then, next to the trickling water, I could tell that Mel wanted to be gently touched. We all need to feel and be felt by another.

Mel leaned into my chest and wrapped her arms around my waist. The warmth of her body contrasted with the coolness of the mountain air. I needed this too. It was comforting to be held. We held each other for a few minutes, and then Mel looked up at me and softly kissed my lips. Her kiss felt better than anything I'd felt in a long while.

"Just friends, right?" she asked as she touched the side of my face.

I nodded. She stood up and walked to the edge of the river, then took off her clothes slowly and deliberately.

This was where my lack of experience showed. Did she want me to do the same? I didn't want to assume or take advantage. Mel looked back over her shoulder, all the shapes and contours of her body visible in the moonlight. Her hand reached out for me, so I joined her. We laughed and then lost our breath as we entered the cold water and then came closer the deeper we went. We swam just long enough to feel clean, and we held each other, then went back to the riverbank where we lay on my shirt. That was when I knew that my reaction to a girl's body was completely natural, and that Travis was right. Life is about experiencing things. I also knew that I would be able to answer Travis's question differently next time, but out of respect for Mel, I would never tell a soul.

Driven

WE LEFT THE RIVERBANK IN A HURRY THE NEXT MORNING. Travis had a sense of urgency to get to the Carry-on Café right when it opened. As we drove, I looked over at the river where I swam with Mel and just smiled. The river was like life, changing constantly. A fog rested on top of the water which started to fade as the sun filtered through the canyon. I hoped this moment, this memory, would always stay in my mind and appear whenever I needed to smile.

Twenty minutes later, we arrived at the café. We all walked in and started looking around. There weren't any customers yet, only the woman behind the counter. The woman had a light blue bandana that covered her entire head with gold earrings that hung from her lobes. She wore a yellow t-shirt that read "Carry-on Café" with a picture of a woman with a backpack climbing a mountain, a cup of coffee in her hand.

"Hey, handsome," the woman said to Travis. "Come over here. I think I have what you're looking for."

Travis moved quickly to the counter. "What is it?"

She opened the drawer next to the cash register and pulled out an envelope. "I'm supposed to read this note to you and your friends."

"Wait!" said Mel. "How do you know it's us you're supposed to read it to?"

The woman grinned, which made her silver nose piercing move upward. "Well, a cute blonde came in here yesterday and dropped an envelope off with this young man's picture." She gestured with a nod of her head towards Travis. "She told me you would be by and it was urgent that you get this note. The girl said it was a matter of 'keeping love breathing,' so here I am trying to give oxygen to the love she described." The woman turned to Travis. "I've never heard someone try to keep love 'breathing' before. You better hang on to this girl."

"I'm trying," Travis sighed. "Can I just see the note?"

"I was asked to read it, so that's what I plan to do." The woman gently opened the envelope, pulled out a piece of light blue paper, and began to read Lux's words, *"I hope you have enjoyed the drive so far. There is so much of this country that you need to see, so I took you on the most beautiful route I could think of. There is so much beauty in this world. Don't ever forget that! You know where I am, and I will be waiting. Meanwhile, have a coffee on me."* The woman pulled twenty dollars out of the envelope and handed it to Travis. "Order some coffee, pick out something to eat, then get the hell out of here and find that girl."

"Cool, I need to charge my iPod anyway," said Devo.

We each had a muffin, and Mel and I got a coffee. Travis wanted to leave right away, but we needed to map out the rest of our route and put it in the phone. There would not be any more clues until we got to San Francisco. The route would take us over the mountains into Utah and then up through Salt Lake City.

"Devo, is that damn thing charged yet?" Travis wanted to be on the road.

"Close," Devo replied.

"I'm leaving in five minutes," said Travis. "You decide if you want to be there too."

Devo stared at him. "You're being a dick."

"I'm just saying. You decide." Travis approached the woman at the counter and tried to hand her the twenty dollars.

"You hang onto your money and go after her. Now get on out of here." She turned to help a customer that had just walked in.

Travis walked out to the Jeep, waving for Devo to follow him, and Devo flipped him off. I was worried that Travis was unraveling. He started the Jeep and put it in gear like he would really leave us if we didn't hurry. What the hell would we do if he freaked out in the middle of the mountains? What do people do to people when they go nuts out here? I figured we would just let him scream to the mountaintops and valleys and let him have a meltdown, but what if he decided to hurt himself? Between the three of us and all the therapy we'd had and the talks with Mr. C, I hoped we could handle it.

After talking to Grandpa yesterday and receiving the note this morning, Travis was determined to drive straight through until we got to San Francisco. He was quiet for the first couple hundred miles, then he turned to me and said, "Your grandpa really pissed me off, but then I realized that I would rather have him know so he could help Lux. Maybe he helped her prepare, so she's safe."

"Yeah, he probably did," I said, trying to reassure him.

"I'm just a little freaked out because I'm not sure why she's doing this. She knows I love her. Why the test?"

"I'm not sure. Maybe she just wants to feel wanted. I think it freaked her out that she was going to college and you were going out west," I responded.

"Yeah, but I just wanted to escape, make some money, and then come and get her."

"People need to be held and cared for though." After I said that, I felt like a geeky romantic.

Travis looked over at me and smiled. "I didn't hear you come back into the tent last night." I didn't answer him, but I grinned.

Travis leaned over and put his arm around me. It was nice to see him come back from that darkness he had been in for the last couple of hours. I hoped he would stay in a good place.

I didn't say anything more about Mel, and I was proud of myself for not talking about it. I wasn't the bragging type, and Grandpa taught me all about respecting women. It wasn't anyone else's business what happened between Mel and me. I peeked back at her. She slept as her hair flowed with the wind. Her face was lit up with the afternoon sun, and sweat beaded her cheeks and upper lip. I was glad that she had said, "Just friends," last night, but I suddenly wanted more. She was leaving when we got back. Her college was somewhere up north, and she wouldn't have a lot of time for hanging out with a sophomore in high school. It made me sad. All of my friends would be gone next year, and I would have no one. Even Mr. C was leaving. I was alone.

Sitting there in the Jeep, I started having anxiety about the whole thing and tried breathing from my belly like Mr. C taught me. Everything was closing in. I tried to write a short story in my head like Grandpa said to do, but nothing was working. The mountains started to come in around me, and suddenly, I felt insignificant and claustrophobic. I made it past Salt Lake City, and then it happened. My freak-out.

Panic!

WE WERE IN THE DESERT WHEN IT HAPPENED. MY BREATHING increased, and I hung onto the roll bar tight, thinking that if I placed my hands over my head that it would calm my breath and stop the dizziness. How do you calm down when you feel like you're dying, like life is falling apart and you're going crazy? I mean really crazy, like you might just freak out a little too much and never make it back. Is that what happened to people that lived in institutions or were homeless on the street? My head was a fucking carnival ride that I couldn't get off.

Travis pulled down a side road off the highway and placed his hand on my shoulder and gave me a slight squeeze. The road seemed like it went for miles without curving, just one straight line. In this car, no one said the obvious things like "Calm down," or "It will be okay," or my favorite, "It will end soon, and then everything will be back to normal." Everyone in the Polar Bear Club knew how this felt. They knew I just couldn't calm down on demand and that everything that made me feel this way would still be here when I finally relaxed. Little words of encouragement do not always help someone with depression or anxiety because the reason why we are the way we are is from years of bullshit that has built up and acts like a circus in our minds. It's the million little thoughts that are like shards of glass cutting up the part of the brain that makes us happy. All we want during those moments is for people not to judge us. To let us work through our panic attacks and depression and the bullshit that we deal with daily. We just want to be understood like people understand cancer or any other disease.

Travis pulled over after a couple of miles, and I jumped out of the Jeep and briskly walked away like I was trying to get somewhere, holding my head, trying to stop the shards of glass from cutting. I breathed deeply and squeezed my hands, then sat down and rocked. It was strange, but rocking back and forth made me feel better than anything. I often wondered if it had something to do with being rocked as a child, because that was when I was happiest. My thoughts weren't corrupted then. Rocking brought me back to innocence.

No one said anything. Nobody chased me, but they were closely watching, making sure I was okay. That's what the Polar Bear Club did for each other. They just let things fall apart because they were going to anyway and then helped pick up the pieces. It took me about ten minutes to finally relax, and when I glanced back towards the car, Travis was sitting right behind me. I didn't know he was there. He just grinned, but tears were in his eyes. We stood up together, and he reached towards me and hugged me. I needed that hug more than anything. It told me that I was okay.

We all cried for each other when we weren't doing well. We knew the pains everyone else was going through. I would never forget the day when Mr. C walked into his office and we were all crying. Not sobbing, never sobbing, because that would be too much. They were gentle cries with slow, fat tears. It was weird how our cries were similar and that they happened for similar reasons. Mr. C didn't say a word.

He just sat down, and tears flowed from his eyes too. We all cried for him that day because we could tell how bad he felt. We saw him earlier in the morning by the front doors, and when we circled around him, Travis asked how he was doing. Mr. C tried his best to cover it up, but depression had set in, and we all knew. That entire session was quiet, and we hoped Mr. C would get through his darkness, but depression doesn't have a timeframe for when it lifts. When the bell rang, we all decided to go for a walk in the nature preserve behind the school. Mr. C always told us that the woods helped him breathe again and find himself. That was when my respect for Mr. C grew beyond just him being a good counselor. He was a part of us.

Mel met me at the side of the Jeep and said, "Welcome back. I was thinking about coming over there and repeating last night to get your mind off it."

As the both of us laughed, she hugged me, then we all got back into the Jeep. Devo reached forward and touched my shoulder, then placed an earbud from his iPod in my ear and leaned in so we could both listen. He didn't say a word, but played "Fix You" by Coldplay. I was surprised at his selection. It wasn't a song from the '80s, but it was his way of telling me that he was there for me. Everyone in the Jeep was there for each other, and we were obviously there for Lux. I was anxious wondering if it would last, and if forever was a true thing.

San Francisco

WE ARRIVED IN SAN FRANCISCO AROUND EIGHT THIRTY AT night. The Golden Gate Bridge was covered in fog and made us feel as if we were driving on a cloud. Mist covered my hand as I held it out the window. We were all exhausted but felt like we were closer to Lux, and our motivation to find her increased our adrenaline. I felt her, I visualized her, and I was overwhelmed to be in the same city as her again. I wondered what her reaction would be when she saw all of us. Would she and Travis start fighting, or would they just be happy to see each other? It was a little crazy, but we were not the types to judge one another's craziness. We just accepted each other as we were. There was a part of me that feared she wouldn't be in San Francisco.

We drove through a section of the city called the Presidio. I'd studied San Francisco on the coffee shop's internet before we left the mountains so I would know the city. I loved reading about places that I wanted to see and fantasized about what they would be like. So far, San Francisco didn't disappoint. The Presidio used to be an Army base, which was interesting in such a liberal city. We drove past the Palace of Fine Arts, all lit up and beautifully golden, and in the bay was Alcatraz, sitting like a gray, stone fortress. We were transfixed because sights like these were rare in the Midwest. We headed for Washington Square. Saints Peter & Paul Church was like a monument that welcomed us into the neighborhood.

It made sense that Lux wanted to meet in North Beach because it used to be a Beatnik hangout. She loved reading Kerouac, Ginsberg, and Burroughs. She would sometimes read us sections of Ginsberg's "Howl" at the diner. Unfortunately, North Beach had been taken over by young, rich techies, but the old Italians and Chinese still lived here along with a few Beatnik types.

We pulled the Jeep up next to Washington Square and looked around as if our heads were on swivels. Even Devo stopped his music. I guess we thought maybe she would just be there waiting for us, waving and yelling, "Thanks for coming to get me!" We slowly drove around the square and looked at every bench. Most were occupied by homeless people trying to sleep. Did she really want us to come here? I was scared.

"Let's get out and walk the park," said Travis. "Mel, you walk this path. Devo, you take the center through the grass. Neil, take the outside walk, and I'll check all the benches and trees to see if she's sleeping."

We didn't say a word. I suddenly became angry that Lux wasn't there waiting for us. Then, panic set in again. What if she thought we would be here by now and had given up? What if there was another clue and we weren't at the end of this bullshit? What if she had been kidnapped or killed? My movements picked up pace and became more urgent. I found myself jogging the square, lapping it several times. Then I started yelling. "What if" questions can drive you to madness.

"Lux!" I ran faster. "Lux, where the fuck are you?" I started grabbing homeless people and turning them over. They stank of booze and body odor. I yelled in their faces, pulling out a picture of Lux and shoving it at them. "Have you seen her?"

"I've seen the top of her head," one man said, trying to be funny. I kicked him in the stomach, making him curl up in a fetal position. Next thing I knew, Travis tackled me to the ground.

"No, Neil!" He held me down as I struggled. My head was next to the man I'd just kicked. His face was in pain, and his yellow, stained teeth showed as he screamed in agony. "He doesn't deserve that."

"You didn't hear what he said when I showed him Lux's picture," I said. "Get the fuck off me."

Travis didn't budge. "I don't care what he said. This man has been hit by hard times, and he doesn't deserve us beating the shit out of him. For all you know, he once had a family, a job, and dreams of his own."

I looked over at the man. He had stopped screaming and just lay there, listening to Travis.

Travis grinned as he continued, "Hell, he could have been one of the Polar Bear Club back home. He would probably meet our standards."

Travis was right. This was just a man down on his luck. Life had given up on him to the point that he had given up on life. He probably could have been one of us. We could one day become like him because, as Travis said, life forgets about the bottom. It seems to focus on those at the top. I rolled over and faced the man as Travis eased up on his grip.

"I'm sorry, sir. I was just upset at what you said."

The man wiped the saliva off his lips that had formed when he screamed. "I was just kidding," he said. "I was trying to get you to leave me alone."

"Why would you want that?" I asked.

"Because when I'm left alone, I'm not ashamed."

"Ashamed?"

"I haven't showered in over a week. My clothes are rags that I found in a dumpster. My teeth are rotted because it's been years since I've seen a dentist. Ashamed is an understatement." He looked away, a dirty tear falling down his face.

"You have nothing to be ashamed about," I told him. "I do have a question, though."

"Go ahead," he said.

"Did you choose to be this way, or is it by circumstance?" I waited for an answer.

"Both," he replied. "I lost my job a few years ago. I was laid off. After that, my wife left me and took my three-year-old son. There wasn't anything I could do. I tried to get another job, but no one would hire me. Then I fell into a deep depression, started drinking, and ended up beating a man half to death for trying to steal my bottle of booze. That put me in jail, which wasn't bad because I could eat and had a place to stay. After that, I was homeless."

"Didn't they help? The jail?" I asked naively. "Didn't they help you find a job or a place to live?"

"Yeah, they gave me a number to call that led nowhere. This is San Francisco. I'm not a priority. I'm just out here surviving on my own day by day."

I looked into his eyes, not sure what to say. "I'm sorry."

"I don't want your sympathy," said the man. "I just don't want you looking at me like I'm the scum of the earth." He pointed his finger to the other homeless people in the park. "Many of these people are here by circumstance, and some are just so crazy that this is all they can do in society."

Travis sat down next to the man and pulled out a picture of Lux again. "Can you tell me if you've seen her, please?" He handed the picture to him. It was the same picture that I carried, which made me feel awkward that Lux gave me the same one she'd given Travis. Her hair was parted to the right, blond, with a purple clip in it. She wore a t-shirt and faded jeans with sandals.

This time, the man examined the picture. He looked up at Travis and said, "Yeah, she's been here the past two days. She comes in the early morning, then around lunch, and then again at night. You just missed her."

Travis looked at me with urgency. "We missed her?"

"Yeah, about an hour ago," the man replied.

"How did she seem? Was she alone? Did she look safe?" Travis quickly stood, his eyes wide.

"She looked safe. Again, I'm sorry I said that thing before. I actually kept my eye on her so no one bothered her. What I noticed the most was how sad she looked."

Travis started to pace, breathing deeply. "We need to find her. We've traveled across the country looking for her. She's . . . my girlfriend."

"Well, she'll be back tomorrow. I'm sure of it," the man said. "You and your friends are welcome to stay here if you want." He pointed to the space around the tree he was under. "It's free." He laughed.

"Which way did she walk?" asked Travis.

The man pointed toward an area that I remembered from the map. It was close to Chinatown. I knew what Travis had on his mind. "I'll go with you," I said.

"No. I need you guys to stay here. I'll just walk around and see if I find her," Travis replied.

"Son, this is a city," said the man. "It's hard to find people in cities. That's why people come here. To get lost."

Travis walked toward where the man pointed. He trudged toward a city that he had no idea about and noises that he hated so much. Travis liked the country and the openness of the land. I watched him scurry away until he was out of sight. Only one thing could get him to enter this place. Lux.

Devo and Mel came and sat next to me. The homeless man looked at us and said, "Well, I didn't know I would have so much company tonight."

I introduced him to my friends, and Devo started talking to him about what music he liked. I could tell the man liked the conversation. I'm sure it wasn't every day that he was asked his opinion about anything. Mel was a little more cautious and stayed close to me, holding my arm.

Mel and I lay against the tree, and she rested her head on my shoulder. I immediately thought back to the river in Colorado. I wanted to do it again. I wanted to do it better and embrace every moment, but a park in San Francisco was not a place to get laid. Though, back in the '60s, that's exactly what people did. Instead, I just put my arm around Mel to keep her warm and continued looking in the direction that Travis went, hoping to see him coming around the corner with Lux on his arm. I wanted this to be over so all of us could go back home, eat at the diner, listen to Grandpa's stories, and just hang out. But, when this adventure was over, everything would be over, so I embraced what I had.

"Do you want to go to the Jeep and cover up?" I whispered to Mel.

She took my hand and led us to the Jeep, and we lay in the back together, a sleeping bag covering us. We kissed gently as I followed her prompts on where and how to move my hands. Mel became my teacher in many ways, and I appreciated it more than just horny teenage boy shit. She helped take the mystery out of being close to a girl.

"Thank you," I said as she kissed my neck.

Mel just looked at me and smiled. "No, thank you!" she said.

"For what?" I asked.

"For treating me nice. For not treating me like a slut and using me to get what you want."

We just held each other until Mel fell asleep. I kept a lookout for Travis and watched Devo talk with the homeless man. Another man joined them, and they sat there like they were long-lost friends. That was Devo's gift. He could talk to anyone about anything and make them feel like they were the most important person in the world. He didn't say much, but he had a gift when he did.

I was startled awake when I heard Travis talking and peered in the direction of his voice. Lux wasn't with him. He sat next to Devo, and now there were five homeless men sitting in a circle, talking. They shared a bottle of booze, which Travis passed on. Devo took a few swigs of it and coughed as he swallowed. I watched them until they all laid their heads down and fell asleep. I guess we aren't much different from each other in this world. We just have different circumstances handed to us.

Lost and Found

THE NEXT MORNING, I WOKE UP TO A SOFT KISS ON MY CHEEK. To my surprise, it wasn't Mel.

"Lux!" I said, then dove out of the Jeep and hugged her. I picked her up off her feet and didn't even know it. I guess I didn't want her leaving again, so I just held her. Mel sat up and wiped her eyes.

"Oh, good. Can we go home now?" she said with a yawn.

I looked over at Travis, who was sitting up with his back against the tree, watching Lux. There wasn't any running toward each other and meeting halfway, embracing like in the movies. It was sort of anticlimactic. Maybe it was because we didn't surprise each other since we were all a little eccentric and acted impulsively as part of our way of living. Lux slowly walked to Travis and knelt down next to him. She leaned in and kissed him, then said, "You must really love me."

"Couldn't you have just asked me?" Travis grinned, grabbing her into his arms.

"Actions are what I respect, not words. Besides, I gave you a nice road trip," Lux replied.

"How long would you have waited?" asked Travis.

I had thought the same thing myself. Mel and I were at Lux's side. All of the homeless men were gone, and Devo still slept.

"Oh, a while," Lux said. "Grandpa called me and told me where you were." I smiled. I never realized how much Grandpa had to do with this. "He's one cool old guy," said Lux. "I told him I needed to find out once and for all how much you wanted to be with me, and he just smiled and helped me plan my route. He also made sure the car was ready and supplied me with food and some money.

"Why would he do that?" asked Travis as he looked toward me. "Why would he help?"

Lux didn't let me reply, but I didn't have much of an answer anyway. "Because he went through the same thing with his wife, except she led him to a small town in Vermont. He told me they slept under the stars in a tent for ten days after that. Then they got married."

Travis looked up quickly when she said that last part.

Lux laughed. "Don't worry, I don't want to get married. All I wanted was to know that you want me. I needed to know that I was more important to you than you working on a ranch in the mountains."

"You always have been," Travis assured her. "Do you believe me now?"

"I do. I guess I believe that all of you love me," Lux said. "I'm sorry I led you on this crazy chase. "

"I'm not," I said with a little too much enthusiasm. Everyone laughed, and Mel just smiled and blushed.

"Where did you stay?" asked Travis. "What if something would have happened?"

Lux looked at me. "Your grandpa knows people all over this country, so I stayed with his friends along the way. Some were

Vietnam vets, and one was a woman who loved to talk about your grandpa." I smiled with pride. "I've been staying with a friend of his a few blocks from here, someone that he knew in the '60s. He and your grandpa came back from Vietnam and told the truth in this park on a stage right over there." Lux pointed toward the church. "He's been here ever since."

Devo finally woke up. "Shit! My battery is dead." He glanced at us. "Hey, Lux," he said while he poked at his iPod, acting like he just saw her yesterday.

This was an unusual occurrence with unusual people in an unusual city. It was then that I truly appreciated our uniqueness. I was glad we were all a bit crazy, at least crazy to the rest of the world.

Talk Doesn't Make It Easier

WE WALKED UP THE HILL TO GRANDPA'S FRIEND'S PLACE. IT was the bottom part of a duplex that had a kitchen, bathroom, two bedrooms, and a small garden within a fence. The upstairs was unoccupied and had one bedroom, a small kitchen, and bathroom. There was not a living room, or much area to move around. His name was Hank Peterson, but he told us to call him Badger. I guess my grandpa gave him the nickname when they were in Vietnam because it was his duty to search holes where the Vietcong hid. He wore a tie-dye shirt that said "Deadhead." His hair was curly and gray to his shoulders, which were broad and strong.

"Your grandpa is the toughest, gentlest, and realest bastard I've ever known," said Badger as he shook my hand. "I practically watched you and your brother grow up through the pictures he sent me." The mention of David made me catch my breath.

We all sat around next to the garden behind the wooden fence. It didn't seem like a city was beyond it. We were far enough up the hill that it was remarkably quiet outside.

"Where did you meet him?" I asked Badger.

"Boot camp," he said. "Your grandpa was a good grunt. Saved my ass more than once." I knew Grandpa was a hero and just never talked about it. He had always been a hero to me. "I called him, by

the way. He said he would call you later and to behave yourself."
Badger smiled, then saw Travis and Lux holding hands and
laughing and whispering in each other's ears. "You think you'll like
it here?"

My heart stopped. Devo and Mel sat up quickly and looked at
Travis and Lux. "What the hell?" said Mel.

"Sorry!" said Badger, his hands up in surrender. "I thought you
told them."

We waited for a response. Lux spoke up. "Badger is letting us stay
here for half the rent, and we're going to find jobs and maybe go to
school." She looked directly at me. She knew this would impact me
the most. One more person leaving my life. Fuck it!

"That's cool," said Devo, nodding. "It's good to move on."

Was he delusional?

"Yeah, you two will probably love it out here," Mel agreed. "I'm
happy for you."

Mel was pissing me off with her enthusiasm. I was the one that
had to be the dick. The one that had to be selfish and tell them I
didn't want them to leave and that I wouldn't make it without them.
I already knew they would probably move on and go to college, but
I thought that maybe after this road trip, we would make a pact to
stay closer together. My childish thoughts were replacing reality.
Everyone looked at me for a response. Maybe they watched to see
if I would freak out. No more Polar Bear Club, no more friends, no
more laughter. After all, laughter is for people who fake life. Crying
is for those that see life for what it really is.

I could have a freak-out right now. I could spaz out in this garden
and run out of the fence for the city. I could leave little notes and see

if any of them would go to the same depths as they did for Lux to prove that they loved me.

I didn't freak out. I handled it with disappointment and encouragement because that was what life was, to keep living through all the bad shit that happened. Hope! It was all about hope, and maybe hope was why Lux and Travis wanted to move away from their old lives.

"I will miss you both so much," I said with a smile, tears building in my eyes. "I love you both and just want the best for you. You have helped me so much that I can't thank you enough." I wiped my tears as Lux moved closer. "You all have made me want to live my life. Before I met you, I was unsure. I thought maybe I would join David."

We were all crying now. Badger excused himself and went inside the house. Devo flipped on his music and blocked everything out. Mel played with a flower, pulling the petals off as tears fell down her cheeks. I could not thank her enough. She offered me companionship, and I learned from her in the most gentle, sensual way that a fifteen-year-old boy could.

Travis and Lux drove us all to the airport the next day. As it turned out, Badger was pretty wealthy and offered to pay for our airfare. His generosity was his gift to Grandpa and to us.

Devo and Mel hugged Travis and Lux and entered the security gate. I hesitated. I wanted to stay with them. They were part of my family now, and I knew the world enough to know that our distance would dissolve our relationship. They would grow with each other and meet new friends. That was expected and part of living a full life, but I was thinking about my loss. How could I enter school knowing that the Polar Bear Club was dismantled, torn apart, never to be again?

"You'll be okay, Neil," said Travis. "We're brothers now, you know."

He hugged me, then handed me a letter. "Read it on the plane." As he stepped back, he smiled and said, "I love you." Those words meant everything to me. We were brothers, and we did love each other. As always, Travis gave me hope. Hope was all anyone really needed to survive.

Lux embraced me softly and kissed my cheek. "You're one of the greats," she said. "Keep being you. Keep being real, and don't change." I wept like a baby on her shoulder, but to my surprise, they were tears of joy. I was truly happy for them. They found each other, and our road trip was proof of that. That kind of loyalty does not come around often. I guess that was why I was happy for them and sad for me. I would miss their loyalty.

I entered the plane and found my seat, Mel next to me and Devo behind me. We didn't speak. I immediately opened the letter:

My dear friend, my brother,

Neil, we have been through a lot together, from the day that we first met when you didn't speak and I was using the psychiatric ward as my home until this crazy trip. That first day seems like so long ago. Let's promise each other that will never happen again. Let's stay out of those places unless we are going there to help someone else. You have a voice, Neil, and I am glad you found it. Use your voice to make this world a better place. I was lost before you came into my life. I had no direction, and Lux and the Polar Bear Club were my only norm. You helped me find a home. You helped me find myself. We are brothers that met as friends. We are a part of each other now, and that will never change. To say goodbye would be to lie to ourselves because, let's face it, we will be together forever. You will do great things.

-Travis

Saying Goodbye

THE PLANE LANDED, AND AS WE MADE IT BACK TO THE GATE, Grandpa was waiting for us. He looked older than I remembered, and it had only been a few days. It's strange how when you see someone daily, then don't see them for a short while, sometimes they seem to change. The one thing I hate but also love about life is that it's constantly changing. Little moments constantly pass us by that we don't even recognize as being important, and then the moments are gone, only to become memories. Those moments make us smile, sometimes for no reason.

Grandpa took Devo home first. When we reached his house, Devo took an earbud out of one ear and kept moving to the music. "I don't care what anybody says, The Cure is a great band." He just nodded to us and then started singing "Pictures of You." I think it was his way of saying goodbye. I wouldn't see Devo very often after that. He went out east and worked in a recording studio. I'm not sure what he did, but once when I visited the diner, his sister said he loved it. Music was the only thing that helped Devo from becoming depressed or anxious. It was his pill, and he took it constantly. I'm glad he found it.

Mel came to Grandpa's house with me since she lived down the street. Mom hugged me, and Grandpa gave me a grin that made me feel like a man, and then I walked Mel home.

"Thank you," she said. "I'm glad you came into my life."

"Why?"

"You treated me with respect. You could have taken advantage of me in Chicago, but you didn't. Shit! That seems so long ago now." Mel moved closer to me and moved my hair behind my ears. I loved it when she touched me. "You just make sure you never change."

"I'm sort of a freak," I said. "I'm afraid."

"You're not a freak, and never let anyone tell you that. You're cool without trying. It's the only way to be cool. What are you afraid of?"

That question haunted me. I was afraid of everything. "I'm afraid I'll never have friends like the Polar Bear Club again. I'm afraid a girl will never be interested in me. I'm afraid of losing everyone. Either you'll forget me, or I'll hear about one of you dying." Mel moved closer, looking up at me, so I continued. "I'm afraid that I'll go completely nuts someday and not come back. I'm afraid that I will never feel happy again." I stopped because I just couldn't continue without breaking into tears. There had been too many tears on this trip already.

Mel just smiled at me, then grabbed my shoulders and pulled herself closer. "You're the bravest boy I've ever met." Then she kissed me.

I was confused. Mel was good at that. She confused the hell out of me. In fact, so did Lux, and so did my mom. Did girls have it in their makeup to keep us confused, to make men think too much so we really don't know what the hell is happening? Mel's gift to me was allowing me to experiment with what it meant to have a girlfriend without us ever dating, which was something that I knew I would appreciate someday.

I would see Mel when she came home for breaks from college. I heard that she tried to kill herself once after a party. She was drunk, and some boys took advantage of her. Mel never protected herself and gave too much of herself to everyone. She didn't deserve any of that. When I went to visit her in the hospital, she just looked at me and said, "There's the only boy that will ever love me." Mel left college and moved out east to stay with Devo after that. I was glad they remained friends. She needed a new life, a new start where no one knew her. I wouldn't see her anymore after that, but I heard she is doing well. Mel and Devo have become a memory, a conversation that makes me smile when I hear their names.

Hope

AUGUST CAME, AND SCHOOL WAS ABOUT TO START. IT WAS registration day, and Mr. C met me at the front door and gave me a big hug. It was good to see him again. He decided to remain a counselor at my school. Selfishly, I was glad because I wasn't sure I could handle him leaving too.

"Welcome back. I heard you had an adventurous summer," Mr. C said, smiling. "That's what happens when you're friends with Travis and Lux."

I got chills when he said their names. I wished they were there with me. "Will we have a Polar Bear Club anymore?" I asked. Would Mr. C find it useful? Would he want to keep doing it?

"Well." He handed me my schedule. I looked at the last hour. It was there. "Even if it's just you, me, and Eric, we'll meet." He put his arm around me as we walked. "I'm sure we can dig up a few more misfits around here."

I was so happy. Mr. C had given me the hope that I needed. It's all a teenager needs from his teachers.

"Eric is back?" The quiet boy who lived for Band would be there. Maybe I would have a friend after all.

I hugged Mr. C and told him I would see him in three weeks when school started. I looked at my schedule several times on the way home to make sure that the Polar Bear Club was actually there. Sometimes just having a place to go was enough.

I took the bus across town to where my old house was. Where David took his life and changed my life forever. I just wanted to see the outside of it again, one more time, and think about how my life had changed since then. The journey that I had been on was nothing extraordinary, but it was my journey.

A young family was outside in the yard. The couple looked to be in their twenties, teaching their son how to walk. They looked so happy and the child so pure, so innocent. I watched them for a while and then left toward the woods.

I entered the forest and hiked to the center, the farthest away that I could get from any civilization in this town. It was strange. The woods seemed so much bigger before. Maybe it was because the rest of my world was so small then. I found one of my old forts and thought about how many times the sticks, dirt, and leaves became my sanctuary. It protected me from everything that I found to be harmful. I sat in the middle of the fort and breathed in the smell of the leaves. As I looked around me, I noticed a small plastic box tucked under a pile of sticks. I opened it and found a stack of baseball cards and three pieces of gum. It made me smile. Another kid was using these woods as their escape.

I walked out of the woods that day never to return. My memory would be my sanctuary from now on. It would also be my curse. As I walked back to Grandpa's, I thought of how much loss we all experience in our small worlds. Sometimes, life is gain and loss, and we blindly move toward a destination where we have no clue what lies ahead. Our compass is so often broken. However, there are memories of people and places that give us hope that life will never be dull. To have an existence that is boring or ordinary would be tragic. Even though there is a great deal of pain along the way, hope of a full life is all that is needed to keep moving forward.

I came home that evening to Mom sipping tea on the porch, Grandpa working on the Beetle in the garage, and a letter addressed to me from San Francisco on the table.

Broken

I STARTED TO JOURNAL AGAIN. IT HAD BEEN A WHILE SINCE I
visited my journal and wrote my thoughts down on paper.

We are all broken.

*Travis, Lux, Mel, Devo, Mr. C, Peter, H, Grandpa, Mom, Dad,
Fred, Badger, David, and me. We cannot do it alone. We walk around
broken every day and need help from others to pick up the pieces. The
crucial pieces that help keep us glued together.*

*I am glad I found others to help put me back together. Maybe along
the way, I helped pick up their broken pieces too.*

Acknowledgements

This book started to breathe in 2014 when I was teaching eighth graders in a rural town in Wisconsin. It found more life over the next couple of years when I was a Dean of Students at a large high school, where my anxiety took hold of me and wouldn't let go. Many of the words in this book were written from a place of darkness and fear that depression and anxiety often brings with it. Finally, when I became a teacher again and started to heal, I found the confidence to send it out and see if the world wanted it. I wrote it to help others understand and heal.

I would like to give special thanks to TEN16 Press, in particular Shannon Ishizaki for taking a chance on publishing my book and making a dream come true, and to Lauren Blue for her editing and guidance through this journey. You helped shape the book into what it is now.

To my students: past, present, and future. You inspire me daily to be a better person and a thoughtful educator. Over the years, I have learned from all of you, and your voices are on these pages.

To those who face the great mystery that is depression and anxiety, never underestimate your strength. Learn from the suffering and build resilience. Use the knowledge that you gain from understanding your own pain and reach out to someone else to help them with theirs. Nevermind the stigmas that we face. They are not important. What is important is to remind yourself that you are not alone.

To Dr. Scott Ritchie, you have been my guide for almost two decades as I learned how to navigate my illness. Without you, my compass would have spun round and round, leaving me without direction. Yes, I sailed the boat, but you helped it launch.

David, I asked, "why" for far too long. Perhaps when we one day meet on the other side, you will tell me. Rest easy, brother.

Karen, my heart beats for you. My love, because I found you, I have found me, and for that I am eternally grateful. There is a gift in the moments we have already had and every second that will follow. Let's continue to breathe them in as we venture on this journey called life. I say venture because we do not know what this current life will bring, and frankly, I don't want to. Instead, we shall explore, finding secrets in each other's eyes, and hopefully one day, if we are so fortunate, hold our aged hands together as we fade away with a content smile on our faces. That would conclude a life well-lived.

Resources for you or someone that suffers from depression:

National Alliance on Mental Illness (NAMI):
nami.org

Teen Lifeline:
teenlifeline.org; 1-800-248-8336 (TEEN)

Teen Mental Health:
teenmentalhealth.org

*Talk to a school counselor, social worker, teacher,
or administrator and get help.*

Resources for you or someone that is suicidal:

National Suicide Prevention Lifeline:
suicidepreventionlifeline.org; 1-800-273-8255

Suicide Prevention Resource Center (SPRC):
www.sprc.org; 1-800-273-8255 (TALK)

The Society for the Prevention of Teen Suicide (SPTS):
www.sptsusu.org

Get help immediately if you are feeling suicidal

CPSIA information can be obtained
at www.ICGtesting.com
Printed in the USA
LVHW041426010920
664636LV00003B/210